Towards the End of the Morning

Michael Frayn was born in London in 1933 and began his career as a journalist on the *Guardian* and the *Observer*. His ten novels include *Towards the End of the Morning*, *The Trick of It* and *A Landing on the Sun*. *Headlong* was shortlisted for the 1999 Booker Prize, Whitbread Novel Award and the James Tait Black Memorial Prize for Fiction. His most recent novel, *Spies*, won the Whitbread Novel Award. His fifteen plays range from *Noises Off* to *Copenhagen*, and most recently *Democracy*. He has also translated a number of works, mostly from Russian. He is married to the biographer and critic Claire Tomalin.

Towards the
End of the Morning

━━━

MICHAEL FRAYN

faber and faber

First published in 1967 by William Collins Sons & Co. Ltd
This paperback edition first published in 2005
by Faber and Faber Limited
3 Queen Square London WC1N 3AU

Photoset by Avon DataSet Ltd, Bidford on Avon B50 4JH
Printed in England by Mackays of Chatham plc, Chatham, Kent

A CIP record for this book
is available from the British Library

ISBN 0–571–22557-8

2 4 6 8 10 9 7 5 3

A NOTE ON THE NEW EDITION

This book seems to have been retitled over the years, by the common consent of almost everyone who has mentioned it to me since it was first published in 1967, as *Your Fleet Street Novel*. No one, for some reason, can remember the title I gave it, though I rather like it still, when I can manage to recall it. The confusion has been made worse because it had a different title in America, *Against Entropy*. I like that one, too; but no one has been able to remember it any better than *Towards the End of the Morning*.

What surprises me a little is that anyone can still remember what the phrase 'Fleet Street' once signified. Fleet Street now is just the dull, busy thoroughfare that connects the City to the West End. When I first arrived to work in it, in the last few months of the 1950s, it was synonymous with the newspaper industry. It referred not just to the street itself, but to the whole close-packed district around it – to a way of life with its own style and philosophy; a world that has now vanished as completely as the Fleet Ditch that gave the Street its name. (The notoriously foul stream was incorporated by Bazalgette into the sewerage system, and concealed in a culvert that runs beneath Ludgate Circus, at the eastern end of the Street; certain parallels with the newspaper industry, however, continued to be visible to its critics.)

It even had its own characteristic smell. Just as Southwark, where my father worked, on the other side of the river, was immediately identifiable by the delicately sour smell of the Kentish hops that were warehoused and factored there, so the alleys and courts of Fleet Street were haunted by the grey, serious smell of newsprint. I catch the delicious ghost of it in my nostrils now, and at once I'm back at the beginning of my career, struggling to conceal my awe and excitement at having at last arrived in this longed-for land.

By that time, actually, Fleet Street was coming towards the end not just of the morning, but of the afternoon as well, and the shades of night were gathering fast. On the Street itself there were only two real newspaper offices left – the modernistic black glass box from which the *Daily* and *Sunday Express* improbably dispensed their archaic patriotics, and the white imperial slab of the *Telegraph*, looking more appropriately like the Tomb of the Unknown Leader-Writer. The London offices of various provincial and foreign papers maintained Fleet Street addresses in cramped rooms up staircases above tobacconist's shops – the *Manchester Guardian*, where I worked, had a few rooms over the Post Office at the Temple Bar end of the Street.

The real life, though, was in the narrow lanes just off the Street, in Fetter Lane and Shoe Lane to the north, and Whitefriars Street and Bouverie Street to the south – in the grimy, exhausted-looking offices of the *Mail* and the *Mirror*, the *News of the World*, the *Evening News* and the *Evening Standard*. The *Observer*, to which I moved in 1962, occupied a muddled warren down in Tudor Street. Other papers had ventured a little further, though they all remained in pubbable range – *The Times* at Blackfriars, the *Financial Times* up the hill by St Paul's, the *Sunday Times* and *Sunday Pictorial* a bleak half-mile away in Gray's Inn Road. The *Sun* and the *Independent* were still undreamed of, and the appearance of anything new in this run-down world seemed as unlikely as the birth of a baby in an old-folk's home. Even when the *Daily Telegraph* did manage to give birth to the *Sunday Telegraph* in 1961 the new infant had a suitably grey and elderly air.

A few terminal cases were still coughing their last in odd corners. The *Daily Herald* up in Endell Street, being slowly suffocated by its affiliation to the TUC; down in *Bouverie Street* the poor old *News Chronicle*, the decent Liberal paper that everyone liked but no one read, and on which I had been brought up, kept going by its rather more successful little brother, the evening *Star*. (A *third* evening! Can you imagine?) On the masthead of the *Chronicle* lingered the titles of a whole succession of defunct and forgotten papers that had been interred in it over the years, like the overgrown names of the departed accumulating on a family mausoleum: the *Daily News*, the *Daily Chronicle*, the *Daily Dispatch*, the *Westminster Gazette*, the *Morning Leader*. I'd scarcely been there a year when the whole vault finally collapsed, taking the *Star* and all the old names with it.

All the same, the forests of the sub-arctic North were still being steadily digested each day through this tangled alimentary canal. Great cylinders of newsprint went swinging above your head from the articulated lorries blocking every side-street. Through grimy pavement-level skylights here and there you could glimpse the web racing on the huge machines thundering in the basements. In every loading-bay there loitered underemployed gangs left over from some earlier industrial age, waiting to pass the product out, bale by bale, hand to hand, like sacks of grain from a mediaeval mill, to the vans that raced the more and more clamorously titled Late Extras and Late Finals of the evenings to the street-corner vendors, then the Irish and country editions of the dailies to the main-line stations. And, wafting from every bay and ventilator and seedy lobby, that intoxicating scent.

Mingling with it was another characteristic smell – the warm beery breath from doorways with titles above them as familiar as the mastheads on the papers themselves. The Mucky Duck, a.k.a. White Swan, where the *Chronicle* and I think the *Mail* drank; the Printer's Devil, favoured by the *Mirror*; the King and Keys, in Fleet Street itself, that refreshed the *Telegraph* opposite. I was passing the King and Keys one day when I was almost killed by a projectile emerging from it like a shell from a howitzer. It was a man being ejected by the management, in a high trajectory that took him clear above the pavement and into the gutter beyond; whoever it was, somebody evidently felt quite strongly that it was time for him to be on his way back to the office. From the windows of the *Guardian* on another occasion I watched a very large and distinguished journalist slowly emerge from Piele's, the pub opposite, totter a few dignified steps, then abruptly sit down on the pavement, where he remained, with a surprised but resigned look on his face, plainly not the shape of person to be able to get to his feet again unaided, until the news got back to Piele's, and a team of rescue workers came straggling out to hoist him up and carry him back inside again for medication.

The *Observer* drank in Auntie's, though I've forgotten whether it had any other name, and even who Auntie was. The *Guardian* had a foot in two camps. One was the Clachan, a rather undistinguished Younger's house grimly decorated with samples of the different tartans, where we drank our best bitter watched by a mysterious official of one of the print unions, who sat on his own at a corner of the bar every day from opening to closing time, wearing dark glasses and referred to in respectful whispers, but speaking to no one, apparently paid by either union or management just to sit there and drink all day.

The other was El Vino's (always so-called, with an apostrophe s, like Piele's or Auntie's, as if it had a landlord called Elmer Vino). This was quite different – not a pub at all, but a wine-bar before wine-bars had been invented, where we drank not bitter but Chablis-and-soda, alongside not trade-unionists but florid Rumpoles from the Temple and the sort of fellow-journalists who had pretensions to be members of a learned profession themselves – ruined scholars who could review you at short notice a book about Lord Northcliffe or Hugh Kingsmill, or knock you out a belligerently authoritative think-piece on the proper constitutional relationship between Crown and Woolsack. Women were strongly discouraged from entering. Any woman who insisted was not allowed to disturb the collegiate atmosphere of the bar itself but was directed to a room at the back furnished with chairs and tables, where Elmer's grand head-waiter would ritually shame her by forcing one of the more elderly and infirm old soaks taking refuge there to give up his seat to her.

There was something symbolic about our alternation between these two different establishments. On the one hand we were simple craftsmen and trade-unionists; on the other we had certain social aspirations. I was a member of the National Union of Journalists, certainly, but my only contact with it by the time I had moved to the *Observer*, apart from paying my dues, was an occasional plaintive note from the Branch Secretary asking why we had no union chapel at the office. I would pass the queries on to colleagues who knew more than I did about the paper's rather idiosyncratic workings, and back the same answer would always come: we didn't need a chapel because we were all, staff and management alike, gentlemen together.

We mostly worked at a rather gentlemanly pace, it's true, by the standards of today's journalists. We didn't have quite such a limitless acreage of newsprint to fill, and we hadn't yet got bogged down in the endless union negotiations that darkened the last days of Fleet Street, before Rupert Murdoch side-stepped them, and in 1986 broke out of that increasingly hobbled and embittered little world to the brutal simplicities of Wapping. Now the rest of the newspaper industry has followed Murdoch's lead, and scattered across London – to the Isle of Dogs and Clerkenwell (where my two former employers have taken refuge under the same roof at last), to Old Street and Kensington High Street – even, at one point, to South London and Heathrow. I don't know who's getting thrown out of the King and Keys these days, but no one, I imagine, with that astonishing ability to drink until the floor tips and still write a thousand words on the shocking decline in standards of behaviour.

Long before newspapers were out of Fleet Street, though, I

was out of newspapers. Leaving behind the small memento that follows, *My Fleet Street Novel*.

The unnamed paper where the story is set is located in one of the Street's more obscure backwaters. From the sound of it I imagine that Hand and Ball Court was on the site of a yard where an early forerunner of fives was played. Perhaps it had been part of Henry VIII's Bridewell Palace, that Edward VI made better known when he turned it into a penitentiary for vagabonds and whores. I can't find it on the current *A to Z*, so I suppose it has vanished in its turn to make way for a splendid new palace of commerce, perhaps also housing a few modern rogues of one sort or another, just as the paper itself has presumably been relocated to a more remote and less congenial environment, if not to the footnotes of media history.

I have been authoritatively informed by some people that it's really the *Guardian*; by others that it's the *Observer*. It doesn't seem to me much like either. So far as I can tell it is itself, as things in fiction so often are, though no one believes it. In which case its editor bears no resemblance to any real editor of my acquaintance? Well, yes, he does, as it happens – to a most distinguished editor, though not one who ever, so far as I know, set foot in Fleet Street, or any of its surrounding byways. So are any of the other characters based on real people? I borrowed a few features, I have to confess – a nose here, perhaps, and an eye there. Some of the characteristics of John Dyson, the head of the department that deals with the crossword, the nature notes, and other miscellaneous features, I took from the wonderful leader-page editor of the *Observer*, John Silverlight, who used to handle my copy, and of whom I was very fond. Gradually everyone in the office but John guessed. He wasn't one to keep a thought to himself, any more than John Dyson is, but he never noticed even when one of our colleagues used to embarrass me by performing lines of his dialogue in front of him – 'Oh, Michael, you write like an angel!', etc. I never owned up, I'm afraid. Not, at any rate, until I wrote his obit a few years ago, just as poor old Eddy Moulton, the ancient who is sleeping out his last years in the corner of John Dyson's office, was no doubt doing of *his* contemporaries.

The story begins with a premature and premonitory night-fall, and I suppose that with hindsight the book does look a bit like a valediction – though in the case of Fleet Street itself, as it turned out, the darkness that settled in was not going to lift in time for lunch. I'm not sure if I think of it like that, however. Dyson is in his thirties, and I see it as being more about . . . well, yes, the later stages of the morning – of *his* morning – and about his doomed attempts to turn back the tide of entropy, the inevitable trend of any system towards death and disorder.

I was in my early thirties myself when I wrote it, so I suppose I was thinking about my own life as well, at any rate unconsciously. What was I worrying about? I can't remember any conscious forebodings. I was happily married to my first wife, with two small daughters. I was still writing a weekly column, but I'd made a start as a novelist and I was already more than half out of journalism, as my characters feel they will have to be before they're forty. Even writing the book was a relatively serene experience, after the difficulties I'd gone through with my first two novels, and I've always had a soft spot for it as a result.

Curiously, it's the ends of the mornings that I remember best when I was writing it – not sudden darknesses in Fleet Street, but sunlit autumn days at home as the first chapters began to take shape, and I went off to fetch my three-year-old daughter from nursery school, my head still humming with all John Dyson's great plans to reconstruct himself along more gentle-manly lines, and all his colleague Bob's helplessness in the face of women and toffees. Writing isn't always the misery that writers sometimes like to make out. Those autumn mornings seem a long time ago now, and there *were* a few complications coming in the plot, for me as well as for my characters.

Now, I suppose, the evening is drawing on, and here am I, no longer fretting away about future events like John Dyson, or awaiting them with dozy fatalism, like Bob, but rambling on about the past like poor old Eddy Moulton. Whatever I was worrying about the first time round, I don't think I saw *that* coming.

MICHAEL FRAYN

The sky grew darker and darker as the morning wore on. By the time the coffee came round it was like a winter evening, and there were lights in all the windows that looked down on Hand and Ball Court. Bob stood at the window of Dyson's department, gazing out dreamily at the apocalyptic gloom, and eating toffees from a paper bag. He was watching the people emerging from the passage-way which connected Hand and Ball Court with Fleet Street. Some of them he knew: colleagues, arriving at their various different times to start the day's work – Ralph Absalom, Mike Sparrow, Gareth Holmroyd. In the strange mid-morning darkness their familiarity seemed slightly ridiculous. It was like seeing one's fellow-countrymen abroad.

Behind his back, John Dyson was heading for a crack-up.

'Oh God!' said Dyson, flinging himself back suddenly in his chair. 'Oh God, oh God, oh *God*! Will somebody put the lights on in here before we all go blind? I honestly think I'm heading for a crack-up in this place.'

Apart from Bob, the only other person in the room was old Eddy Moulton, who was sitting over a tatter-edged Victorian newspaper file, picking out items for a daily column called 'In Years Gone By.' He was long past retiring age, and not expected to pay any attention to Dyson. In any case, he was asleep.

'Bob!' said Dyson plaintively. 'Will somebody for God's sake put the lights on?'

'All right, John,' murmured Bob automatically, not moving, still intent upon the dark figures in the court.

'Oh God!' said Dyson. He had a staff – Bob and old Eddy Moulton were his staff – and he had to jump up and down all the time switching the lights on and off himself! No wonder he was overwhelmed by work. No wonder that by four o'clock in the afternoon he would be literally dizzy, literally overcome by a sensation of drowning in work, so that he had to loosen his tie and undo his collar. Now that he had put the lights on he could see clearly just how much work there was waiting on his desk. There was copy waiting to be subbed, galley proofs waiting to be corrected. There were complimentary tickets for the National Provincial Bank's performance of *The Pirates of Penzance*, and for an undergraduate production of *Sweeney Agonistes*, passed on to him by the Reviews Editor in case he was interested. There were invitations to Citizenship Forums and Cheese Tastings passed on to him by the News Editor and the Features Editor, and invitations to try new golf-training machines and indoor ski slopes, sent along by the Sports Editor. Dyson's department was the drain into which the last spent dregs of the world's commercial largesse fell after being sieved and filtered by everyone else on the paper, so that it was Dyson who had the labour of writing the letters of refusal. He did not like to tell his colleagues to stop passing on their unwanted perquisites, because occasionally they involved free airline trips abroad, which he and his department accepted.

Most urgent of all, there were notes and memoranda scribbled on pieces of coarse office copy paper. They were from himself to himself. 'Ring Muller abt t buzzards piece,' they said. 'Ask Sims abt t libel poss of sayg chem frtlisr klls hdghgs.' 'Check w Straker on immac concep VM.' 'RING MORLEY FIND OUT WHERE T HELL COPY FOR FRI IS.'

But how could he ring Morley to find out where the hell his copy for Friday was? Every time he stretched out his hand to pick up the phone it rang in his face.

'Hello,' he sighed into it. 'Dyson . . . Yes . . . Good . . . Bless you . . . Bless you, bless you . . . Wonderful . . . Perfect . . . Bless you.'

And scarcely had he had time to put it down and mutter 'Silly tit' before it was ringing again. It was an awfully bad day for Dyson, as he told Bob from time to time, when he had a moment.

'Somebody wouldn't like to ring Morley, would they,' he pleaded, 'and find out where the hell his copy for Friday is?'

The words broadcast themselves about the empty air, their urgency fading by the inverse square of the distance.

'Bob!' he said.

'John,' said Bob politely.

'I said somebody wouldn't like to ring Morley, would they, Bob?'

Bob slipped another toffee into his mouth. Reg Mounce, the appalling Reg Mounce, was just crossing the Court, kicking sourly at the paving stones as he went, just in case inanimate matter was in some way capable of sensation.

'I'm a bit tied up at the moment, John,' said Bob absently. 'Got some writing to do in a minute.'

Dyson stood up, trying to get the work on his desk into perspective by gazing down upon it from a great height. Supposing the phone didn't ring for a minute; whom should he call first? Morley, perhaps – then Sims might be back from court. . . . No, he'd have to ring Straker, because this was the day Straker had a committee at twelve. But Straker would go on for at least ten minutes about immaculate conception, and he would probably miss Morley.

The phone rang again.

'Oh God,' he groaned. 'Hello; Dyson . . . Ah, I've been trying to get hold of you all morning . . . Yes – I've been trying to get hold of you all morning . . . Exactly – I've been trying to get hold of you all morning . . .'

By the time he put the phone down he couldn't remember what it was he had been worrying about before. The state of the rack, no doubt; that was what he worried about most of the time. He looked anxiously at the rack of galley proofs behind him. He had only seven 'The Country Day by Day'

3

columns in print, and he had sworn never to let the Countries drop below twelve. He had a 'Meditation' column for each of the next three days – unless Winters had made a cock-up about immaculate conception, in which case he had only two and a half pieces – but he should have had a running stock of fourteen Meditations. He would have a blitz on Countries; he would have a blitz on Meditations. But then what about the crosswords? He counted them up miserably. God Almighty, he was down to his last eight crosswords! Day by day the presses hounded him; with failing strength he fed them the hard-won pieces of copy which delayed them so briefly. On and on they came! They were catching him up!

He sank back into his chair and banged the palms of his hands against his forehead.

'I honestly sometimes wonder how I'm expected to carry on,' he said. 'I slave and slave to keep this department going! I work my guts out doing three men's work! I literally work myself into the ground! But what happens? I get no co-operation! I have to try and stagger through with half the staff I need! I have to share a secretary with Boyle and Mounce and Brent-Williamson and half the paper's specialists! I'm heading for a crack-up, I really am!'

Bob put the bag of toffees away in his pocket.

'All right, John,' he said. 'I'll give Morley a buzz if you like.'

Dyson stopped heading for a crack-up. 'Bless you, Bob!' he said. 'You're a poppet, you really are. I'm sorry I went on about it like that. I know how busy you are. We're all busy. We're all under strain. I'm sorry, Bob.'

Bob hunted through the mess of telephone numbers scribbled on the old blotter propped up against the end of Dyson's desk.

'It's Gerrard's Cross 5891,' said Dyson. He got up and walked across to the window, where he stood wriggling his fingers impatiently, as if playing an invisible bassoon. 'You dial GE 4. I'm not trying to get at you personally, Bob. You know that. It's the frustrations of the job.'

Bob dialled GE and then F for frustrations. He pressed the receiver rest down and began again.

'I don't know how you always manage to seem so calm,' said Dyson. 'Doesn't the job ever get you down, too?'

Bob dialled GE 2. Perhaps certain aspects of working with Dyson were a little 2 much for him, he thought. He started again.

'I toil all the hours God made at this job,' said Dyson bitterly, 'and somehow I feel I never quite get on top of it. It's like trying to fill a bottomless bucket. You just about get next week's stuff straightened out – and already it's gone, it's used, it's forgotten, and the week after's on top of you.'

'May I speak to Canon Morley, please?' said Bob into the phone.

'Television, that's the answer, Bob. Make a name for yourself with a little spare-time work in the evenings on the box, and you can dictate your own terms. If people like Brent-Williamson and Mitchell Farjeon can do it, I don't see why I can't. I know at least as much about Indonesia, say, as Brent-Williamson does about books.'

He yawned, and looked at his watch.

'Well, I'll leave you in the chair, Bob,' he said. 'I've got to slip along to Bush House now to do a talk for the West African service. If anyone wants me, tell them I'm on my way up to the composing room.'

Bob nodded. Dyson put on his overcoat, and folded away his spectacles in his inside breast pocket to stop them being rained upon. He looked dark and nervous and almost forty.

'Hello?' said Bob into the phone. 'Is that Canon Morley?'

'Be cross with Morley,' said Dyson. 'Copy by first post tomorrow or else. I'll be back in time for lunch.'

The bang of the door as Dyson went out woke old Eddy Moulton. He had been dreaming about a journalist he had known in the old days called Stanley Furle, who had never gone anywhere without his gold-knobbed cane and a carnation in his button hole. One day Stanley Furle had fallen down the basement steps of the Falstaff and given himself a black eye on the knob of the cane! Old Eddy smiled at the thought of it. He dipped his pen in the ink and began to copy out in his close, careful longhand a report which had been published exactly a hundred years ago on Thursday week, about a boiler bursting in Darlington with the loss of thirteen lives. Nothing much surprised old Eddy Moulton, but he was taken aback very slightly to find that night had fallen already.

Various members of the staff emerged from Hand and Ball Passage during the last dark hour of the morning, walked with an air of sober responsibility towards the main entrance, greeted the commissionaire, and vanished upstairs in the lift to telephone their friends and draw their expenses before going out again to have lunch. Furtively among them came a short, rather fat man in a shapeless raincoat and a shapeless trilby hat. He kept his eyes cast down upon the gleaming dark pavements, as if he were trying to avoid meeting other people's gaze, or treading on the gaps between the paving stones. He did not walk across the middle of Hand and Ball Court, but shuffled along close to the walls, surreptitiously feeling them as he passed. He was the sort of man who calls at newspaper offices carrying sheaves of brown paper on which he has written down messages from God or outer space setting forth plans for the spiritual regeneration of the world.

He slipped through the swing doors while the commissionaire was looking the other way, got past the inquiries desk with his head turned slightly to one side so that his face was hidden by the sagging brim of his hat, and shuffled into the lift among a crowd of typists, messengers, and accountants from the wages department. His face was shiny and mottled, with wire-framed spectacles which rode up an inch above his left ear. He looked out of place among the crisply laundered shirtsleeves of the accountants and the elegantly skimpy suits of the messengers. He kept his head half turned away from them all, pretending to be absorbed in the brass plate which carried the name and address of the makers of the lift. He got out at the fourth floor and began to walk quickly along a corridor with a worn maroon carpet, past offices with heavy doors painted dark brown. The corridor lights were inadequate; there was a vaguely wartime air about the place. Somewhere a man was talking to himself, or on the telephone. 'Um,' he said gloomily, over and over again. 'Um . . . Um . . . Of course . . . Of course . . . Um . . .' Two men with their hands in their pockets, both smoking pipes, came down the corridor in the opposite direction, talking about what had happened after old Harry Stearns had told Bill Waddy what he thought about the paper's treatment of Mitchell Farjeon. The man in the shapeless hat turned aside and stood close up against one of the brown office doors, as if awaiting a summons to enter, until the men had passed by and disappeared, leaving only a trail of laughter and tarry Balkan tobacco smoke.

At the end of the corridor he came to a door with the letter G painted on the woodwork, in enamel yellowing with age. He tapped on it deferentially with his finger tips.

'Come in,' said a woman's voice.

He opened the door to exactly the diameter of his stomach and squeezed through. Inside the room a large woman with a flat, placid face was sitting at a desk.

'Good morning,' he said shyly, taking his hat off.

'Good morning,' she replied, no less shyly.

He closed the door carefully behind him, smiling deferentially, tiptoed across the room to an inner office, and edged himself into it. There was the sound of a key being turned.

The large woman at the desk picked up the house phone and dialled a number.

'Mr. Dancer?' she said. 'The Editor is in.'

Mounce, the Pictures Editor, was busy putting the fear of God into his staff. He had plenty of the fear of God to hand, but just at present only one member of his staff to put it into, a small, meek photographer called Lovebold, some twenty years older than himself. There were a great many pictures in the Pictures Department. The ones around the walls were almost exclusively of naked women, some of them supplied as advertising material by freelance agencies and firms selling photographic products, others clipped out of the magazines to which Mounce subscribed. The photographs intended for publication in the paper were laid out on tables. These were of restored cathedrals, Cotswold villages, sunsets over lakes, seagulls in flight, small children gazing at clowns, and of patterns of light and shade formed by steel girdering, frost, moving traffic at night, sparks from welding, arrangements of cogwheels, and sunshine on old stone. Mounce was looking at a sheaf of prints which Lovebold had just brought down from the darkroom. They showed patterns of light and shade formed by the rigging of sailing-boats.

'What's all this crap supposed to be?' he asked insultingly.

'I thought it was the sort of crap you wanted,' said Lovebold.

'Well, it's crap.'

'I thought we were supposed to be taking this sort of crap.'

'It's still crap.'

Mounce looked through the photographs once again, then handed them back to Lovebold with a grimace. 'All right, then,' he said. 'Take them away and put some captions on them.'

Lovebold looked slowly through the pictures in his turn. 'I was thinking of something like "Symphony in Rope," ' he said diffidently.

'Jesus!' said Mounce.

'What do you think, then?'

'I don't think anything. If "Symphony in Rope" is the best you can dredge up out of your stinking little mind, put "Symphony in Rope" on them.'

'Or how about "Symphony for Strings"? Do they have symphonies for strings?'

'How should I know? They're a spotty lot of pix, anyway. I don't care what spotty caption you put on them.'

'How about "String Symphony"?' suggested Lovebold. 'Like "Spring Symphony"?'

Mounce walked up to the other end of the room without replying. He sat down at his desk with his back to Lovebold and began to sort through a stack of agency pictures.

' "String Symphony"!' he said after a little while. 'God give me patience! If this was a real newspaper, and not a rest home for old gentlemen, I'd scare the living shits out of you lot. If this was the *Express*, and not just a load of old toilet-paper, I'd have fired you and your snotty little friends as soon as I set eyes on you.'

'I'll go and do the captions,' said Lovebold, edging towards the door.

' "String Symphony"! God give me strength!'

'You tell me what you want, Reg, and I'll do it.'

Mounce swung round in his chair indignantly.

'Oh, thanks!' he said. 'I'm not your wet nurse, you know. I'm not your private arse-wiper. Try and use a bit of initiative, sonny! You wouldn't have lasted a week on the old *West Midlands Post*. You know what I did once on the *Post*?'

'You mean when you tried to get through a police cordon by saying –'

'I mean when I practically breezed through a police cordon by saying I was the Home Office pathologist! Know how I got my job on this paper?'

'You just walked in off the street –'

'I just walked in off the street and told them to give it to me! Still, I'm wasting my breath telling all this to a pinhead like you.'

Mounce had re-immersed himself in the agency pictures. Very quietly Lovebold faded through the door and closed it behind him.

'Lovebold!' shouted Mounce. 'Come back here, Lovebold!'

Lovebold came back into the room, sighing noiselessly.

'Lend me a fiver, will you?' said Mounce.

Lovebold sighed again. 'Can't, I'm afraid, Reg,' he said.

9

'Come on!'

'I haven't got a fiver on me, Reg,' said Lovebold, pulling a single pound note out of his back pocket and showing Mounce the empty lining.

Mounce took the pound. 'Don't give me this crap,' he said. 'Show me what you've got in your other pockets.'

'Oh, come on now, Reg. Be reasonable.'

'Let's see what you've got in your jacket pockets, for a start.'

'All right,' said Lovebold wearily. He took a small, tightly-folded bundle of notes out of his breast pocket and counted off four.

'You can't fool Uncle Reggy,' said Mounce.

Lovebold fetched an expenses chit, while the matter was still fresh in Mounce's mind, and wrote down at random on it two nights expenses in Wolverhampton, with lunches and entertainment for contacts, adding up to £6 8s. 4d. He gave it to Mounce to sign.

Mounce folded his hands and closed his eyes. 'For what we are about to receive,' he said, 'may the Lord make us truly thankful.'

A bluff, friendly man-to-man relationship with your staff, he reflected as he scribbled his signature; that was the way to do it. A bit of bluster – one's staff respected it. A little turning of the old blind eye – they loved you for it. And if they ever took it into their heads to let you down you could always get them the boot for fiddling their exes.

Towards lunch-time the sky grew lighter again, and when old Eddy Moulton woke up just before one o'clock he had the impression that it was the following day. The days went very fast when you were old, he reflected. He began to copy out a piece of political intelligence about the intentions of Lord Derby.

It was the noise of Dyson coming in that had awakened him.

'Did somebody manage to get some copy out of Morley?' asked Dyson. He sounded very cheerful. His arrival seemed to bring the bustle of the outside world into the room.

'Promised for tomorrow,' said Somebody, looking up from a book he was reading for review. 'How did your thing go?'

'Oh, marvellously! I adore broadcasting; I really feel in my element. Do you know, Bob, I'm always sorry to get to the end of the script. I'd like to go on all day.'

He hung up his coat, and rubbed his hands together vigorously, full of smiles.

'I feel completely recharged, Bob,' he said. 'A tremendous sense of psychic energy. This afternoon I'm going to have a blitz on crosswords.'

He sat down at his desk and began to stack papers together and shuffle the stacks into a different order.

'As a matter of fact, Bob,' he said, 'I'm getting quite a following in West Africa. The producer had a letter this week from some girl in Conakry, of all places, asking for my photograph. Of course, I shan't send her one.'

'Why not?'

'Do you think I ought to, Bob? Perhaps I should. You think I should, do you?'

'I don't see why not.'

'Well, you know, it seems a bit film-star-ish. I don't know whether I've got time to mess about sending pictures of myself out.'

Bob yawned. 'How about some lunch?' he said.

'All right. I mean, it's not as if I had a publicity manager. I am rather pushed. But you think I should?'

'Sure. Where shall we go? The Gates?'

'If we must, I suppose. Perhaps it would be rather mean to disappoint her. Eddy, we're going to the Gates. Will you keep an eye on things?'

One by one and two by two the sober, responsible men emerged from the main door again to go out for lunch. The Foreign Editor, the Literary Editor, the Diplomatic Correspondent, and the Rugby Football Correspondent made up a

11

party to share a taxi to the Garrick. Mr. Dancer, the Chief Sub-Editor, went to a workmen's café in Whitefriars Street. The senior advertising men, swishing rolled umbrellas, strolled grandly off to sip hock at EI Vino's. The Editor shuffled out, unnoticed by anyone, and caught a number fifteen bus to the Athenaeum.

At the Gates of Jerusalem, just round the corner from Hand and Ball Court, Bob and Dyson found Bill Waddy, the News Editor, with Mike Sparrow, Ralph Absalom, Ted Hurwitz, and Andy Royle. It was that sort of set which went there. Gareth Holmroyd, the Assistant Industrial Editor, was buying stout for Lucy from the Library and Pat Selig, the woman's page sub. Round the far side of the bar Mounce was talking to a girl with brown eyes and straight blonde hair. He raised his glass to Bob and Dyson and winked. It was the sort of pub where you'd expect to find the Waddy-Absalom-Hurwitz set, and Gareth Holmroyd, and Mounce leaning over some rather plain girl.

Bill Waddy was telling a story.

'Anyway,' he said, 'I said to this bloke in the colonel's pips, "Where the blazes are we?" John, Bob, what are you drinking?'

'No, no,' said Dyson. 'Let me get these.'

'No, no, I'm in the chair.'

'No, no, I insist.'

'No, no, certainly not. Mrs. Dunfee!'

Mrs. Dunfee, busy pouring more vodka for Mounce's girl, gave no acknowledgment.

'Anyway,' said Bill Waddy, 'so I said to this chap, who let me say was in the uniform of a full colonel, "Where the dickens are we?" '

'Yes?' said Mrs. Dunfee.

'Oh . . . two more bitters, please, Mrs. Dunfee. Pints?'

'Half for me, please, Bill,' said Dyson.

'Half for me, too,' said Bob.

'Two halves, Mrs. Dunfee. Anyway, so I said – this bloke was in the uniform of a full colonel, I should point out –'

'Two-and-twopence,' said Mrs. Dunfee.

'I said to him . . . I've only got a pound note, I'm afraid Mrs. Dunfee . . . I said to him –'

'You've got the twopence.'

'So I have. Anyway, so I said to him –'

'Thanks, Bill,' said Dyson, picking up his beer. 'Cheers.'

'Cheers,' said Bill Waddy.

'Cheers,' said Bob.

'Cheers,' said Bill Waddy. 'Anyway, so I said to this bloke –'

'Where was all this, Bill?' asked Dyson.

'Well, that's just what I asked this laddie in the colonel's uniform.'

'Oh, I'm sorry, Bill.'

'I said, "Where the hell are we, colonel?" And *he* said, "I haven't the faintest idea!" '

'Fantastic,' said Dyson. 'Bob, can I get you a sandwich?'

Bob and Dyson drifted over to the sandwich counter.

'Perhaps I could ask Mounce to get one of his people to take some pictures of me,' said Dyson, gazing absently across the bar at Mounce.

'He's such a tit,' said Bob.

'Bob, why don't you do some broadcasting? We could easily fix something up for you at Bush House.'

'I don't think I'd like it, thanks, John.'

'You'd love it. I get a terrific kick out of feeling I'm known in parts of West Africa. I'll tell you something I've never told anyone, Bob: I'd like to be one of those terrible people you see airing their views about life on television.'

'So you keep saying, John. I think it's a horrible idea.'

'But think of it in practical terms, Bob! A hundred guineas an appearance and no script to write!'

'Even so.'

Dyson looked at Bob admiringly.

'There's a saintly streak in you, Bob,' he said, 'which I've noticed before. And of course you write like an angel. Another half?'

* * *

By half-past two most of the sober, responsible men had returned to Hand and Ball Court, walking a little more slowly now as the day began to tell upon them. By three o'clock a certain amount of writing was being done. Bob was writing a book review for the *New Statesman*, Dyson a radio-script on oil prospecting for the schools' programmes. Locked away in his office on the fourth floor, the Editor was also writing. The room was chaotic. The raised surfaces were all covered with wrinkled page proofs and sheaves of yellowing galleys, the floor with stacks of books and with old framed photographs which had fallen off the walls. They were of former editors and ranked groups of schoolboys, dons, and officers. On a table in the corner stood a number of silver cups won by various athletics and boxing teams got up among the paper's staff; the Editor's raincoat and hat had been thrown down on top of them. The desk had disappeared beneath papers a long time ago. The Editor had abandoned it and moved to a table against the wall, where he was typing very rapidly with two fingers on a small old-fashioned portable.

Mr. Dancer [he wrote]. PRIVATE AND CONFIDENTIAL.
I have been giving further thought to the eternal problem of how we may best *put the skids under* our friend Mounce. As I have stressed before, I have no experience of summoning employees to my office and telling them that they are fired, and after long and careful consideration I must tell you that I see no prospect of finding the courage to start – particularly not with Mounce, whom I find very frightening indeed. Besides, it would be against the whole spirit of this office, where we have always laid great stress upon security of employment. But in the case of Mounce, who has turned out to be our greatest mistake since Pavey-Smith (do you remember Pavey-Smith? He got the canteen manageress with child, obtained a refrigerator by fraud, charged dinner for

14

eight at the Savoy to the paper, and then – mercifully – absconded with three months' salary in advance), I believe we should be justified in adopting *guerilla tactics*. That is to say, I think we might try *persecuting* him, within the limits imposed by our consciences and by ordinary discretion, in the hope that he will spontaneously resign, and disappear from our lives, taking with him what, if we are careful, need be only a comparatively small amount of the firm's money. As to *how* we should persecute him, I must confess that I have no idea. I am sure you will be able to think of something suitable; the world has come very low if a Chief Sub-Editor cannot think of discreet ways of making a man's life a burden to him. I have great faith in your abilities in this direction, and I shall give you full backing in any scheme, provided that it does not involve (a) my coming face to face with Mounce, (b) physical violence, (c) putting ourselves in any morally false position, or (d) giving any appearance thereof. I await your thoughts on the matter with impatience.

The Editor folded the letter up, crammed it into a small brown envelope on which he wrote 'B. D. Dancer Esqre.' and pushed it through a sort of serving hatch to his secretary in the outer office. During office hours the passing of notes through this hatch was his only form of communication with the world.

'I always feel so sleepy in the middle of the afternoon,' said Dyson in the middle of the afternoon, yawning, and leaning back in his chair with his hands linked behind his head. 'I must cut out this beer for lunch. My system can't take it, at my age.'
    'Neither can mine, at my age,' said Bob, yawning also.
    'How old are you exactly, Bob, as a matter of interest?'
    'Twenty-nine.'
    'My God, you're young! My *God*, you're young! Do you know how old I am, Bob? Have a guess.'

15

'Thirty-seven.'

'I suppose I've told you, have I?'

'Yes.'

Dyson rocked his chair back on its rear legs and gazed at the ceiling for a long while, yawning from time to time.

'Do you keep a stock of photographs of yourself, Bob?' he asked at last. 'To send out to producers and editors and so on?'

'No. I don't do much freelance work, John.'

Dyson pursed his lips and shook his head slowly.

'When you get to my age, Bob,' he said, 'with a wife and children, and a mortgage, you'll be working all the hours God made. Saturdays and Sundays. Morning, noon, and night. I can scarcely lift my eyes from my desk from one day's end to the next. I honestly sometimes wonder how long I can stand the pace. A journalist's finished at forty, of course.'

He went on staring at the ceiling, occasionally blinking thoughtfully, and yawning, and sometimes opening his eyes very wide, as if to exercise the skin around them. Bob brooded over his book review. 'Mr. Berringer knows his New York,' he wrote. A wave of honesty passed over him, and he altered it to 'Mr. Berringer appears to know his New York.' The wave of honesty was succeeded by a wave of professionalism, and he altered it back to 'Mr. Berringer knows his New York.' He put a toffee into his mouth.

'You'll rot your teeth sucking those things all the time,' said Dyson, without taking his eyes off the ceiling, hearing the familiar rustle of cellophane and the faint slopping of salivaed membranes. Bob did not reply. Old Eddy Moulton smacked his lips too in his sleep.

'God, I was going to have a blitz on the crosswords this afternoon,' said Dyson.

He yawned twice in succession.

'God, I can scarcely keep my eyes open,' he said.

At five o'clock Dyson got restless. He jumped up and began walking up and down the room. The whole building was at last fully alive. The sub-editors' room was full. The copy-takers' typewriters were clattering. The leader-writers were writing leaders. There were queues at the tea-trolleys.

Dyson went out and bought the evening papers.

'I feel I must know what's going on in the world,' he said, perching himself on the corner of his desk to study them. 'Don't you feel that, Bob?'

'No.'

'I read all the papers every morning. I'd feel a definite sense of anxiety if I missed a single one of them. You don't read any of them, do you, Bob?'

'I read the cricket scores.'

'You're a shit, Bob. I don't know how you can bear to work in newspapers. Of course, you write like an angel.'

He fell silent, reading.

'Listen to this,' he said suddenly. ' "Darkness at Noon for Londoners. Freak weather conditions brought darkness to Central London streets this morning. Lights went on in shops and offices all over the City and West End, as the sky grew black. By mid-morning it looked as if night had fallen." '

He looked up at Bob expectantly.

'I know,' said Bob. 'I looked out of the window.'

Dyson started to read the paper again, grinning. 'You're a real shit, Bob, aren't you?' he said admiringly.

Just after eight o'clock the glass in all the windows started to vibrate. Here and there light shades and other thin metal fixtures burred faintly, or ticked, or rattled. In Dyson's department, deserted, and lit only by the yellow sodium light coming in through the windows from the street-lamps in Hand and Ball Court, a ruler sticking out over the edge of old Eddy Moulton's desk moved itself slowly sideways until it over-balanced and fell on the floor.

The great presses in the basement were running for the first edition.

17

2

When Dyson had read the boys a story and kissed them good night, he settled himself in an armchair in the living-room to wait for dinner, and gazed up at a section of plaster which had broken away in the corner of the room and peeled back a large triangle of wallpaper. He had painted the wall only a month or two before, which made its decay particularly irritating.

'God strikes again,' he said bitterly.

'What?' said his wife, coming to the door in apron and rubber gloves, holding a mixing bowl.

'Jannie, you didn't pick at it or pull at it in any way, did you?'

'Pick at it or pull at it? How could I possibly pick at it or pull at it? I can't even reach it to stick it back.'

She disappeared back to the kitchen.

He wanted to say, you might have been trying to get cobwebs down with a broom, but he knew she wouldn't be able to hear in the kitchen. God, it irritated him when Jannie asked a question, and then walked out of earshot before he could reply! It was one of her most infuriating habits.

She was back in the doorway again.

'If you want to know,' she said, 'it's the damp getting in through that bald patch under the children's window where the stucco's come off. The plaster's sodden.'

Dyson sat back in his chair and drummed his fingers gloomily on the arm. God had his eye on the house, there was no doubt about it. Slowly but surely he was gathering it to his bosom. He was coming in through the walls as rain, up from the ground as rising damp, down through the chimney as birds, and moving in mysterious ways throughout the fabric as dry rot, green mould, mice, and earwigs. Dyson won brief tactical advantages with Polyfilla and emulsion paint, only to find that God had accomplished some vast strategic infiltration behind his back. The sad truth, Dyson realized, was that it was an unfair fight. If God had been prepared to start square, and spend most of his time and energy, like Dyson, on keeping up the crossword stock and explaining the rudiments of British political life to Africans, Dyson could have given him a real run for his money.

The Dysons had bought an old house deliberately, when Jannie was carrying their second child, after long and shrewd reflection. They did not want to live in the suburbs, in an ugly suburban house with uncongenial suburban neighbours, miles from town. They decided to find a cheap Georgian or Regency house in some down-at-heel district near the centre. However depressed the district, if it was Georgian or Regency, and reasonably central, it would soon be colonized by the middle classes. In this way they would secure an attractive and poten- tially fashionable house in the heart of London, at a price they could afford; be given credit by their friends for going to live among the working classes; acquire very shortly congenial middle-class neighbours of a similarly adventurous and intel- lectual outlook; and see their investment undergo a satisfactory and reassuring rise in value in the process.

In the early years of their marriage, while they had still been content to live in a rented flat, they had often noticed the sort of place they now had in mind. Driving about London they had passed innumerable Georgian and Regency terraces which needed only a lick of pastel-shaded paint to make them habit- able. But now that they were actually looking for them a curious thing became apparent. The houses had vanished. It was like trying to return to a place one remembered from one's childhood; the innumerable terraces could not be found – the appearance of the world had subtly altered. There were Georgian and Regency houses, certainly, but they were occupied by the rich already. There was no shortage of slums; but they were not Georgian or Regency slums, and in any case the prices already seemed to have gone up beyond what they could afford in anticipation of the middle-class invasion, improbable as that Armageddon seemed in those flowerless grey streets where abandoned motor-cars squatted on flat tyres, bleeding their rusty insides and torn upholstery into the gutter around them. The houses they had seen belonged not to the real world at all, but to the world one glimpses out of the corner of one's eye, which vanishes when one turns to look.

Little by little they made concessions to themselves, swinging from each last concession to reach the next. They decided that they were prepared to settle for an Early Victorian house, provided it was central. Then they agreed that they were prepared to go a little way out, provided they could find an Early Victorian house. Like Tarzan swinging himself from branch to branch through the jungle, Dyson and his wife swung themselves farther and farther out from the centre of London, and farther and farther on through the nineteenth century, until they arrived at the year 1887, and number 43 Spadina Road, s.w.23. Here the descending curve of demand at last met the unyielding base-line of supply. Looked at in one way, what they had acquired was an ugly suburban house with uncongenial neighbours, miles from town, which had cost all the money they could raise by mortgage, plus all the savings and borrowings they had intended to use for modernization and repair. But they didn't look at it in that way. And in any case, the uncongenial neighbours would soon be driven out by the great influx of congenial architects, journalists, civil servants, and university lecturers who would come flooding in to follow the Dysons' example, and who would float the whole district off the bottom and up to the £2500 a year mark.

But the middle classes did not come to Spadina Road, s.w.23. Number 41, the house next door to the Dysons', continued to be occupied by Mr. Cox, who was a lorry-driver, and by Mr. Cox's wife and three children, his sister and brother-in-law and their three children, another sister who was a bit soft in the head, and Mrs. Cox senior. Number 45, on the other side, went not up but down. It was owned by two elderly sisters. One of them died, the other was put in the asylum, and the house was bought by a West Indian landlord who broke it up into flats. Dyson was entirely in favour of both the working classes and West Indians. All the same, the particular West Indians and members of the working class living next door to him seemed to be very hard to get to know. And he couldn't help feeling that the refusal of the middle classes to follow his example and move to Spadina Road was a reflection on his judgment. He invited friends and colleagues out at the weekends to see for themselves the delights of the district. They agreed that s.w.23 had a village-like atmosphere and a distinct character of its own. They agreed that if you cut through the back-streets to the Tube, and the District Line was running normally, you could be in Fleet Street in under the hour. They agreed that Ecosse St. George was a wonderful West Indian name, and that Ecosse St. George and his wife Princess were wonderful characters to have for neighbours. But they did not move to Spadina Road.

A man described as a surveyor moved into number 84, it was true. The Dysons invited him to dinner as soon as they heard, and told him all he needed to know about the district – where the only good butcher was, what to do about the little boys who came in at night and shat in one's basement area. But it became apparent that whatever it was the man surveyed, he surveyed most of it through the bottom of a glass. He was on his way down in the world, like Spadina Road itself. He did not paint his house a pastel colour, and after a couple of evenings of watching his eyes become more and more like unfocussed brown poached eggs, Dyson began to feel that the tone of the street had been higher without him. There was no doubt about it; God was leaning on Spadina Road, s.w.23.

'Incidentally,' said Jannie, reappearing in the doorway, 'they've been throwing stuff over the wall again.'

Dyson jumped to his feet, the adrenalin instantly flushing into his bloodstream.

'Which of them was it?' he demanded excitedly.

'I didn't see them – I just found it there.'

'You didn't touch it?'

'No.'

'You left it exactly as it was?'

'Yes, of course.'

'When I go out there now I'll find it *exactly* as it landed?'

'Yes, yes, yes. It's just beyond the second apple-tree.'

Dyson rushed out into the garden, without stopping to find a torch. It was a long, thin garden, set with blighted, infertile fruit trees which cowered between the yellow brick walls like sick dogs in an exercise yard. Dyson stumbled over loose bricks in the rank grass. There was a vague, yellowy urban nightglow in the air, and Dyson found what he was looking for at once. He got down on his hands and knees to examine it more closely, scarcely aware of the wetness of the grass. Old tin cans – twenty or thirty of them. Old Long Life beer cans. Dyson clenched his fists, and snarled aloud with rage. Not loudly, but definitely aloud.

He wouldn't have it. God knows he was kicked around by everyone, but he wasn't going to have his own garden treated as a tip. Positive action was going to have to be taken. But against whom? That was the question. Was the stuff coming from the Coxes' side or the West Indians'? The garden was so narrow it was impossible to tell.

He didn't think it was the West Indians. He didn't know, of course. But he didn't want to be the sort of man who went round believing that his West Indian neighbours were throwing old beer cans into his garden. That wasn't the sort of person he was at all. If by some chance it *was* the West Indians, then tact was called for. A friendly word of advice, no more – and he didn't want to raise the matter with them at all unless he was absolutely sure.

But if it was the Coxes . . . Well, by God, he wasn't putting up with this sort of nonsense from the Coxes! He'd asked Cox about it point blank, and Cox had denied it. But that proved nothing. If it was the Coxes he would get an injunction. He would damned well go round and post a load of rubbish through their letter-box.

He examined the position of the cans carefully. They were slightly nearer the West Indian wall, but that proved nothing in itself. They were quite widely scattered. Now that was interesting. They would scarcely have been thrown over one by one; someone must have brought them out of the house in a box, and shot them over in one load. Since they were now scattered it argued a long trajectory. And as Dyson peered at them in the faint jaundiced light it seemed to him that they were to some extent radiating out from an epicentre on the Coxes' side. They were! They had hit the ground on the Coxes' side first – he could see some sort of darker mark in the grass! – and bounced towards the West Indian side, scattering as they went!

In an access of justified rage, now that he could permit himself some really justified rage, Dyson scooped up as many of the cans as he could and flung them back over the Coxes' wall. Some of them rang out against stones or bricks as they landed. The noise made Dyson hesitate. He had flung enough back to teach the Coxes a lesson, he decided; he would put the rest in the dustbin. He bent down to gather them up. But at that moment he thought he heard the Coxes' back door open. He decided that it would be better to collect up the rest of the cans in the daylight, when he could see what he was doing, and he straightened up and walked briskly back to the house. In his haste he missed his footing on the second of the wooden steps up to the kitchen door, and trod on the first with unnatural heaviness. It collapsed beneath his foot, with a scrunch of considerable self-satisfaction, as if God had been waiting for that little opportunity for some time.

* * *

Bob crept upstairs and let himself into his flat as quietly as he could, in the hope that Mrs. Mounce wouldn't hear that he had come in. She didn't always hear; it was worth a try. The flat was dark and cold. He took off his shoes and walked softly about in his overcoat, turning on the Anglepoise light over the desk, and various lamps made out of old brandy bottles. He found a cold, dusty shilling behind the jar of multicoloured spills on the mantelpiece and lit the gas-fire. Then he drew the curtains and put a long-playing record of someone's dreaming strings on the gramophone, with the volume turned down very low. He looked round the room. It honestly didn't look too bad.

What did he have in stock to go with the chops for dinner? Still in his overcoat and socks, he went across and opened the kitchenette up to look. His gaze wandered vaguely along the shelf. The shelf was lined with old newspaper, and the sight of the newspaper, still greyly excited about the daily trivia of six months before, made him feel suddenly dismal. My God, he thought, I must find another flat, I really must. He lit a cigarette, and got down the tin of brown sugar. He drifted across to the mirror over the bookcase and looked at his reflection, holding the cigarette in his left hand and eating a spoonful of sugar with his right.

He looked a bit tired, he thought. Been getting a little too much sleep recently, perhaps. Coming home and watching the television, instead of refreshing mind and spirit at the cinema. He was also getting a little paunchy, a little soft around the face. He ate another spoonful of sugar and smiled experimentally. He had rather prominent eyelids, which came down when he smiled and made him look even sleepier than usual.

It was terrible to be getting paunchy at twenty-nine. He had been young all his life; and now suddenly youth seemed to be leaking out of him. He ate another spoonful of sugar. He'd have to go swimming at the St. Bride's Institute in the lunch-hour occasionally with Ralph Absalom and that crowd. A few lengths a week – soon get the weight down. But my God, he thought, to find the fabric was beginning to need attention already, with another forty or so years still to go!

There was a soft scratching at the door. Mrs. Mounce *had* heard him come in. He ate some more sugar and looked at himself sombrely in the mirror.

'Bob?' said Mrs. Mounce quietly.

Bob sighed.

'Bob?' said Mrs. Mounce, rather anxiously.

He went across and opened the door.

'Hello,' he said, with polite surprise.

'Bob, darling,' said Mrs. Mounce, holding a cigarette in her specially sophisticated way, with the whole flat of the hand upraised beside the face, as if for a one-handed salaam. 'Am I disturbing?'

Her bright little brown eyes looked past him into the room to see if he had a visitor.

'Come in,' said Bob.

'I really just looked in to see if you could possibly spare me some matches, darling,' she said, gliding across to the armchair and immediately curling herself up in it with her legs beneath her. She was wearing trousers, noted Bob with relief. Mrs. Mounce's knees and thighs were beginning to exercise a definite hold over him.

'I wouldn't say no to a drink, sweetest,' she said.

'There's nothing to drink,' said Bob. 'You can have a spoonful of sugar, if you like.'

'*Sweetest!*' she protested.

Bob pulled the chair away from the desk and sat down on it back to front, like a cautious lion-tamer. He nibbled another half spoonful of sugar.

'Reg working late?' he said.

'He's away overnight on a business trip.'

'Oh.'

'Did I hear a naughty note in your voice, darling?'

'No.'

25

'Because I shall have my door bolted and barred, sweetest, never you fear. I'll tell you that now.'

'Oh, yes?'

'I know you men.'

She laughed, and blew out smoke knowingly. Bob licked a few loose grains of sugar off the back of the spoon.

'There's not much you can teach me about men, darling,' she said.

'No?' said Bob absently. He was wondering exactly how old she was. About forty, he would have supposed, but in rather better working order than he was himself. She was slight and spry, with beady brown eyes. She had sharply pointed breasts, or at any rate a sharply pointed brassiere, and a sharply pointed nose, around which the rest of her face gathered itself expectantly, the upper lip lifting to reveal two sharp upper incisors like a beaver's. She smoked almost continuously, the right hand poised in its salaam, the left hand brought across the body to support the right elbow.

'I've had such an awful day, darling,' she said.

'Really?' said Bob. The room was getting quite warm. He took off his overcoat and hung it up behind the door, then lay down on the bed, which served as a divan, with his cigarette and his tin of sugar.

'Don't you want to hear about my awful day?' she asked.

'Yes, yes,' said Bob. 'Tell me about your awful day.'

'Try and look interested, darling.'

'I am looking interested.'

'There's no earthly reason why you should have to listen to my troubles, of course, if you don't want to.'

'I do.'

She thought. 'Well, we've got the builders upstairs doing one or two tiny things which I should have thought could have been finished in a week, and they've been up there *seven* weeks now, and still not a *sign*! Dotty's been peering out of her door all day, as if it was *my* fault! As if *I* wanted them hanging around for two months – as if *I* asked them to hammer on the pipes!'

26

Bob let it wash over him, murmuring sympathetically from time to time, and spooning individual grains of sugar out of the tin to crunch. Mrs. Mounce always had the builders in, and Dotty was always peering out of her door, a single, doubtful eye at the crack, because she owned the house, and no doubt wanted to keep some faint track on what was happening to it. Dotty's real name was Avdotya, Mrs. Avdotya Stypulkowski, but people didn't want to make fools of themselves by going round calling someone Avdotya, and anyway she was rather dotty – rather old and rather Polish, and not entirely able to understand what was going on around her. Certainly she couldn't understand what was happening to her house.

The house was divided into seven furnished flats – one in the basement, and two on each of the other three floors. Mrs. Stypulkowski lived in one of the ground-floor flats herself, and Bob in one of the pair on the first floor. The Mounces had first come to the house at Bob's suggestion, when Reg arrived from the provinces to become Pictures Editor. The ground-floor flat next to Dotty's was empty; they had moved in gratefully. Then gradually they had begun to colonize the house. First of all they had annexed the flat on the first floor, next to Bob's. Then they had taken over each of the top-floor flats in turn. How they had got rid of the previous tenants Bob did not know, nor what arrangements they had come to with Dotty about the rent. Were they really paying her the full rent for all four flats? Or had Mrs. Mounce talked her into accepting a wholesale price? It was Mrs. Mounce who was the driving force behind this expansionism. Her husband was scarcely ever there; more and more often he was away for odd nights and whole week-ends, on freelance jobs, perhaps to pay the extra rent. What did she want with four flats? She didn't sublet them. She never had friends to stay. She had no children – she told Bob once that she was unable to conceive. She went up and down the common stairs all day with a bunch of Yale keys, letting herself in and out of her colonies. Dotty stood with her door on the ground floor open a crack, watching her silently. A regular force of builders lived in the house almost permanently, moving slowly from flat to flat. They seemed to specialize in hardboard work. They installed hardboard partitions, covered up mantelpieces with hardboard panels, constructed hardboard kitchen units. They turned one of the second-floor flats into a den for Mr. Mounce by installing a hardboard hi-fi unit and a suite of hardboard desks. They converted the first-floor flat next to Bob's into a hardboard bar, with concealed lighting behind hardboard pelmets. On Sunday mornings when Mr. Mounce was at home Bob would sometimes be invited into the bar for a drink. Reg would stand behind the counter and dispense vodkas, then lean over it like a philosophical barman and talk about what a lot of crap it was that people talked these days, while Bob and Mrs. Mounce perched up on cocktail stools, their knees tangling and untangling a foot or two in front of Reg's nose, and all around them Mrs. Stypulkowski's original furnishings mouldered on unchanged. Occasionally the Mounces gave Saturday-night parties, to which they invited a number of other couples rather like themselves – large, melancholic men with small, bright wives – who all got drunk very quickly. The small, bright wives shrieked with laughter and showed their suspenders. The large, melancholic men leaned heavily on the small, bright wives and felt their bottoms. Bob, who was always invited, usually left at about this point, conscious that it was not suitable entertainment for the young. Once when he got back to his flat he found that he had left the door open and that a large, melancholic man and a small, bright wife were lying on his bed. He apologized for intruding and went out for a walk while they finished. In the hall he found Dotty peering through the crack of her door. Silently, accusingly, the single troubled eye followed him down the stairs. 'I'm sorry,' said Bob helplessly to the eye. It was he who had brought the Mounces into the house. One day, he knew, the white-faced wholesale butcher in the basement would be edged out. Sooner or later he would leave himself. After that it would not be long before the hardboard men moved into Dotty's flat, to turn it into a sewing-room or a rumpus-room, and Dotty found herself out on the pavement with her three cats, her silver crucifix, her late husband's sword and medals, the active sympathy of the Polish Ex-Combatants' Association, and no house.

Bob became aware that a question had been asked. He took the sugar-spoon out of his mouth.

'I beg your pardon?' he said.

'I said, have you eaten, darling?' said Mrs. Mounce.

'No.'

'*Sweetheart*! You must be *starving*!'

She jumped out of her armchair and snaked across to the kitchenette, rolling her bottom importantly.

'What are you going to do?' asked Bob anxiously.

'I'm going to cook your supper, pet.'

Bob sat up quickly on the edge of the bed. 'I don't know about that,' he said.

'Just put your feet up, darling, and tell me what there is.'

'Well, look, I don't know about this.'

She came twinkling across, seized his legs, and put them back on the bed. She leant over him threateningly, and Bob lay back, frightened of putting his eye out on her nose or one of her breasts. Also, he was painfully hungry.

'There's a couple of pork chops in my overcoat pocket,' he said, 'and you'll find a tin of peas or a tin of sweet corn next to the saucepans.'

He gazed at the ceiling. Mrs. Mounce turned the television on, and the booming of impartial expert voices filled the room, drowning the dreaming strings on the gramophone. Through the noise Bob heard her singing as she worked – the first few lines of 'Jealousy' over and over again. The old grease in the bottom of the grill-pan melted, and released its familiar aroma. From time to time she emerged from the kitchenette, and glided about the room, her cigarette still up by her right ear, a fish slice in her left hand, her bottom catching the light inordinately.

'Oh God,' said Bob gloomily. There was a stack of *Vogue*

and *Queen* magazines on the bedside table. He picked one of them up, and began to study the advertisements for under-clothing and support garments. The women in the photographs all appeared to combine education and breeding with stunted pelvic development. Their eyes were soft and remote with the contemplation of spiritual things, and they seemed unaware of Bob's sleepy libidinous eyes following them as they wandered through the long summer grass in nothing but their matching sky-blue underwear, or magnolia pink roll-on and crossed arms. They didn't have bottoms. Well, all right, they had bottoms, but bottoms with sunken cheeks and spiritual expressions. A woman like that to grill his pork chops, thought Bob, and he would be reasonably content.

Dyson and his wife drank half a pint of bottled beer each with dinner, as they usually did. 'Our only luxury,' said Dyson, 'our one self-indulgence.' The warm pool of light shining down on the table enclosed them both against the darkness. They sat for a long time over their coffee, leaning their elbows on the table comfortably, gazing at the cheese, or at the dark green casserole which had contained the stew, or at each other, saying little.

'Gawain walked into a tree on the way home from school,' said Jannie, cutting another sliver of cheese to nibble. 'He said sorry to it.'

Dyson polished an apple on his sleeve, thinking about Gawain.

'I think half this dreaminess of his is just a performance, you know,' he said. 'He's playing up to us.'

'I think that's nonsense.'

'Well, he always tells us about these incidents, doesn't he? He thinks he's a clown.'

'He tells us just to reassure himself that we don't mind.'

'But we do mind.'

'But we don't let him see that we mind.'

Dyson put the first apple back in the bowl, and began to

polish another one. Ah, Gawain, Gawain! He was a thin, fragile child, who often walked about as if in a trance, his mouth slightly open, his eyes gazing into the distance, unaware of voices calling him or objects in his path. He seemed to get on all right in the Infants' School, but Dyson was afraid he would start to be teased when he moved up into the Junior School the following year. Dyson blamed himself for calling the boy Gawain. It was scarcely surprising that a child called Gawain – or at any rate a child with parents who had the sort of attitudes that went with choosing the name Gawain – should turn out to be dreamy. Dyson saw that now. The intention had been romantic; to recall in the grey wastes of winter London those russet-autumn green-spring days when he and Jannie had been reading English together at Cambridge. 'Sir Gawain and the Green Knight' – fertility symbolism – Green Men peering slyly through the lush Middle English forest – Courtly Love – the red-brick maidentowers of Newnham embowered in green summer lawns and burnished prunus – days of longing and possibility. Dyson now made sporadic attempts to reform Gawain by calling him Garry, but it was futile. One look at Gawain and you knew his name couldn't possibly be Garry. Dyson was unable to suspend even his own disbelief.

He put the second apple back and picked up a third.

'How about Damian?' he asked. 'How was he?'

Jannie sighed.

'Jack, Jack, Jack all day,' she said. 'Was it Jack who pulled the wallpaper off? Will Jack come and eat all our food up? After lunch Jack went away to stay with his Granny for a fortnight.'

'Perhaps we'll have a break while he's away.'

'No, he came back from his Granny's at teatime.'

The name Damian had turned out to have an entirely different effect from Gawain. It had made the younger boy rather earthy and coarse. 'Damian' had come to signify for Dyson bulging, polished red cheeks, and slow, hoarse laughter. Damian was an imaginative child; but what he imagined was extremely boring. More than anything except perhaps eating he enjoyed running jokes, which ran for weeks, until every possible permutation and application had been exhausted. From somewhere – perhaps from something that Gawain had said, or from hearing about Jack Frost, or Jack Sprat, or Jack the brother of Jill – he had evolved an all-purpose Jack, a formless, characterless, pointless personage to whom he attributed deeds and sayings of stupefying dullness, in a daily soap opera which often ran without respite from breakfast to bedtime. Jack's doughy presence had loomed over the family's conversations for months. Not that Damian was unresponsive to the views of the critics. 'Isn't it about time we packed Jack in now, Day?' Dyson had said once in exasperation, after listening all one Saturday afternoon to an account of what Jack had in his stomach. 'We're all sick and tired of him.' 'Jack's packing in now,' Damian had said thoughtfully at intervals since then. 'Jack's sick and tired. Jack's sick and tired all over the floor. Jack didn't have time to be sick and tired in the pot, so do you know, Mummy, Jack did be sick and tired all over the floor.' Already Dyson could see the name Damian Dyson on the spine of some thick volume embodying a lifetime's diligent pedantry, or an endless, worthy novel about feuds and forbidden passions through seven generations in a Norfolk rush-cutting community.

'We should have called Damian Gawain and Gawain Damian,' he said.

'Poor Damian,' said Jannie. 'I feel so sorry for him sometimes.'

'Do you remember when we used to meet for coffee in that seedy milk bar in Market Square? After your supervisions with that terrible man in Caius?'

Jannie smiled, looking at the cheese-board and tapping it softly with her knife.

'Ah, then,' she said.

Morning mist, thought Dyson, padlocks in bicycle baskets, cinemas showing old Marx Brothers films.

'I saw Dick Hemming today,' he said. 'At Bush House.'

'Dick Hemming?'

'Stand-up hair, bushy eyebrows. Perhaps you never met him. In Jesus.'

Jannie put down the knife and leaned her cheeks on her fists. She gazed at her husband intently.

'He went into the BBC,' said Dyson. 'I see him sometimes when I go to Bush House.'

'We've known each other almost half our lives,' said Jannie.

Dyson gazed back at her. It was odd to think that she was his wife. It seemed such a generalized, public category of being, dissolving her into wifeliness, allying her with good-wives, midwives, and fishwives, shutting her off in a dour sorority united in its complaints against the husband class. It was hard to think what she was like, she was so familiar. She was – well, she was Jan, she was Jannie. Looking at her, Dyson felt free and yet secure, like a small ball-bearing which has been placed upon a very wide, shallow dish, wandered easily about for some while, approaching the edges but always turning back, and eventually found its way, as if by its own sure instinct rather than by external forces acting upon it, to settle in the very centre.

'I can outstare you,' she said.

Dyson dropped his gaze for an instant. 'I thought I might get one of Mounce's people to take some pictures of me,' he said. 'Did I tell you the BBC had a letter from a girl in Conakry asking for a picture of me?'

Jannie said nothing, but after a while she began to laugh, still leaning on her fists and still gazing at him.

'Well, they did,' said Dyson.

'How's Bob?' said Jannie.

'Bob's well.'

'You'd better bring him back to dinner tomorrow night. He hasn't been this week.'

'I don't suppose he'll starve.'

'I'll get a joint.'

Rather thoughtfully, Jannie began to gather up the plates.

'Did it get dark here this morning about eleven o'clock?' asked Dyson suddenly.

'I suppose it did,' said Jannie, her mind on something else.

'It was as black as night in the City. There's a bit in the evening paper about it. I'll fetch it for you.'

'Poor Damian,' said Jannie. 'He even bores Gawain.'

'Very nice,' said Bob, finishing up the last spoonful of fruit salad. 'Very nice indeed.'

Mrs. Mounce might have her shortcomings, he reflected, but she certainly knew how to open a tin of fruit salad. She sat at the table opposite him, watching him eat, with a whimsical smile on her sharp little face, from time to time turning her head, drawing down the corners of her mouth, and taking another pull at her cigarette.

'You enjoyed it, did you, darling?' she asked.

'Yes. very nice. Thank you.'

'The pleasure's mine, sweetest. There's nothing a woman enjoys more than cooking for a man. Especially if he really appreciates his food.'

'Yes. Well, thanks, anyway.'

She blew out smoke between her teeth.

'If I'd known what time you were coming in,' she said, 'I'd have cooked din-dins for both of us. I could have done something really nice. Do you like crispy noodles? And prawn balls in batter? And fried spare ribs? There – you didn't know I could do Chinese cooking, did you, sweets? Oh, yes – I've cooked Chinese food for experts. Do you know Mr. Carlsson, who runs Carlsson Syndication Services? He's a *very* big man in Far East syndication. You should get to know people like that, darling, they could help you to get on. Anyway, I gave him chicken in almonds, sweet-and-sour prawns, crispy noodles, and bamboo shoots, and you know what he said? He said, "Glenda, darling" – because he's not a stuffy old stick-in-the-mud like you – he said, "Glenda, darling, I know the Far

34

East intimately – Hong Kong, Singapore, the lot – and I have never, *never*, tasted such exquisite Chinese cooking." '

'Ah,' said Bob. He got up, put the dishes on the draining-board for the cleaning woman to do in the morning, and threw the various empty tins into the rubbish-bin. Mrs. Mounce slid sinuously across to the armchair and curled herself up to watch the television, where a girl with long blonde hair was busy shooting a solemn-faced man in a dark overcoat.

'I'd ask you downstairs,' she said, 'but my darling hubby would be livid if he found out I'd been having men friends in. He's jealousy incarnate, you'd never believe.'

She gazed at the screen, narrowing her eyes against the smoke she was blowing out. Bob lay down on the bed and belched discreetly. He remembered that he had a letter from Tessa in his pocket, which he had picked up off the hall table on his way upstairs. He took it out and slit the envelope.

'What's that?' asked Mrs. Mounce.

'A letter.'

'From anyone special?'

'No.'

He unfolded the thick wad of blue paper, each sheet densely covered with neat round handwriting. He turned to the last page. It was numbered twelve. He sighed, and turned back to page one. *The Rectory, Staple Tarland, Somerset,* it said. *Tel. Staple Tarland 17. Monday.*

'Bob my darling, Bob my dearest,' began the letter. 'I miss you most dreadfully, really dreadfully, much more than I ever thought possible. It's now three whole weeks since you were here, 21 days 19 hours and 12 minutes to be exact, and it seems like three centuries. There is really nothing else to say . . .'

'Do you like jealousy in a woman?' asked Mrs. Mounce.

'No.'

'I think it's nice for someone to be jealous, within reason. You know where you stand.'

'. . . really nothing else to say,' said the letter, 'but I will recount the boring chronicle of my days so you can see just how much your silly T. does miss you. Honestly, I mope about the house like a sick cow. Mummy says I have become impossible to live with, and even Daddy has noticed. He says it must be love, so you can see he notices more than you give him credit for. I mean, he knows I'm having An Affair with you, but he's no idea exactly *quelle affaire* it is.'

Bob felt a familiar sensation, as if he were shrinking inside his clothes, or sinking slowly through the surface of the earth. He tried to fight it off, and skipped a couple of paragraphs.

'Mummy says I must go to the Rothensteins' on the 30th, if only out of common courtesy, and that I shall enjoy it once I get there. I say phooey to that, because I know I shall be unutterably bored without YOU there to Entertain and Delight me, but I suppose I shall have to go in the end, even though it means going back to college a couple of days late, and there are exams this term (Social Dynamics, World Literature, and History of Ideas I – groan, groan!). Anyway, they (the Rothensteins, that is!) live near Taskerton, and have Pots and Pots of Money. Well, Daddy has thought of one of his Awful Romantic Ideas, that A and I should make up a party with the two Gillington boys and *ride* over! I ask you! Can you imagine A and I riding side saddle in our ball-gowns!?'

Not only could Bob not imagine it, but he couldn't remember which one A was. The Rectory was full of Tessa's sisters, all kindly and romantic and fond of animals, and all called A or V or G or B. It was like a department of the Secret Service.

'But Daddy says V could take our dresses over in the car, since her pony Jester is lame anyway, and anyway she despises riding as much as I feel I ought to in this day and age, though I must confess that as you know I do get a tiny guilty sneaking pleasure out of it.'

Bob laid the letter down. He couldn't conceal it from himself; he was embarrassed. All Tessa's letters made him sweat with embarrassment. She wasn't like that to talk to. But then she wasn't as articulate when she talked. Her handiness with the pen might mean that her letters tapped the real Tessa within. Could he in all honesty continue an affair with a girl who wrote letters like this?

'Bad news?' asked Mrs. Mounce.

'No,' said Bob. 'Yes and no.'

He turned over a couple of sheets and took a sounding on page five.

'I think you must have made quite an impression on Daddy during your visit here. He didn't mention you at all until last Saturday, and I thought he must have forgotten about you altogether. Then suddenly out of the blue, while we were having tea, he asked which school you had been to. I had to say I didn't know, because strange to say you've never told me, and he said H'mph. And I said but you'd been to Cambridge, and he said Ha. Which coming from him is high praise, or at any rate a sign of some interest. You know how hard it is to get him interested in anything these days except the Liberal Party and German theology. No, I'm making him sound like some grouchy old eccentric, and he's really a very sweet and saintly man, and I *adore* him, second only to you. Incidentally, which school *did* you go to?'

He skimmed through a few more pages, trying to see if they contained anything he was supposed to do something about – an invitation, a question which needed to be answered, a rendezvous. Tessa's letters always made him anxious. Somewhere in that sea of words there might be some vital message bobbing about that he was failing to pick up. One evening she would arrive at the front door of his flat – he knew it. His face would fall in astonishment. 'Oh Bob!' – 'Oh God!' – 'Oh Bob, I *did* write!' He felt a flutter of indigestion at the thought.

'It's a funny thing about jealousy,' said Mrs. Mounce. 'I'm quite broad-minded about Reg, but I *can* be as jealous as a cat, darling, believe me.'

Bob tracked backwards again through the text. Somewhere there should be an acknowledgment of his last letter. It had been rather an amusing one, he thought.

'. . . wonderful to get your letter. I carried it around un-opened for at least an hour, inside my shirt, next to my heart. What a sloppy thing to do! Really I am a dreadfully sloppy person, not fit to know you. What does "sirjaspery" mean? I looked it up in the Shorter Oxford, but no sign. You wrote: "Oho then my proud beauty, he cried in sirjaspery tones." I think it must mean something like syrupy, with overtones of jasmine and raspberry. Am I right? And who is Captain Cosmo, master of the space-ship Staphylococcus? Is he a character I ought to know about? Or did you make him up? Oh, I feel such a fool reading your letters, and so unworthy of you. How can you bear to put up with me? I tried to read *Miss Lonelyhearts* as you suggested, but it was so miserable I gave up. I'm ploughing through *A Face in the Crowd*, which I must say is very interesting in its revelations about what goes on in "the communications industry." I've even got the library to get me *U.S.A.* by John dos Passos, but it's so enormous I can't imagine ever getting through it. It would take me all year just to read the books you mentioned when we happened to be talking about American literature. I shall *never* have read anything like as many books as you, however hard I try. Sometimes I despair. This is the *only* way I regret being nine years younger than you. You'll always be nine years ahead of me in reading and in knowledge of the world. Do you mind, dearest Bob? I *know* you mind. I *know* it irritates you when I don't understand, or don't recognize an allusion. Oh, I am a stupid child, and I'm sorry. Sometimes I'm almost sorry we met, I know I must irritate you so much . . .'

Bob put the letter down and stared at the ceiling, overcome with sadness and shame.

'What I'm going to do, sweetest,' said Mrs. Mounce, 'is to get a spare key to this flat from Dotty.'

'Oh?' said Bob, thinking about his unworthiness.

'Then I can slip in before you get home from the office sometimes and have something ready for you.'

Bob went on thinking.

'A man needs someone to look after him a little, darling. Someone to spoil him occasionally.'

Bob sighed.

Mrs. Mounce jumped out of the armchair and dimpled across to the bed. 'You don't sound very grateful, sweety pie,' she said, making a reproachful moue. She sat down on the edge of the bed.

Bob pulled his knees up to make room for her, and she leaned on them, her cigarette hand still aloft. Bob looked away, feeling low.

'I think he's a tiny bit scared of me, chaps,' she said. 'I think he thinks I've got wicked designs on him.'

Bob tried to smile. Mrs. Mounce pushed her chin forward teasingly.

'Don't worry, darling – I shan't bite you,' she purred. She sucked in cigarette smoke, and let it out slowly, gazing at him through it with half-closed eyes.

'Or perhaps I will!' she said suddenly, and in the same moment leant forward and sank her teeth into Bob's leg, just above the knee.

'Arrrrrgh!' he shouted, springing up. The bite was astonishingly painful.

Mrs. Mounce had jumped up, too, and was streaking away to the door, laughing.

'I thought that might wake you up, sweetheart!' she said. 'Night night!'

Dyson lay in bed, glancing through the book reviews in the *Statesman*, waiting for Jannie to come to bed and turn the light out. 'Glyn's slow disintegration and inevitable breakdown are magnificently handled . . . Magda, abandoned by her lieutenant, goes to live with a senescent baron in his crumbling Schloss in the Thüringer Wald; the atmosphere of decay and elderly lust is picturesquely conveyed . . . Riki's growing sense of isolation and despair is convincingly done, but her final breakdown seems a long time coming . . . ' Dyson relished the reviews, the texture of the sheets, and the softness and warmth of the bed. Outside 43 Spadina Road the world was senescent, disintegrating, despairing, and everyone was on his way to a breakdown. Inside, it was soft and warm and linen-sheeted, and everyone was in the pink of mental health. Jannie moved slowly about the room in her pyjamas, vaguely shifting heaps of clothes about. The whole room was full of heaps of clothes – his, Jannie's, the children's; some put out for cleaning, some for sending to the refugees, some to be decided about. We must get another chest of drawers, he thought luxuriously. It gave him great pleasure to see all the clothing about the room. Hundredweights of it – and all provided out of his earnings. Shirts, socks, dresses, stockings; silver dance shoes and thick winter overcoats – all quarried by his own labour. The bed itself; the butter downstairs in the refrigerator; the electricity they burned so casually; the telephone; the complex structure of beams and bricks and slates that housed it all; he, John Dyson, thought by some as a boy to be rather a fool, had got it all. Had got it by his sheer ability at maintaining the crossword stock, at checking points of theology and country lore, at explaining the intricacies of British politics to West Africans with lucidity and wit and some small measure of personal charm. Life was rich and satisfying.

Slowly Jannie got into bed, sighing at the clothes, and switched the light off. He put his head on her shoulder, and for a while she stroked his eyebrows. He wondered if he had Jannified her at all by calling her Jannie, as he had Gawained Gawain. As a girl she had been Janice, and no one had tried to shorten it. Janice Atterbury. He thought of her going off to school each day on a green double-decker bus, a Janice among Janices, a Janice Atterbury among Janice Leighs, Vivienne Williamses, Heather Marshalls, and Sandra Thompsons. Janice, you can share my crayons if you promise you won't let Heather have them. Janice Atterbury is a stuck-up pig. Atterbury, J. D., did useful work at left back, but must mark her man and tackle more aggressively. Janice Dorothy

40

Atterbury has satisfied the Examiners in German (Written and Oral), Pianoforte (Grade v), Ballet (Intermediate), and Life Saving (Royal Humane Society Bronze Medal) . . .

He started to laugh, shaking the bed.

'What is it?' said Jannie, half asleep.

'You as a schoolgirl.'

'Oh.'

And then he had come on the scene to corrupt it, knocking on her door (J. D. Atterbury, it said on the card) in Newnham on those gusty spring afternoons. Jan, I just happened to be passing by, so I thought I'd look in. But don't you find Sir Gawain's predicament intensely *moving*, Jannie? Have you thought about what would *happen* if we ever have a Tory government again, Jan? Doesn't the name Bunk Johnson mean *anything* to you, Jannie?

John Dyson and Jan Atterbury – the names went together, as everyone in their circle quickly came to see. John Dyson and Jan Atterbury – John and Jan. The names went together like Huntly and Palmer, or Fortnum and Mason. It was difficult for everyone, in the summer term of their second year, to get used to saying Jan Atterbury and Lionel Marcus. It was like finding Fortnum and Mason had become Fortnum and Freebody. Nevertheless, people managed it, in time. Even Dyson grew accustomed to it. Lionel and Jan, or rather Jan and Lionel, since easygoing, amiable Lionel was always a pace behind . . . They haunted his last year, like the prospect of getting a third, and his failure to shine as a speaker in the Union.

Dyson thought he had been awake, until he turned over, when he realized he had been asleep. And then the arrangement of names had been Belinda Charles, Jan Atterbury, and Margaret LeRoy, next to the bellpush of a flat in West Kensington. And then, after a long time in which many things had happened, some unhappy, some too embarrassing to recall, some meaningless, the names John and Jan Dyson had emerged. There was surely a chasm between Janice Atterbury and Jan Dyson. Those strong hands . . . those serious and sometimes sad brown eyes . . . Whereas he himself, he felt, had scarcely changed since the age of seventeen or eighteen . . .

His mind cruised slowly down into sleep, like a bubble drifting across the surface of an eye. A remote metallic clattering half-penetrated his consciousness, disguising itself in a suite of dreams. It was the noise of the Long Life beer cans being thrown back into the Dysons' garden.

3

Dyson's awfully bad day was followed immediately by an awfully good one.

For a start, a producer in one of the commercial television companies rang him quite early on in the morning and asked him to appear in a programme. Dyson could scarcely contain himself. He walked up and down the office frowning furiously with pleasure.

'This is exactly what I've always wanted, Bob!' he said. 'Do you realize that? This is exactly what I've been waiting for!'

'I know,' said Bob. 'Congratulations, John.'

'Of course, it probably won't lead to anything. One obviously mustn't set too much store by it. I shall probably make a terrible cock of it.'

'I'm sure you won't, John.'

'I have had a lot of experience in radio, of course. That must count for something. I have been consciously preparing myself for an opportunity like this, Bob. I haven't been waiting idly.'

He gazed out of the window, his hands behind his back, clapping the palms together.

'What sort of programme is it?' asked Bob. 'Something about Indonesia?'

'Indonesia?'

'Isn't that your great speciality?'

'Well, I know something about Indonesia. I know something about a lot of things. I'm a *journalist*, Bob.'

He sat down at his desk, very pleased with his calling, then almost immediately jumped up and began to walk about the room again.

'It's a discussion programme about race,' he said. 'Apparently they want someone with actual experience of living in a multiracial community.'

Bob stared at him. 'I didn't know you'd lived in a multiracial community, John.'

'Bob, you know we have West Indians living next door to us! We have four West Indian households in the road. You know that, Bob.'

'Oh, I see. How did the television people find out?'

'Well, the programme's being produced by a man called Jack de Sousa. Our wives were at Newnham together – we had the de Sousas out to tea one Sunday. As a matter of fact they almost decided to buy a house in the road, they liked it so much. Anyway, Jack wants me to take part in a discussion about the problems involved. Apparently the chairman's going to be Norman Ward Westerman. Have you seen him on television, Bob?'

'No.'

'He's *marvellous*, Bob. He's someone I really do feel the most tremendous respect for.'

It took some time before Dyson had simmered down enough for Bob to return to his work. He was writing a letter to Tessa.

'My darling Tessa,' he wrote, then remembered that very soon he was going to break the affair off. He tore the paper out of the typewriter and took a fresh sheet. 'Tessa darling,' he began, then remembered her letter, felt ashamed of himself, and took another sheet. 'My darling Tessa,' he began. He gazed out of the window for some minutes, wondering what on earth to say. Then he typed: 'How the Giant Dyson subdued the Tyrant Cox,' and underlined it.

'Now when Dyson returned from his labours in the City,' he wrote, 'where his education and literary accomplishments had been the wonder of the citizens, and his conversational stamina had severely taxed the strength of even his most loyal friends, he discovered that the seigneur of the estate adjoining

44

his, the cruel and tyrannous *Cox*, had been laying waste the district, and terrorizing the inhabitants, with a fearful bombardment of old beer cans. Stopping only to refresh himself with a hurried snack, consisting of 47 packets of Smith's potato crisps, 3,287 stuffed cocktail olives, and four or five cartloads of broken cake and biscuits left over from the children's tea, Dyson hastened forth and challenged Cox.

' "Ha, Cox!" he cried in a terrible voice. "Come forth, Cox, or by St. Eulalie I'll slap a writ on you! Where are you, you mother-fixated turdsmith, before I knock your grimy spectacles off and stuff an injunction down your shirt-front! Come out, you paraphrenic pissmain, you subanthropoid snotspray, or by St. Archibald I'll tread on your heels and lay an information with the Sanitary Inspector about the state of your drains!'

'But the tyrant Cox, not recognizing the force of these arguments, remained where he was. Whereupon Dyson put his nose down Cox's chimney and sneezed with such panache and violence that the tyrant was blown out of the larder window, and fell to earth in Trinity Road, Balham. Dyson at once rushed after him, pelting him with the old beer cans and whatever else came to hand, which included: Tetley's tea-bags, ex-U.S. Air Force sparking plugs, overdue library books, rubber reducing garments, and genuine reproductions of Old Masters. Without pause for breath Dyson chased him throughout the length and breadth of the land; videlicet, through Clapham North, Clapham South, and Clapham Common, Mitcham Lane, Mitcham Village, and Mitcham Junction, Collier's Wood, St. Helier, Thornton Heath, and Norbury, paying no attention whatsoever to traffic lights or belisha beacons, and frequently going the wrong way up one-way streets . . .'

But by this time another nice thing had happened to Dyson.

'This is an awfully good day for me,' he said, putting the phone down and rubbing his hands together. 'You'll never guess who that was on the phone.'

'No?'

'Sir William Paice!'

'Oh.'

'You know, the unit trust man. You must have heard of him, Bob! He's a very well-known amateur ornithologist. You remember, he married old Glenormond's daughter.'

'Someone I know?'

'Oh, *Bob*! Lord Glenormond, the shipping man. Oh God, Bob, don't you take any interest at all in the upper classes?'

'Well, you know . . .' said Bob, finding a soothing bag of peppermints in his pocket, and slipping one discreetly into his mouth.

'But Bob, they're *fascinating*! I should have thought a writer like yourself would have found them absolutely absorbing.'

Bob rattled the peppermint against his teeth with the tip of his tongue.

'I mean,' said Dyson, 'not for any snobbish reasons. But just as a sociological study I find them absolutely *fascinating*. Anyway, I've persuaded Sir William Paice to write us some "Country Day by Days." Rather a coup, I think.'

Bob returned to his letter.

'Now when they reached Sydenham,' he wrote, 'Cox snapped off the spire of St. Wendy and All Angels, and turned, and fetched Dyson a terrific blow on the funny bone . . .'

'Sir William's initials are W.G.R.P.,' said Dyson thoughtfully, brooding over the *Who's Who* he kept on his desk. 'How do you think he'd like to be credited on the column, Bob? Just plain W.G.R.P.? Or Sir W.G.R.P.?'

'Search me,' said Bob.

But Dyson wasn't listening, in any case. 'Oh God!' he cried, jumping up excitedly, and beginning to stride up and down the office all over again. 'This is such a good day for me!'

Old Eddy Moulton gazed thoughtfully at the piece he was copying out, roused by the sudden shriek of Dyson's chair being pushed back. He had been dreaming about someone he had not thought of for years and years – a character called Stanley Furle, who had fallen downstairs at the Press Club one night and blacked his eye on the silver knob of his cane!

'He was tight at the time, of course,' said old Eddy to Bob, shaking his head and smiling. 'He was as tight as a tick, poor fellow.'

Bob's own phone rang.

'Hello?' said Bob.

'This crap's from you, is it?' said a cross voice.

'What?'

'Don't give me that crap. This load of crap's your idea of a joke, I take it?'

'Is that Reg Mounce?'

'Don't give me that crap.'

'Reg, what are you talking about?'

'Bob, don't give me that crap.'

'I don't know what you're talking about, Reg.'

Mounce hesitated. 'It was you who sent me this crap, wasn't it, Bob?'

'What crap, Reg?'

'You know what crap, Bob.'

'Reg, I honestly don't know what on earth you're talking about.'

'You know, all right.'

'No.'

Mounce hesitated again. Bob could hear him sucking in air through his teeth.

'Well, *some* bastard sent it,' he said.

'Not me, Reg.'

'Well, it was *some* bastard.'

'Yes, but not me, Reg.'

'The bastard.'

Bob waited.

'If I catch the bastard . . .' said Mounce.

There was another pause.

'The bastard,' said Mounce finally.

He rang off.

'What the devil was all that?' asked Dyson, as Bob slowly put his receiver back.

'Search me.'

Dyson's phone rang.

'Hello, Dyson . . .'

Dyson frowned as he listened to the voice at the other end, and raised his eyebrows at Bob.

'What crap?' he said. 'Look, is that you, Reg? . . . Well, what crap, Reg? . . . Yes, but *what* crap? . . . Look, for God's sake, Reg, *what* crap? . . . Well, Reg, how do I know whether I sent you the crap if I don't know what crap it was? . . . Yes, but what did the bastard do? . . . Yes, yes – but what crap was it that the bastard sent you? . . .'

Dyson put the phone back.

'Well?' said Bob.

'Search me,' said Dyson.

Dyson's awfully good day got better and better. Just before lunch one of de Sousa's assistants at the television company rang to say that Lord Boddy had agreed to take part in the programme.

'Who's Lord Boddy, John?' asked Bob, when Dyson reported this to him, walking up and down the office once again.

'Oh God, Bob, you're impossible! You must know who Lord Boddy is!'

'I'm sorry, John.'

'Eddy, Bob doesn't know who Lord Boddy is! Are you awake, Eddy? Eddy? Anyway, Bob, Lord Boddy's an extremely well-known man. He's the second baron, isn't he? Wasn't his father given the title by Ramsay MacDonald for something to do with the League of Nations?'

'I don't know, John.'

'I think he was. Anyway, the present Lord Boddy is tremendously interested in things like the colour problem – he sits on committees and Royal Commissions, and so on.

Apparently there's also going to be a Mrs. Somebody-or-other who's a social worker. And someone coloured, of course.'

'Anyway, congratulations, John.'

Dyson picked up the *Who's Who* and studied it in silence for some moments.

'His father was Edward Boddy, before he got the title,' he announced. 'The present Lord Boddy's Christian names are Frank Walter. Married, with two sons. Publications: *The Case for Disarmament* (1939); *Let Victory Be Ours;* (1942); *The Russians – Our Comrades!* (1945); *World Communism: A Study in Tyranny* (1949); etcetera, etcetera . . . *Race: The Challenge Within* (1963) . . . oh, and (edited) *The Man in the Tweed Plus-Fours* (The Diaries and Letters of the First Lord Boddy).'

'I see,' said Bob. 'Why don't we go out and have some lunch before the phone rings again?'

'All right, Bob. Listen – this is interesting. His clubs are the National Liberal and the RAC.'

'What's interesting about that, John?'

Dyson snapped *Who's Who* shut and tossed it down on his desk. 'You're a shit, Bob,' he said, grinning. 'Eddy, we'll be in the Gates.'

There was the usual crowd in the Gates of Jerusalem – Bill Waddy, Mike Sparrow, Ralph Absalom, Andy Royle, Ted Hurwitz, Gareth Holmroyd, Lucy from the Library, Pat Selig – but today they had crystallized around Mounce. Mounce kept shifting about from foot to foot, restless with irritation.

'Well, *some* bastard sent it,' he kept saying.

People were passing round from hand to hand a grubby sheet of quarto copy paper with something typed on it.

'Seen this?' said Bill Waddy, handing it to Dyson and Bob as they joined the circle. 'Some joker sent it to Reg. He found it on his desk when he arrived this morning.'

It was a letter, in the form of an office memorandum:

Editor to R. Mounce. PRIVATE AND CONFIDENTIAL.

After giving the matter considerable thought, and taking advice, I have come to the conclusion that you would be wise to begin looking round with a view to making other arrangements. I do not feel that this office can give sufficient scope to your talents. Three months' notice is customary with us, as you know, but if you were particularly anxious to leave sooner I believe you would find us reasonably accommodating.

You have, I understand, a week's holiday entitlement outstanding. This would of course be paid in full. Or, if you preferred, you could take it as a holiday, and leave a week sooner than otherwise arranged.

'It was in a little brown envelope addressed 'R. Mounce Esqre.' just the way the Editor does it,' said Ted Hurwitz.

'I'd like to get my hands on the bastard,' said Mounce.

'One of your photographers, perhaps?' suggested Dyson.

'We thought of that, of course,' said Bill Waddy. 'But none of them can even spell, can they, Reg?'

'The bastards,' said Mounce.

'He's got the Editor's style exactly,' said Gareth Holmroyd.

'That's why we think it must be someone who does get communications from Room G,' said Bill Waddy.

'The bastard,' said Mounce.

'It could have been quite serious,' said Andy Royle, 'if this had been an office like the *Daily Express*, where people actually are sacked.'

They all sipped their beer thoughtfully.

'Hey, listen,' said Dyson, seizing the opportunity.

'Same again for everyone?' said Ralph Absalom, seizing it too.

'I'm going to be on television,' said Dyson.

'I think it's my round,' said Mike Sparrow.

'Tchah, tchah, tchah! Same again for you, Lucy? Pat?'

'I'm going to be on the box.'

'Have a pint this time, John.'

'With Norman Ward – no, just a half, please, Ralph – with Norman Ward Westerman – that's my glass by your elbow – and Lord Boddy.'

'Old Frank Boddy,' said Gareth Holmroyd. 'No, I won't, thank you, Ralph.'

'Go on.'

'No, I won't.'

'It's a sort of discussion programme.'

'Change your mind. Be a devil.'

'I said it's a sort of discussion programme, Gareth.'

'No, I really won't, thanks, Ralph. What was that about a discussion programme, John?'

'It's about the colour problem, with Lord Boddy.'

'Oh, I didn't see it.'

'The bastards,' said Mounce, looking into his beer and swaying slightly.

'Do you think one ought to join a club, Bob?' asked Dyson, leaning back in his chair and yawning. Things were very quiet in the office.

'What sort of a club?' said Bob. 'You mean a night club?'

'Bob, you're a treasure,' Dyson yawned and laughed at the same time, then became thoughtful again. 'The point is, I could very easily get myself put up for the Garrick. Or the Savage. Or the Travellers', even. What do you think, Bob? One does need somewhere one can go. Somewhere one can take people. I mean, if one does a certain amount of work in television, as one is likely to do if one is in our position . . . Well, supposing I wanted to have a quiet talk with a producer, say, to outline an idea I had for a programme. Or supposing, just for the sake of example, Lord Boddy and I happened to get on rather well next Friday, and I wanted to invite him to have lunch with me somewhere. Where could one go?'

'Why not the Gates?'

'Oh, Bob, for heaven's sake!'

'Well, what's wrong with a restaurant?'

Dyson gazed at the window, wrinkling up his nose judiciously and pursing his lips.

'I don't feel a restaurant would be right, somehow,' he said. 'It would be a little too *voulu*. Do you see what I mean? One's guest would know one was going out of one's way to entertain him, as if one wanted something out of him. Whereas at one's club one could sit in an armchair reading the paper while one was waiting for him to arrive. One could walk into the dining-room with him in a rather mundane sort of way, as if one did it every day. It would be more like asking him to drop in at one's home.'

'Why don't you ask him to drop in at your home, then, John?'

Dyson sighed. 'Well, you know, Bob. These days, when one doesn't have servants, with one's kids around, and broken toys, and this and that . . . Incidentally, I nearly forgot – Jannie told me to bring you home for supper tonight. Is that all right?'

'Yes, very nice. Thanks, John.'

Dyson looked back towards the window. 'Or perhaps the Oxford and Cambridge would be the right one,' he said. 'It is rather a nice place, you know.'

He drifted across to the window, clapping his hands together behind his back, and stood gazing down at the people crossing Hand and Ball Court. From time to time he yawned absent-mindedly.

'Do you think one should get one's suits made for one?' he said eventually. 'Perhaps one should take a little more trouble about these things if one's in the public eye.'

But Bob was absorbed in what he was writing. Dyson yawned again, became conscious of it, and tried to beat it out with his hand.

'God, I was going to have a blitz on "Thoughts" this afternoon, too,' he said. 'Somebody wouldn't like to give me a hand, would they? How are you placed, Bob?'

'Bit tied up just at the moment, John,' said Bob remotely, not looking up from his typewriter.

Dyson yawned again, uncontrollably. 'God oh God,' he said. 'I must knock off this beer at lunchtime. It's really wrecking me.'

'And when,' wrote Bob to Tessa, 'Dyson and his comrades sat down to carouse, the good ale wet their wits and loosened their larynxes, and they talked merrily and disputed learnedly far into the afternoon. What are you drinking, old alebladder? – No, it's my round, old weepbooze. – By St. Septimus, I'm in the chair! – My shout, by St. Cynthia! – No no, by St. Yoland, I insist! – Well, a half, then, by St. Sholto! – By St. Tib, I've come out without my money! – By St. Almeric, that's three pints, two Guinesses, one tomato juice, and five ham sandwiches! – No, by St. Trixy, it's four ham sandwiches, three sausage rolls, four draught Guinesses, and a bitter lemon! – And a packet of crisps, by St. Ruby! – And two packets of crisps, by St. Bogislaw! – That was half-a-crown I gave you, by St. Lorinda! – By St. Cecil it was a florin! – By St. Hilarion, I wish I were lunching at the Oxford and Cambridge!'

4

Jannie instinctively hid her cigarette behind her back when the kitchen door opened; John hated to see her smoking while she cooked. But it was not John – it was Bob. She brought the cigarette out again.

'Jannie,' said Bob, 'is there anything I can do?'

'Not really, Bob. You can stay and talk to me if you like, though.'

Bob drew one of the rush-bottomed chairs out from the great dining-table in the middle of the kitchen and sprawled in it. The room was full of the fat, brown smell of *gigot aux haricots*. It was a dish which Jannie often cooked for Bob. He was a glutton, and the rich heaviness which the golden-crusted beans absorbed from the exhalations of the mutton touched some deep chord in him. John hated the dish.

'Can't peel the potatoes or anything?' Bob asked.

'No. What's John up to?'

'He's reading the paper. Very good about him getting on the television. Are you pleased?'

Jannie leaned against the edge of the dresser, smoking and looking down at Bob. She bit her lower lip anxiously. 'I suppose so,' she said. 'I don't know.'

'He's as pleased as Punch about it. He's been bouncing about the office all day like a rubber ball.'

'You don't think he's going to make a terrible fool of himself, do you, Bob?'

'He'll be all right, Jannie.'

'I can't bear the thought of sitting here watching him. I don't know how I shall manage to look at the screen.'

Bob picked up one of the knives laid out for dinner and scored along the grain of the table with it. 'How are the boys, Jannie?' he asked.

The worried look on Jannie's face softened. She began to laugh. 'Poor old Bob!' she said.

'No,' said Bob, 'I'm very fond of them.'

Jannie smiled at him, wondering if he could even remember how old they were. When he came at week-ends he played with them vigorously, until they screamed and wept with over-excitement. He was very good with them, as the phrase went. But Jannie was used to friends, particularly childless ones, who were good with the children to the point of dedication, and who a month later called Gawain Damian and Damian Adrian, or who sent the six-year-old Gawain a pull-along elephant for his birthday, and gave Damian a velvet party frock, in the belief that he was called Deborah and was a girl.

'They're fine,' she said. 'How's Mrs. Mounce?'

'Well,' said Bob, 'things aren't too good at the moment. She cooked me dinner last night. Just marched in and set to work. There was nothing I could do about it.'

'I think you ought to watch out for that woman, Bob.'

'I know. I know. But what can I do?'

'She'll land you in trouble.'

'You really think she's after me, Jannie?'

'What do you think, Bob?'

Bob sat back in his chair, playing with the pepper-mill, grinding a little pile of pepper into his left palm. He was like an old cushion in the chair, thought Jannie, a plump, shabby, comfortable old cushion. With his fisherman-knit Marks and Sparks sweaters, and his broad suede shoes, and his mild, sleepy eyes, he fitted into the background of 43 Spadina Road so well that you hardly noticed him.

'She bit me last night,' he said, dragging up his trouserleg and showing her the line of tiny red marks. Jannie stared at them, trying to imagine the scene – Bob, retreating backwards round the room, and Mrs. Mounce, on all fours, snarling and barking, snapping at his trousers.

'How on earth did it happen, Bob?'

Bob shrugged. 'She just suddenly bit me,' he said.

'But what led up to it? Something must have led up to it.'

Bob sighed. 'She said, "I won't bite you." Then I suppose she changed her mind.'

'Honestly, you are a bit wet sometimes, Bob.'

It occurred to her that she hadn't made the salad. She began to wash the lettuce, while Bob made the dressing, hunting luxuriously through her spice cupboard for the oil and vinegar.

'How's Tessa?' she asked.

'Fine. Do you think a little cinnamon would help?'

'No. Does she know about all this business?'

'All what business?'

'Mrs. Mounce.'

'No, no. How about tarragon?'

Bob was always evasive about Tessa, which made Jannie suspect that he might be serious about her. It also made her want to find out more about the girl, and gave her a terrible desire to tease Bob about her.

'When she comes to London,' said Jannie, 'she can always have the spare room here, you know.'

'That's very kind of you, Jannie.'

But of course, thought Jannie, feeling foolish, Tessa would stay with Bob. Now Bob would think she disapproved.

'I mean,' she said, 'only if she wants to.'

'Yes, yes,' said Bob. He sounded embarrassed.

'I mean . . . Oh, you know what I mean.'

'Yes, Jannie. I'll put some sugar in the dressing, shall I?'

'I mean, there's a bed here if ever she wants it.'

'Sugar, Jannie?'

He was holding the sugar-jar up questioningly. She gazed at it for some moments in silence, thinking about a flat in Manchester where she and John had spent a ghostly week one winter before they were married. It had belonged to a man called Flowers, and they had gone to Manchester just because he had offered them the flat. It had been bitterly cold. They had stayed in bed most of the time. In the afternoons they had walked around the cold, grimy streets. She had a picture of sooty red brick, quiet, empty streets with grey winter haze at the end of them, little corner shops with paper decorations left over from Christmas, gritty smoke blowing down from the chimneys. It had been just after Christmas; she had worn a new pair of fur mittens her sister had given her. She could remember standing by the window of the flat and crying, but not why she was crying, or indeed much else. Except that the mattress had smelt musty, and that as they lay in bed through those long cold mornings they could just see the spire of the Congregational church through the window.

'Half a teaspoonful, Bob,' she said.

'What were you thinking about?'

'Oh, things. It's funny how . . .'

She put the lettuce in a bowl and dried her hands, staring unseeingly at the loose tile above the sink. The grittiness of the coal smoke coming down on those gaunt January afternoons was still in her nostrils. She could hear the rising engine-note of the Corporation buses as they pulled away from the stop at the corner, coming from nowhere either of them had ever heard of, going on through the gathering winter dusk to destinations equally obscure.

'How what, Jannie?' asked Bob, taking a teaspoonful of sugar from the jar and slowly licking it up.

Jannie pulled another of the chairs out from the table and sat down. 'How you suddenly remember something very vividly,' she said, 'and you think for a moment you've really got hold of it. But then . . .'

She hesitated again, dismayed by the difficulty of delineating such fleeting, unshaped feelings in words.

'But then,' she said, 'when you try to think what it is you've got hold of, it's not very easy to say.'

Bob took another teaspoonful of sugar. 'What was it

that you were remembering, Jannie?' he asked.

'Oh, a bleak time. A lot of things you remember like that are moments of desolation. Sometimes I wonder if one really knew they were so desolate at the time.'

She watched Bob as he took another spoonful of sugar. He followed her gaze, saw what he was doing, and quickly pushed the sugar jar away.

'Sorry,' he said. 'I didn't realize I was doing it.'

'You'll get fat, Bob.'

'I've got fat.'

She rested her chin in her cupped hand. 'Do you get on with women better than men, Bob?' she asked.

'I get on fairly well with everyone, to tell you the truth.'

She examined him curiously. He was definitely plump.

When he turned his head to look at her the flesh folded underneath the jawbone into the beginnings of a double chin. He was so different from John in every way that it was amazing to think the human race could contain them both. She thought of her husband shaving in the morning, in trousers and vest. Dark, gaunt – almost emaciated – leaning forwards anxiously towards the mirror as if afraid his reflection might suddenly vanish altogether.

'What's Tessa like?' she asked.

'Oh, you know . . .' said Bob, a little uneasily.

'Dark or fair?'

'Dark.'

'What colour eyes?'

Bob frowned. 'I think they're brown,' he said, playing with the pepper-mill again.

'And she's attractive?'

'Oh, yes.'

'How old is she?'

'Oh, about twenty.'

Jannie felt she wanted to laugh. 'Why haven't we seen her here?' she asked.

'She hasn't been up to London yet. She's at a kind of college of citizenship in Bath.'

'You go down there?'

'Well, they're a bit tough about letting them out. It's a sort of finishing school, really.'

She couldn't prevent herself from bursting out laughing. 'Bob, Bob, Bob!' she said.

'What?'

'You. Carrying on with someone at a finishing school.'

'I know.'

John came into the kitchen, holding three half-full sherry glasses. 'I found a drop in a bottle at the back of the knitting cupboard,' he said. 'What are you two up to out here?'

'Oh, flirting,' said Bob, with a sigh.

'Charming,' said John.

'Got to earn my supper,' said Bob.

Bob and Jannie teased Dyson all the way through dinner, and he became more and more irritated.

'It's not just the money,' he said, stabbing at his beans and sending a scattering of them across the table. 'Though I may say that I shall be getting twenty-five guineas next Thursday for doing nothing but sit around in a television studio for half an hour, instead of beating my brains out all week-end to write a script for the BBC Overseas Service and getting ten guineas for it.'

'I thought you told me you'd be getting a hundred guineas a time if you were a television personality, John?' said Bob.

'So I shall, Bob,' said Dyson irritably, 'if I make a success of this and begin to make a name for myself. And that's the real point. It's not just the money.'

'Though you don't despise the money,' said Jannie.

'Though I don't despise the money, certainly.'

He stopped suddenly and took another mouthful of lamb.

'What is it, then?' said Jannie.

'Well,' said Dyson, chewing hard, 'I must admit that I

should like to make a name for myself, just for its own sake.'

'Oh, John!' said Jannie, laughing. Bob grinned silently.

'All right,' said Dyson. 'You may laugh if you like. But I'm thinking purely of the practical advantages.'

Bob and Jannie laughed again.

'Look, Jannie,' said Dyson seriously. 'Do you remember when we wanted to get Gawain into Almeira Road school, and we couldn't, because all the middle-class parents in s.w.23 were trying to get their kids into Almeira Road, and we live just over the zoning boundary? Well, do you honestly think the answer would have been the same if I'd been Norman Ward Westerman or Lord Boddy?'

'You mean you'd have been able to pull strings?' said Bob.

'*I* shouldn't have pulled strings – other people would have pulled them for me! "If we had Lord Boddy in the Parent-Teacher Association," they'd think, "we might have a little influence at County Hall." Or they'd realize that it might be rather agreeable to say to visiting parents, "That's Noel Westerman – you know, Norman Ward Westerman's son. He's a scamp – aren't you, Noel?" Pat-pat on Noel's well-connected head.'

Bob and Jannie gazed at him.

'Listen, if I wasn't just John Dyson, but The John Dyson, people wouldn't even waste their time asking me to do ten-guinea talks for the Overseas Service – they'd know I'd be fully occupied doing pieces for *Playboy* and *Esquire* at a thousand dollars a time, and going on television at a hundred guineas an appearance. It's a matter of purely practical economics.'

'You sound very impassioned, John,' said Bob.

'Well, I *am*, Bob. I *am* very impassioned. Look, I don't want to be so famous that I have to write autographs all over the place, and can't travel by bus in case I'm mobbed. Moderation in all things. But if I was The John Dyson, do you think crowded restaurants wouldn't be able to find a table for me? If I was The John Dyson, don't you think I'd have a better chance of getting theatre seats? I know you two think I'm a tit, going on like this. But I have a serious point here.'

'Eat up your meat, John,' said Jannie. 'You haven't put a mouthful in for the last ten minutes.'

'I have a serious point,' said Dyson, 'and that is that nowadays it's not excellence which leads to celebrity, but celebrity which leads to excellence. One makes one's reputation, and one's reputation enables one to achieve the conditions in which one can do good work.'

'You do talk a lot of shit sometimes, John,' said Bob mildly.

'It's not shit, Bob! Look, take me. Let's be honest with ourselves; I'm a small but vital link in the business of producing one of the most important daily newspapers in the world. But shouldn't I do better work if I weren't driven from pillar to post to supplement my salary? Well, *shouldn't I?*'

'John, love,' said Jannie, 'do eat up. The rest of us have finished.'

'Or take you, Bob,' said Dyson. 'You're a writer.'

'*I'm* a writer?' said Bob

'I didn't know you were a writer, Bob,' said Jannie.

'Bob is a *marvellous* writer!' said Dyson, his voice almost breaking with emotion at his own generosity. 'Perhaps a *great* writer.'

'But I haven't written anything,' said Bob uneasily. 'Have I?'

'Exactly! *Exactly!*' Dyson leaned forward in great excitement. 'And why haven't you written anything? Because you're slaving away in that little office all day doing stupid, piddling little jobs for me! That's why!'

'Oh, I shouldn't say that.'

'I drive you hard, Bob. I realize that. I make you work like a dog. He writes like an angel, Jannie! And I make him work like a dog! I drive you hard because I drive myself hard, Bob.'

'Really, John, you're very reasonable . . .'

'No, no, I'm a slavedriver and I know it. But don't think I don't understand what it costs, because I do. I know you both think I'm an egotistical shit, going on about wanting to be

61

famous. But it's not just for myself. I want *Bob* to become well known, too, so that he can liberate himself from *me*.'

'What about me?' asked Jannie. 'Do you want me to become famous and liberate myself from you?'

Dyson put down his knife and fork, frowning, his exaltation all turned to dust. 'All right, pick holes,' he said sulkily. 'All right, I haven't got my ideas completely worked out and watertight. I know that.'

He pushed his plate away.

'Aren't you going to have any more?' asked Jannie.

'It's too rich for me – it always gives me indigestion. I don't know why you keep serving it.'

Jannie cleared the plates away, catching Bob's eye for a moment and pushing her bottom lip up in mock guilt. Bob looked quickly away, trying not to smile. Dyson sat pouting and rubbing his hands together, glaring down at various parts of the table.

'Shall we take our puddings into the next room and watch television?' suggested Jannie.

'Why don't we?' said Bob.

'Load of shit,' said Dyson.

'There might be a discussion about the colour problem,' said Jannie

'Oh, very sarcastic.'

'It's the old movie tonight,' said Bob.

'Oh, go and switch it on then, Bob!' said Jannie.

'Condescending lowbrows,' said Dyson sourly. 'High-brow lowbrows. No – not even genuine highbrow lowbrows. Middlebrow highbrow lowbrows.'

The old movie sent Dyson to sleep. Bob looked round to say something to him, and there he was, in the flickering bluish light from the screen, with his head back and his mouth open.

'We shouldn't have insisted,' said Bob.

'No, he must have been enjoying it,' said Jannie. 'He always goes to sleep when he's enjoying something. Open another bottle of beer, Bob.'

'Will you have some?'

Jannie was absorbed in the film again.

'I'll have a sip,' she said eventually. 'What's the name of the girl who's playing the reporter? I don't mean Myrna Loy, do I?'

'No, no,' said Bob, pouring the beer. 'I know who it is. I'll think of her name in a minute.'

He settled back in his armchair with his beer, full of mutton and beans and well-being. He felt as though there were a space for him in the universe, and he exactly filled it.

'I don't mean Carole Lombard, do I?' said Jannie.

'No, no. The name's on the tip of my tongue.'

White telephones were brought to night-club tables. Stars were surrounded by reporters as they emerged from stage doors. Tycoons snarled. Eyes sparkled mistily. There were skyscrapers and luxury suites.

Life was suspended . . .

Once Damian cried out in his sleep, and fell silent again. Once Dyson snorted, and Jannie leaned over and stroked his hair. 'It's not Jean Arthur, is it?' she said.

'No. I think the brother's the bloke who was in *The Philadelphia Story*.'

'Was that the one with Katharine Hepburn?'

'No – the one with Katharine Hepburn was the one with Cary Grant.'

From somewhere outside at one point there came a distant rumble and chinking, like old milk bottles clashing together.

'Is that the rubbish coming over the wall?' asked Bob.

'I suppose so.'

'Shouldn't we wake John up and tell him?'

'He'll find out soon enough.'

Bob opened another bottle of beer.

'Poor John,' said Jannie.

* * *

Dyson drove Bob home in the old Standard Vanguard, through the dank, dead streets of the inner suburbs, yellow under the sodium lights. Bob felt comforted by their calm and familiar variety. Yellow high streets, with yellow electrical shops, and in the windows of the multiple tailors blank-faced dummies leaning discreetly forward in eggily dark worsted. Yellow Victorian mansions, with their front gardens asphalted over to make yellow parking areas for the flatholders' yellow cars. Now it was mercury vapour country. Bluish second-hand car lots; sagging bluish fences; bluish Unitarian churches; small bluish factories, some Odeon-fronted, some glassed and rectilinear, but set at odd bluish angles to their surroundings. Now they were back among the sodium, passing yellow pre-war flats – Keeps, Courts, and Mansionses, with yellow gables and yellow weatherboarding.

There were few people about, but many cars. As soon as they got within range of Dyson everyone seemed to drive badly. They overtook him when he wasn't expecting it; they pulled up at the side of the road and trapped him behind them; they got in front of him at traffic-lights and then decided to turn right. 'Oh, for God's *sake!*' snarled Dyson, snatching at the wheel, thumping the accelerator up and down uncertainly. He sat forward tensely in his seat, as if he found it difficult to see the road, and frequently wiped at the windscreen with his handkerchief. At one point something heavy fell off or out of the dashboard on to Bob's foot and rolled away beneath the seat with a metallic ring. Dyson peered down into the darkness after it, driving the car steadily out across the white line in the middle of the road.

'Don't worry about that, Bob,' he said. 'That's always coming off. Incidentally, Bob, those brown patches on the wings aren't rust, you know.'

'Which brown patches, John?'

'I thought I saw you looking at them before we started. They look like rust – it fooled me at first. But it's rather interesting – it's brown undercoat. It's quite remarkable when you come to think about it. The car's fifteen years old, it stands out in all weathers, and the undercoat's still intact.'

'Remarkable.'

'Of course, it's not just the paintwork. Everything was built to a slightly higher specification then. They hadn't learned to cut quite so many corners. It's worth remembering, Bob, if you ever buy a car.'

Dyson swung left into a main road, looking over his shoulder to watch out for traffic from the right, and drove over the edge of the kerb. The thump of the back wheel coming back into the gutter brought Bob's window down.

'Jam it with that wedge of paper,' said Dyson. 'I suppose some damned fool left a brick lying in the gutter.'

In the middle of a yellow common the engine died, and the car rolled jerkily to a halt.

'That's funny,' said Dyson. He pressed the starter. He pressed it again. He went on pressing it until the starter-engine ground to a halt. Then they sat in silence for some moments.

'George God strikes again,' said Bob.

In a sudden access of enraged energy, Dyson jumped out of the car, slammed the door violently behind him, and wrenched the bonnet open. Bob followed him apprehensively. Dyson was glaring into the hot, oily darkness of the engine as if he were about to smash it to pieces with his bare hands.

'Perhaps it was that bump we went over,' said Bob hesitantly.

Dyson straightened up and transferred his glare to Bob. 'Do you know anything at all about cars?' he asked curtly.

'No, John.'

'Then be a good fellow, will you, and try not to make imbecile remarks.'

Dyson bent over the engine again.

'If you want to know,' he said, 'it's probably the points. Or something to do with the plugs.'

He put his hand into the engine, touched something hot, and sprang back a pace.

'*Christ!*' he hissed, sucking his knuckles.

'John,' said Bob, 'may I ask a very naïve question? Are you sure it hasn't just run out of petrol?'

'Oh, shut up, Bob,' said Dyson, peering into the engine and trying to see what it was he had touched.

'But would it perhaps just be worth looking at the petrol gauge?'

Dyson straightened up slowly. 'Look, Bob,' he said. 'I'm extremely tired. I'm extremely angry. I'm extremely likely to hit you. Every single thing without exception has gone wrong today. It's been the most awful day of my life. And now you pester me with idiot suggestions about something you know nothing whatsoever about.'

He plunged back into his contemplation of the engine. Bob did not like to remind him that up till then it had been an awfully good day for him, on which every single thing without exception had gone right.

He crept inconspicuously back to the dashboard, switched on the ignition, and looked at the gauge.

'The gauge doesn't work,' snapped Dyson. 'I know precisely how much petrol I've got because I know precisely how much I've put in and precisely how many miles I've been. I put in two gallons on Saturday, and I can tell you for a fact there's at least quarter of a gallon left. I hope that satisfies you.'

When Dyson was hidden beneath the bonnet again Bob tiptoed round to the boot and eased it open. Beneath a heap of old rags and newspapers and raincoats he found an empty petrol can. He put it under his overcoat, gently closed the boot, and tiptoed away along the yellow pavement in search of a yellow garage.

'I'm not waiting for you,' shouted Dyson when he was about fifty yards away. 'As soon as I've got the car going I'm off.'

Dyson undressed quietly in the dark, so as not to wake Jannie, sighing loudly in the hope that it would. As he got into bed she rolled over towards him and put her arms round him.

66

'What time is it?' she asked sleepily.

'Half-past one,' said Dyson. 'I ran out of petrol.'

She ran her hand down over his chest and stomach, and seized him softly and irresistibly by the roots.

'No, Jannie,' he said, 'No, really . . . No, honestly, I'm terribly tired . . . No, honestly, Jannie, I shall be absolutely deadbeat tomorrow as it is . . . Now, Jannie! . . . *Jannie*! . . . Well, look, Jannie . . . Well, I suppose . . . Just . . . Oh, well . . .'

5

Dyson made thorough preparations for his television appearance. All week-end he drove about the outer suburbs with Jannie and the boys, calling on relatives and letting fall the news in the course of conversation.

'The poor old souls like to know what one's doing,' he explained to Jannie, as they jerked along in the traffic stream between aunt and aunt.

At the office during the week he found circumstances made it necessary for him to ring most of his influential friends and acquaintances – Sims, the paper's tame lawyer; Sir William Paice; Brent-Williamson, the Literary Editor; Huysmanns at the French Embassy. 'I hope you'll be watching the box on Thursday night,' he said to each of them in a humorous voice. 'What? Well, *I'm* going to be on . . . Yes! Isn't it preposterous? Ten-forty-five on the commercial – some ghastly programme called *The Human Angle*.'

Bob's gaze disconcerted him. He would turn his back on him while he was talking, or look down smiling into the mouthpiece.

'It's naughty of me, I know,' he would say as he put the phone down. Or: 'I'm sorry, Bob. I'm behaving outrageously.'

And he would dial another number.

He also gave some serious thought to how he should look. Should he lean forward passionately and denounce things? Or should he sit back in his chair and smile calmly at the idiocies of mankind? He rehearsed a calm smile in front of the mirror at home; it looked like an apologetic grin. He tried an expression of passionate commitment; it came out

68

indistinguishable from defensive surliness. Either way, his finger-tips became moist with sweat at the thought of producing the expression in front of the television cameras.

There was also the question of what he was going to say. He began to note down suitable thoughts and epigrams on pieces of office copy-paper, not really with the intention of learning them off by heart, but with the idea that he might put them in his jacket pocket and touch them from time to time during the programme to give himself reassurance, knowing that if the worst really came to the worst he could take them out and refresh his memory.

'T prob of t multi-racial soc,' he wrote, 'is in ess merely t mod versn of t time-hon prob of unitg tribes in nationhd.'

The real problem was to avoid the obvious. He was not being paid twenty-five guineas to tell people what they could manage to think out themselves for nothing.

'T troub is,' he tried, 'tt we aren't prej *enough*! Shd educ ourselves to be dply & bttrly prej – agnst prej!'

He tried it over uneasily in front of the mirror. If one of his deans or canons had written it in a Meditation he would have read it out to Bob in a mock clerical voice, and deleted it, snarling. However, this was a television programme, not a newspaper article. Different criteria applied.

The trouble was that they would all agree with each other. They would all sit round deploring racial prejudice and suggesting how to avoid it. Perhaps he should try to play the devil's advocate? He noted down one or two cautiously controversial points. 'Mst try to undrstnd att of man whse hse val falls. – Ind ckng delightfl but hly fragrnt. – Mst admt I pers h diff in undrstndg next-dr neighbr's Eng.'

He would keep the liberal thoughts in his left-hand pocket, he decided, and the provocative ones in his right-hand pocket. Then he would be able to put his hand immediately on what-ever he required. And jokes, of course – he'd need jokes. He could keep a list of jokes in his inside breast pocket. The idea of race opened up a few humorous possibilities. Something about the three-legged race, perhaps, or the egg-and-spoon race? Bn estab by scientists tt all races are of eql intell, except prhps egg-&-spn race. Something along those lines. Professionalism, that was what counted – thorough, serious preparation for even the most informal and evanescent of undertakings.

Whenever Dyson's phone rang that week it was the television company. Could he give them a few facts about himself for the company's press release? They hoped that he would be able to join the other participants for dinner at the studios beforehand. A car would be sent for him at seven-thirty. The final members of the team had now been settled – Miss Ruth Drax, a social worker, and Mr. Lewis Williamson, a barrister from Trinidad. The car would be coming at eight. A list of likely topics of discussion was on its way to him by post. The car would now be calling for him at seven.

Every time the phone rang Dyson's fingers became moist with sweat. So did Bob's. Every time Dyson looked at himself in the kitchen mirror, trying to imagine it was a television screen, his stomach and Jannie's stomach turned over in unison. Jannie was beginning to doubt whether she actually would be able to bring herself to watch the programme.

'Would you like to go round and hold Jannie's hand on Thursday night, Bob?' said Dyson at the office one morning. 'I'd be awfully obliged if you would. She's in a terrible state about the whole thing, poor poppet.'

'I'm in rather a state about it myself, John,' said Bob.

'You can hold each other's hand, then. I'm in a frightful state about it, too, and there's no one to hold my hand. It's funny – I never get in a state about doing radio programmes. Do you, Bob?'

'I don't do radio programmes, John.'

'Of course you don't. I get a few qualms just before the green light comes on. Nothing to worry about, though. But I must admit, when I think about Thursday night I feel absolutely sick with nerves. Do you do any television, Bob? I can't remember.'

'You know I don't, John.'

'You're very sensible, Bob. Take my advice – stick to good old steam radio.'

Bob had troubles enough of his own.

'Bob my darling,' wrote Tessa. 'What a strange letter you wrote me! I know it's very stupid of me, but I couldn't understand what it was supposed to be about at all. Did John Dyson really have a fight with a man called Cox, or did you make all that up? It was all like something you read in a book. My private idea, which I hardly dare mention in case I've got it all wrong, is that you were copying the style of some book or other to see if I would recognize it. Darling Bob, don't be cross if I haven't got it right, but is it one of your beloved American writers? Is it supposed to be someone like John dos Passos or James Joyce?'

And Mrs. Mounce was crowding him closer and closer. She had got a key to his room out of Dotty, as she had threatened. She came and went while he was out, tidying up, laying the table for his evening meal, and no doubt reading his letters and looking in his drawers to see if he had a rupture belt or kept a stock of contraceptives. She left dishes she had cooked for him, with notes underneath them. 'Have a good nosh darling,' said the notes, or: 'Sorry Bob I broke the milk jug, I will get you another.' 'Have borrowed one of your Frank Chacksfield records, promise faithfully not to scratch it.' And, under not a dish but his pillow, folded into his pyjamas: 'How's the bite Bob, sorry but you did ask for it sweetie.'

Bob stayed away from home every evening, pursuing old Hitchcock films he had seen before to art cinemas in Kilburn, Tooting, and Putney, and eating cheaply in Indian and Cypriot restaurants. But she usually heard him creep in, however late it was, and came scratching on the door just as he had got his trousers off, or just as he was scraping her uneaten steak-and-kidney pie into a polythene bag to throw away at the office next day. It embarrassed him to receive her in his dressing-gown. It embarrassed him still more when she arrived dressed

71

for bed herself as well, a complex bundle of diaphanous night-wear from the midst of which her poised cigarette arm stuck out oddly, like an awkward projection emerging from some ill-wrapped Christmas parcel.

'I hope you're not shy, darling,' she said, kicking off her high-heeled slippers and snuggling sensuously down into his armchair. 'You've caught me in my frillies.'

'I'm sorry,' said Bob.

'Still, I'm sure you've seen girls in their frillies before. Haven't you, Bob?'

Bob made some small, noncommittal noise.

Mrs. Mounce blew out cigarette smoke provocatively, narrowing her eyes against its sting. '*And* without, I bet, sweety pie. Oh, you don't have to tell me. I know you're not one of these lily-white mother's boys. I can tell a real man when I see one, believe me. I could tell you a thing or two, darling, I really could. I may look like a demure little wife who sits at home minding the house, but darling, I could tell you one or two things that would make your ears stand up on end.'

She was going to get him finally, he could see that. She was going to edge him into a situation where it would be openly discourteous to refuse her, and nothing in his education or his upbringing had prepared him to be discourteous to anyone, least of all a woman. He felt a terrible queasy emptiness in his stomach at the thought; it was as bad as the prospect of Dyson's going on television. Worse, Mr. Mounce had begun to look at him oddly. Or so it seemed to him. When he met him in the office, or on the stairs, his habitually offensive glance seemed to have a new dimension of thoughtfulness. One Saturday morning Bob came face to face with him as he emerged from the communal bathroom on the first half-landing. 'I want to have a little chat with you sometime, Bob,' he said. Bob was numbed with fear. To be actually accused point blank by an outraged husband! He had never dreamed that it would happen to him.

He went out immediately, and stayed out for the rest of the

week-end. He had an idea that he would find himself another flat, and he actually called at a number of agencies in the Bayswater area and asked for their lists. The prices were unbelievable. Small bachelor flats were offered at £500, £650, £1,000 a year; plus £1,600 – £2,000 – £2,500 for furniture and fittings. Where did the people who could pay such prices come from? What jobs could they possibly have? How could there be so many of them? Some advertisements asked for only 'a reasonable figure to cover F & F.' But how much was that? He could offer them – what? – not more than fifty or sixty pounds altogether. Was that a reasonable figure? He didn't have the nerve to ask.

He gave up flat-hunting and went to the cinema. After the cinema he had tea, walked the streets for an hour, had a couple of Guinesses in a pub to keep out the sharp evening air, and ate a biriani. Then he went to a party. There was a party almost every Saturday night given by someone in his circle of friends. It was that sort of set. A motheaten sort of set, as he frankly recognized – indeed, as they all frankly recognized – left over from Cambridge, and out-grown and abandoned by all its more enterprising members. The remaining half-dozen or so clasped the last tattered shreds of the undergraduate life around them to keep out the cold winds of the world. The party that night was like all their parties. Old Dave Meadows put old Brubeck records on the gramophone. Old Mike Ramsden got out his guitar and sang old Tom Lehrer songs. Old Ian Strachan locked himself in the bedroom with old Caroline Pickthorn, and old Peter Staithes pissed out of the window and threw empty bottles down into the basement area. On Monday morning they would all disappear into the Shell Centre and Unilever House and various grim out-departments of the BBC, yawning rebelliously.

Bob sat up till three drinking red table wine from a bottle marked Red Table Wine, and talking to old Janet Moss about life and death and their relations with their respective parents. Then he dozed in an armchair for a few hours, until he was too cold and stiff to bear it any longer, when he got up and made tea for everyone, and discovered that there was nothing to eat for breakfast.

Sunday went by in a haze, long and grey and unreal. He sat over breakfast in a cafeteria for a long time, reading the Sunday papers. He walked round Kensington and Earl's Court and Chelsea until his feet were sore, met old Mike Ramsden and old Caroline Pickthorn for drinks, had lunch on his own in a spaghetti house, walked again. Afterwards, he remembered that Lots Road power station had smoked whitely into a grey sky, and that along the Embankment a cold wind had been whipping off the river, driving spread-eagled pages from an old newspaper before it and wrapping one of them round the legs of a tall, frail man in a tweed overcoat.

After tea he dozed through an old Peter Sellers film at the King's Road Classic, dined off a biriani, dozed through an old Tati film at the Baker Street Classic, and crept upstairs to his flat just in time to meet Mounce coming downstairs from his den.

'Ah,' said Mounce. 'The prodigal returns. I want to have a word with you, lad.'

'All right,' said Bob. He gave up. He had no fight left.

Mounce unlocked the flat which had been converted into a bar. He switched on the strip lights behind the bottles, and the electric fire, and poured out two large glasses of whisky. Bob perched on a bar stool, still wearing his overcoat. It was cold in the room, and the air smelt musty and unbreathed.

'The point is this, Bob,' said Mounce, leaning across the bar towards him and swilling the whisky round in his glass, 'I'm away a lot, as you know. I've got to be. I'm a married man – I've got responsibilities. You know what I mean, Bob?'

'Yes,' said Bob, remembering from his childhood just how much it hurt to be punched on the nose.

'The point being that while Dad's out earning the housekeeping, certain things could conceivably be occurring behind

74

his back. I'm not saying they do. But you know what I'm driving at?'

'Yes,' said Bob. Or perhaps Mounce would punch him in the eye. A flash of light – then darkness – the sight perhaps permanently damaged.

'I mean,' said Mounce, 'I'm not going to give you a lot of crap about being pure as the driven snow myself. I'm not saying that. All the same, there are limits. There are some stinking limits. I don't know whether you'd agree with me on that?'

'Oh, yes,' said Bob. 'Yes. Yes, indeed.'

Mounce swilled his whisky round moodily for some time, as if trying to think what to do next. If he just suddenly hits me without warning, thought Bob, I shall almost certainly go straight over backwards with my feet still caught up in the bar-stool, and split my skull open on the floor.

'Do you see much of Glenda while I'm away?' asked Mounce.

'No,' said Bob eagerly. 'Oh no. Scarcely at all.'

'You never drop in on her?'

'Never!'

'You never ask her in for a drink?'

'No!'

Mounce frowned. Oh God, thought Bob. It's all just about to happen.

'You are a rotten sod, Bob,' said Mounce.

'Honestly, Reg . . .' began Bob, trying to get one foot down on the floor behind him.

'No, you're a rotten sod, Bob.'

'I assure you, Reg . . .'

'You're a rotten, stinking sod. You might just ask her in once in a while. You know, hold her hand and cheer her up a bit. Keep her out of trouble. Do you see what I mean?'

Bob took a long draught of whisky, spilling some of it down his chin.

'I never thought of it that way,' he said.

Dyson had expected to find the television studios a blaze of activity in the middle of the evening viewing hours, and humbly anticipated that he would himself be treated as a completely unimportant part of the machine – jostled indifferently in the corridors by actors, musicians, and cameramen, sighed at offensively in the studio by the technicians and professionals. But when he stepped out of the Humber Snipe which had been sent to pick him up he found that the building was in darkness and apparently deserted. The only light he could see was in the lobby, and the only person in the lobby was an anxious girl with a clipboard who was waiting to greet him personally, and who seemed personally grateful for his skill in getting himself found and driven there by the company's chauffeur. She led him along deserted, echoing corridors; nothing was happening in the whole enormous building, he realized, but the tiny preparations for this one tiny programme. All the rest of the evening's television was pre-filmed, pretaped, or provided by other companies.

The preparations for *The Human Angle*, Dyson discovered, were going forward in a room on the first floor furnished with a sea-blue fitted carpet, a number of discreetly abstract paintings, and a walnut sideboard. A dozen or so well-bred men in dark suits – some of them, noted Dyson with interest, wearing Brigade ties – were standing about drinking gin and smiling agreeably at each other's jokes. A selection of them pressed forward upon Dyson deferentially, introducing themselves, fetching him drinks and salted peanuts. Like the girl with the clipboard, they seemed consumed with gratitude and admiration for his skill in getting there. 'You got here all right, then?' they asked anxiously. 'The driver found you all right? You found your way upstairs without any difficulty?'

The only person in the room Dyson recognized was de Sousa, the producer, and he seemed to be the least important of them all. There was a woman – presumably Miss Drax, the social worker, and a man with rather dark skin – clearly

Williamson, the Trinidadian barrister. Dyson never caught the names of any of the others, or found out what they did, apart from drinking the company's gin with a reassuring deftness. Dyson assumed they were the company's directors, bankers, and financial advisers; they all had an air of unassuming integrity and human dignity which in Dyson's experience was acquired only by daily contact with very large sums of other people's money. He liked them, he discovered. He liked their deference and he liked their gin, and within ten minutes he was explaining to them exactly how the daily supply of cross-words in a newspaper was maintained. They were fascinated. *'Really?'* they said. 'How extraordinarily interesting!' Dyson began to feel that everything was going to be all right. His pockets were full of remarks to make, and a bottle of bismuth in case he got nervous indigestion. He began to feel that he would not need either.

Lord Boddy arrived. He was a large, slow-moving man with bushy grey eyebrows and dandruff on his shoulders.

'I must tell you, Lord Boddy,' said Dyson deferentially, 'how very much I enjoyed that collection you did of your father's papers. Of course, I'm a great admirer of all your books.'

'Really?' said Lord Boddy, pushing up his eyebrows with no less deference in return. 'It's very good of you to say so. Most kind, most kind.'

Deference bred deference. Lord Boddy, grasping his gin-and-tonic in his right hand and talking about the greatness of Asquith, put his left hand in his trouser pocket. A moment later Dyson realized that all the men listening to Lord Boddy had their left hands in their trouser pockets, too. His own left hand, he discovered, was in his trouser pocket. He took it out hastily, lest Lord Boddy notice it and jump to the conclusion that Dyson was mimicking him, and transferred it to his jacket pocket. At once Lord Boddy did the same, and one by one, as they listened and nodded, everyone else followed suit. Embarrassed, now that he had noticed what was happening, Dyson removed his hand from his jacket pocket and slipped it inconspicuously behind his back. Boddy, describing very slowly and emphatically how Asquith had died just before he could meet him, put his own hand through the same manoeuvre, and one by one all the other spare left hands disappeared behind their owners' backs, too. Mutual deference could scarcely be carried farther.

And yet, when Norman Ward Westerman arrived, it was. Dyson could imagine Lord Boddy and the executives gathered around him putting deference aside from time to time in order to get on with the gardening, or to discipline some delinquent guardsman. But Norman Ward Westerman was deference made flesh. When he bent that famous craggy face and strong jaw down from its natural elevation to the level of ordinary human beings it was not to advance any opinions or tell any anecdotes of his own. It was purely to bring his ear reverentially into line with the mouth of whoever was speaking. 'Exactly,' he murmured. '*Exactly*.' And Dyson knew from the depth of humility and reverence in his inflection that he was getting a larger fee than even Lord Boddy. Dyson felt awed by him. He felt awed by Lord Boddy, for that matter, and by the company in general. He felt awed by himself. They were all gods, gathered in godly discourse.

They moved into the next room and sat down to dinner. White-jacketed waiters tiptoed reverently around them, pouring hock with the frozen scampi, a claret with a fruity, full-bodied label to go with the reheated roast lamb. 'Thank you,' murmured Dyson with heartfelt respect to a waiter at his elbow. 'Thank you, sir,' said the waiter. 'Thank you,' said Dyson.

'Or take Baldwin,' Norman Ward Westerman was saying to Lord Boddy. 'I find him . . . an enigmatic figure. Would you think that was a fair assessment, Frank?'

'Oh, indeed. Indeed, indeed, indeed. I think that's a very fair assessment of him. It's rather interesting you should mention Baldwin, as a matter of fact, because I never met him.'

'Didn't you? That's extraordinarily interesting.'

'No, I never met Baldwin.'

'You interest me, Frank, because I didn't know that at all.'

One of the financial figures was leaning deferentially across the table towards Williamson. 'You don't happen to know a man called Firmead, do you?' he said.

'Firmead?' said Williamson deferentially. 'Curiously enough I don't believe I do.'

'*David* Firmead, to be precise.'

'Curiously enough I don't believe I've ever met him.'

'He was in Trinidad for some time last year. Something to do with oil, I think.'

'*Really*? How very interesting.'

'I just thought you might have run across him. Awfully nice man. We were at school together.'

'Really? That is most interesting.'

'Married a terribly nice girl. Lives near Guildford.'

'How extraordinarily interesting.'

The financial figure turned his head slightly to include Miss Drax in the conversation. 'You don't know him, do you, by any chance?' he asked. 'A man called Firmead, David Firmead?'

'As a matter of fact,' said Miss Drax, 'I don't think I can honestly say I do.'

'Awfully nice man,' said the financial figure.

Dyson felt he had grasped enough of the general principles of the conversation between Boddy and Westerman to risk joining in himself.

'I find *Halifax* a curiously intriguing figure,' he said when there was a pause. 'I don't know whether you'd agree?'

Westerman swung round in his chair to give Dyson his full attention.

'I think that is an awfully good point,' he said. 'Halifax is a figure who intrigues me, too. Do you find Halifax at all intriguing, Frank? Or do you feel that there's nothing really interesting about him?'

'No, I think as Mr. Dyson says, Halifax is an extraordinarily intriguing figure. Most *extraordinarily* intriguing. But do you know, Norman, in all the years that Halifax held office I never met him once.'

'*Really*?' said Westerman. 'That is absolutely fascinating.'

'Not once.'

'That is most incredibly interesting,' said Dyson.

The meal went by like a dream. Dyson felt as though that small room, surrounded by the dark emptiness of the studios, was the one speck of warmth and life in an unpeopled universe. Of course, there were other subsidiary settlements if one stopped to think. Somewhere in the building was a room where a hired chef was unfreezing the scampi, reheating the meat, and opening the giant economy can of fruit salad. Somewhere there was a studio with five black leather armchairs waiting. But the real richness of life was concentrated here – brilliant conversation, warm mutual esteem, a man who had not known Baldwin or Halifax, and good claret warmed by discreet waiters on some radiator well out of sight. This, realized Dyson with a sense of homecoming, was where he belonged; this was the way of life for which his character and education had fitted him.

'Norman,' said de Sousa as the coffee and brandy were being poured, 'I wonder if we ought perhaps to have just a tiny natter about the programme.'

'I think that would be an awfully good idea, Jack,' said Westerman. He took some cyclostyled papers out of his pocket and looked at them. 'Well, as I understand it, Jack – tell me if I'm wrong – we open with the credits on telecine. Right?'

'Right,' said de Sousa, lighting a small cigar.

'Then we come up on me in the studio. I say, "Good evening. The film you're about to see is the record of a remarkable experiment in blah blah blah . . ." '

'All on Autocue.'

'All on Autocue. Then we have the film. Then we come back to me in the studio and I say, "The film you have just seen was an attempt to blah blah blah. Now we have here in the studio tonight four people who are vitally and personally concerned with the problems of living in a multiracial community. On my right is Lord Boddy, who was a member of the Royal Commission on blah blah blah . . ." '

'And you go right round the table.'

'And I go right round the table. Then I'll turn to you, Frank, and say, "Lord Boddy, what do you think of the experiment we have just seen? Do you think it holds out a ray of hope among the problems which perplex us all so sorely today?" '

'I say blah blah blah,' said Lord Boddy.

'You say blah blah blah. Then we all join in blah blah blah. Then when I get the sign from the studio manager I wind up and say, "Well, then, the conclusions we seem to have reached tonight are blah blah blah." '

'All on Autocue,' said de Sousa.

'All on Autocue. I think that's all fairly well tied up, isn't it, Jack?'

'I think so. Is everybody happy?'

'Indeed, indeed, indeed,' said Dyson. 'I don't think I've ever enjoyed myself so much in my life.'

They trooped down to the studio for the line-up, taking their glasses of brandy with them. A little of the festive warmth seemed to die out of the air as they took their places around the low coffee table in the corner of the great hangar. Williamson kept clearing his throat. Miss Drax smiled unhappily about her. Even Boddy, who had been telling Westerman as they came down the stairs how he had been at Bad Godesberg in 1938 just two days after Hitler and Chamberlain had left, trailed away into silence. Only Dyson lost none of his elation. When the studio manager asked him to say something to check the microphone levels, he recited the first few lines of *The Wreck of the Deutschland* with appropriate gestures. It seemed to amuse the studio crew. Really, he thought, this was his evening.

By the time they had been to make-up, and tramped back

up the stairs to have another drink, a definite uneasiness was beginning to settle over the whole company. The men with the Brigade ties and their friends were running out of potential mutual acquaintances to describe. Miss Drax seemed to have caught the frog Williamson had had in his throat. Williamson, coming back from his second trip to the lavatory, passed Boddy on the way out for his third. Westerman, shuffling the cyclostyled papers about in his hands, dropped his glass and filled his shoes with brandy. Dyson watched them all with amazement. He himself was greatly excited, but not nervous in the least.

'The public just don't realize,' said Williamson to him gloomily, 'the terrific amount of work that goes into making one short half-hour of television.'

'Work?' said Dyson. 'It's pure pleasure. I've never enjoyed anything so much in all my life. I'm absolutely bubbling over. I simply can't wait to get on.'

'Good God,' said Williamson.

One of the financial figures, still smiling deferentially, poured them both more brandy. 'I wonder if you could try and keep the bottle away from Lord Boddy,' he said quietly. 'I think perhaps he's had almost enough.'

How interesting it was, thought Dyson, how extraordinarily intriguing, to find that out of the whole team the only one who was actually turning up trumps was himself.

'I think perhaps we might go down now,' said de Sousa.

'I shan't be able to watch,' said Jannie, as the film sequence in the first half of John's programme unreeled meaninglessly in front of her. 'Honestly, Bob, I shan't be able to watch. I know something awful will happen. Oh Bob, supposing he's had too much to drink?'

'He'll be fine, Jannie,' said Bob. 'Stop fussing.'

Jannie gripped the arms of her chair, trying to stop herself jumping out of it. 'What on earth's this stuff they're showing us now?' she demanded irritably.

'It's the film they're going to discuss.'

'Oh God, I know he's going to make a fool of himself. I know it, I know it, I know it!'

When the film ended, and the face of the chairman appeared again, she put her hand over her eyes, unable to watch the screen. The chairman was introducing Lord Boddy. She had a vision of John sitting hunched up in his chair, as he did at home sometimes when things were going wrong, all dark and gaunt and unhappy. Oh, poor John! Poor John! But where was he? The chairman had been introducing people for an eternity, and still no sign of him. Perhaps he was ill. She imagined him standing in some white-tiled institutional lavatory, suffering from nervous nausea. Had he taken the bismuth with him? But better for him to be in a lavatory somewhere than for him to be sick on the programme! Please God he wouldn't be sick on the programme! Of course, they would turn the cameras . . .

'And on her left,' said the chairman, 'is Mr. John Dyson, a journalist and broadcaster who lives . . .'

And there he was! Involuntarily she reached out and gripped Bob's hand. And what in the name of God was John up to? He was smiling and waving!

'What's he doing?' she cried, agonized, as the picture cut back to the chairman. 'It's not that sort of programme!'

'I don't know whether you noticed,' said Bob, 'but he was smoking.'

'Smoking?'

'Didn't you see? He had a cigarette between his fingers.'

'Don't be crazy, Bob. John hasn't smoked since he was an undergraduate.'

'Well, he's smoking now, Jannie.'

'Oh God!' said Jannie, holding Bob's hand very tight. 'I shan't be able to watch, Bob!'

'You're all right now, Jan. Lord Boddy's set for the night.'

But someone was saying something at the same time as Lord Boddy, making him falter and finally stop in midstride. The cameras hunted round the team, trying to locate the intruder.

They were all smoking, observed Jannie, but John, as she saw when the camera finally settled on him, was smoking more than most. He was smoking and talking simultaneously, taking little melodramatic puffs between phrases.

'If I might butt in here,' he was saying (puff). 'If I might possibly butt in a moment . . . (Puff, puff) I should just like to say that I find what Lord Boddy is saying extraordinarily interesting. *Extraordinarily* interesting.'

He took another energetic puff, and blew out a dense cloud of smoke at the camera as Lord Boddy resumed his discourse.

'Oh God,' said Jannie.

'Sh!' said Bob.

Dyson was back in the conversation again. 'That is fascinating,' he was saying. 'Most fascinating. I find that absolutely fascinating.'

Jannie squeezed Bob's hand so hard that he flinched. 'Poor John!' she said.

When Miss Drax's turn to speak came, Dyson was fascinated by her thesis, too. 'Indeed!' he kept murmuring. 'Indeed, indeed!'

'Why is he behaving like this?' cried Jannie. 'Why is he smoking, and waving his arms about in that awful way?'

'He waves his arms about at the office sometimes,' said Bob. 'I don't object to that.'

'But why does he keep saying things like "extraordinarily interesting" and "indeed, indeed"? I've never heard him say anything like that before.'

'I've never heard him say "indeed, indeed," I must admit.'

Williamson was talking. Dyson turned out to be extraordinarily interested in his views, as well. 'Indeed,' he murmured. 'Indeed . . . indeed . . . Oh God, indeed!'

Jannie sank down into her chair, trying to work out who would be watching the programme. All John's family, of course. All *her* family. Her parents had invited the neighbours in to see it, too. Her friend Belinda Charles – she'd rung up to say she'd seen John's name in an article about the programme in the paper. Out of nowhere the idea came to her that Lionel Marcus might be watching. Please God, not Lionel Marcus!

'John Dyson,' the chairman was saying, 'do you, as a journalist, agree with the suggestion that what we need is for the press to take a firm moral lead and play down all news to do with race relations?'

Dyson did not answer at once. He frowned, then leaned forward and stubbed out his cigarette thoughtfully in the ash-tray.

'He's got a sense of timing, anyway,' said Bob.

'I can't bear it,' said Jannie.

Dyson sat back and put his finger-tips together, as if about to deliver his verdict. But at the last moment he changed his mind, and instead leaned forward again and took another cigarette out of the box on the table.

'Oh God, Bob!' said Jannie.

Dyson picked up the table-lighter, and with an absolutely steady hand lit the cigarette. Then he snapped the top of the lighter down, drew in a mouthful of smoke, and let it out again slowly and meditatively.

'I think it's an extraordinarily interesting idea,' he said.

Jannie put her spare hand over her eyes as if shielding them from the sun, and closed out the sight of her husband.

'You're exaggerating, Jannie,' said Bob.

Later he said: 'People who don't know him wouldn't get the same impression at all.'

Later still he said: 'Honestly, Jannie, nobody watches this sort of programme apart from the relatives of the performers.'

It seemed to Jannie that the noise of John blowing cigarette smoke out almost drowned the conversation. She kept her hand over her eyes until at last Westerman halted the dis-cussion and summed up. He paused before saying good night, and a voice from off-screen cut in at once.

'That is absolutely fascinating, Norman,' it said.

Jannie put her head on Bob's shoulder and wept.

* * *

Dyson walked up and down the bedroom in his overcoat, making large gestures, and trailing in his wake the cosy smell of digested alcohol. Jannie lay in bed, looking at him over the edge of the covers. It was after midnight.

'Honestly, Jannie,' said Dyson excitedly, 'I astonished myself! I simply didn't know I had it in me! How did it look?'

'Very good, John.'

'Really? You're not just saying that?'

'No, John.'

'I actually *enjoyed* it, Jannie, that was the thing. I was amazed! The others were all shaking with nerves! Even hardened television performers like Norman and Frank. But honestly, I could have gone on all night. I didn't use my notes at all.'

'I thought you didn't.'

'Didn't touch them – didn't even think about them. I was absolutely in my element! How did I come over, Jannie?'

'I told you – very well.'

'I didn't cut in and argue too much?'

'I don't think so.'

'I thought perhaps I was overdoing the controversy a bit?'

'No, no.'

Dyson stopped and gazed at Jannie seriously. 'I feel I've at last found what I really want to do in life, Jannie,' he said. 'It's so much more alive and vital than journalism. Honestly, Jannie, I'm so exhilarated!'

He began to stride up and down the room again, smiling at himself. He glanced in the mirror as he passed it and straightened his glasses.

'What did Bob think?' he asked. 'Did he think I was all right?'

'He thought you were fine.'

Dyson stopped again, smiling reflectively.

'Frank Boddy is an absolute poppet,' he said warmly. 'He really is. Oh, Jannie, I adore television! I can't tell you! You really think I looked all right?'

Later, as he was crawling about the floor in his under-clothes, looking under the bed for his slippers, Jannie asked, 'Why were you smoking, John?'

He straightened up and gazed anxiously over the end of the bed at her. 'You thought it looked odd?' he said.

'No, no.'

'You don't think it seemed rather mannered?'

'Of course not, John. I just wondered how you came to think of it.'

Dyson smiled with pleasure as he remembered. 'It was sheer inspiration on the spur of the moment,' he said. 'I just saw the box of cigarettes lying there on the table, and everybody else smoking, and I just knew inside me with absolute certainty that I should smoke, too. I think it absolutely *made* my performance.'

He fell asleep almost as soon as the light was out, and woke up again about an hour later, his mouth parching, his whole being troubled with a great sense of unease. What was occupying his mind, as vividly as if it were even now taking place, was the moment when he had said, 'That is absolutely fascinating, Norman,' and then realized it was supposed to be the end of the programme. Had he *really* done that? How terrible. How absolutely terrible.

He sat up and drank some water. Still, one little slip in an otherwise faultless performance . . . Then with great clarity and anguish he remembered the moment when Westerman had put his question about a moral lead from the press, and instead of answering at once the idea had come to him of leaning forward and judiciously stubbing out his cigarette. It had been scarcely a quarter smoked! He lay down in bed again slowly and unhappily.

All the same, when he had finished stubbing the cigarette out he had given a very shrewd and pertinent answer . . . No, he hadn't! He'd taken another cigarette! In absolute silence, in full view of the whole population of Britain, he had stubbed out a quarter-smoked cigarette and lit a fresh one!

He turned on to his right side, then he turned on to his left, wracked with the shamefulness of the memory. It was strange; everything he had done on the programme had seemed at the time to be imbued with an exact sense of logic and purposiveness, but now that he looked back on it, all the logical connections had disappeared, like secret writing when the special lamp is taken away.

And what about the time he had interrupted Lord Boddy, and then realized that all he had wanted to say was that it was interesting? *Extraordinarily* interesting . . . Had he *really* said that? He himself? The occupant of the tense body now lying obscurely and privately in the dark bedroom of a crumbling Victorian house in Spadina Road, s.w.23? Was that slightly pooped gentleman with the waving arms who had (oh God!) told Lord Boddy that his views were absolutely fascinating, and (oh God oh God!) lit another of the television company's cigarettes with their silver butane table-lighter every time he had seen the red light come up on the camera pointing at him – was that exuberantly shameful figure really identical with the anguished mortal man who now lay here stretched as taut as a piano-string in the dark?

'Jannie,' he groaned. 'Are you awake, Jannie?'

There was no reply. He turned on to his right side. He turned back on to his left. He hurled himself on to his face. Still, Westerman and Boddy and Williamson and Miss Drax sat around in conversation with him. He went through his whole performance second by second, from the moment Westerman had introduced him and he had *waved at the camera*, to the moment Westerman had summed up, and he had told him it was *absolutely fascinating*. He went through it again and again, trying to improve it slightly in his memory, in the face of an increasingly hostile reception from the other four. By the time morning came he was convinced he had been wide awake the whole night, though by that time he had remembered with the utmost clarity that the whole performance had taken place not in a television studio at all but in an enormous public lavatory, with Sir William and Lady Paice among the large crowd around the coffee table, and that his final humiliation was to discover at the end of the programme that he had been sitting on one of the lavatory seats throughout, with his trousers down around his ankles.

6

Raindrops trembled on the office windows, coalesced, and ran down, leaving paths like silver snail tracks against the lightness of the sky. Dyson watched them absently, grimacing as he bit each of the finger-nails on his right hand trim in turn. Bob sat sucking toffees, and watching Dyson from behind his hand. Old Eddy Moulton, who was awake and in an unusually forthcoming mood, looked at Dyson and Bob alternately as he talked.

'I knew Stanford Roberts,' he said. 'But then I knew most of them. Walter Belling, Stanley Furle, Sir Redvers Tilley – you name them, I knew them. Stanley Furle carried a cane with a solid gold knob – never went anywhere without it. The knob unscrewed and the inside of the cane was hollow. Stanley used to keep it filled with Scotch – three solid feet of Johnnie Walker. One night he was at the old Blackfriars Ring. At the end of every round off came the gold knob and up went the stick. He was with a man called Naylor – not Freddie Naylor of the *Mail*, but Allington Naylor, who later worked for A. W. Simpson on the *Morning Post*. A. W. Simpson was one of the great ones. So was Allington Naylor. So was Stanford Roberts, for that matter. Real journalists. Real professionals. Stanford could turn you out an impeccable paragraph on any subject you liked to name at the drop of a hat. He'd have done a par about the lead in his pencil if you'd asked him – a stick and a half – a column – whatever you needed; and all of it full of wit and erudition.'

Dyson went on staring at the raindrops, saying nothing.

'Honestly, John,' said Bob, 'you were great. I don't know what you're worrying about.'

Dyson gave no sign that he had heard.

'Anyway,' said old Eddy Moulton, 'when Stanley Furle came out of the Ring at the end of the evening, he fell down the stairs and blacked his eye on the knob of his cane! I was in the Kings and Keys the night J. D. Maconochie told Bentham Miller that O. M. Pargetter's Tibetan Terror story was a hoax. Oswald hadn't been nearer Tibet than the end of Folkestone pier! I was in the Feathers the night Sandy MacAllister punched Laurence Uden on the nose for saying that Stanford Roberts had been drunk at poor old Sidney Cunningham's funeral.'

'Come on, John,' said Bob. 'Cheer up.'

'In fact,' said old Eddy Moulton, 'Stanford *was* drunk at Sidney Cunningham's funeral. I met R. D. Case afterwards – he was on the *Westminster Gazette* at that time – and he told me that Stanford was so drunk that he'd almost fallen into the grave! Apparently he'd just been caught in time by George Watson-Forbes, who later wrote a remarkable series of articles in the *Daily News* on the Home Rule question.'

Dyson stirred himself, and sighed. 'Would somebody ring Morley, Bob,' he said, scarcely opening his mouth to let the words out, 'and ask him where his copy is? I can't face talking to him today.'

'Now don't be silly, John,' said Bob. 'Jannie and I both thought you were tremendously good.'

'The last job I went on with Sidney Cunningham,' said old Eddy Moulton, 'was an explosion in a gas-main at Newark, which killed thirteen people. I travelled up from King's Cross with Sidney, Daryl Bligh of the *Graphic*, K. B. D. Clarke of the *Times*, "Tibby" Tisdale of the *News*, Stanford Roberts, of course, and I think we had Norton Malley with us, who would at that time I suppose have been on the *Morning Post*, though he later went back to the *Irish Times*. Anyway, the day after we all arrived in Newark, Tibby announced that it was his birthday, and Stanford had the idea of hiring a private dining-room at the Ram . . .'

Dyson suddenly turned on old Eddy Moulton, silencing him with the sourness of his expression. 'You never went on a gas-main explosion in Newark, Eddy,' he said irritably. 'You're getting mixed up with one of your "In Years Gone By" columns.'

Old Eddy Moulton stared at Dyson, his mouth slightly open.

'You did a fifty-years-ago about a gas-main explosion in Newark the week before last,' said Dyson. 'Don't you remember?'

'I went to Newark on the story, too,' said old Eddy Moulton.

'You're getting mixed up, Eddy.'

'That was my own story I put in the column,' said old Eddy Moulton stubbornly.

'Oh, for God's sake, Eddy!' snapped Dyson. He jumped to his feet and walked quickly out of the room, slamming the door behind him. Old Eddy Moulton looked at Bob, who looked away.

'I was only trying to cheer him up,' said old Eddy Moulton. The rain had almost stopped, but various projections over the pavement in Fleet Street dripped on Dyson as he passed, wetting the lenses of his spectacles and making it difficult for him to see where he was going. He had decided to show himself to the crowd, and take the plunge into the humiliation that was awaiting him.

He walked with self-conscious haste up the south side of the street towards Temple Bar, staring into the face of everyone coming the opposite way, challenging them to give any sign of their pity and contempt. It was difficult to know whether they recognized him or not. Every time he removed his glasses to wipe the rain off them he could see that everyone was taking advantage of his short-sightedness to stare at him and grin and point. But as soon as he got his glasses back on again, they had all smoothed the hazy, unfocussed grins off their faces and seemed intent on their own affairs. Several times he swung round suddenly to see if people were turning to stare at him from behind. They seemed not to be, but it was difficult to be sure that they had not simply managed to turn away again in time. Outside the Lord's Day Observance Society he caught the eye of a tall girl with a red face, who looked quickly away. He jerked his own head away almost as fast, galvanized by the shock of embarrassment. That had been recognition, all right! That had been a pointed enough comment, by God! Or had she thought *he* was staring at *her*? He stopped, confused, by the bus stop opposite the Protestant Truth Society, and gazed unseeingly at the list of routes. Suddenly he realized that everyone in the queue was staring at him with frank interest and uninhibited hostility. This was it, then! They hated him! He had tried to rise above them, and had fallen back among them, there to be hated once for his attempt, and twice for his failure! He hurried away, his heart beating fast, shocked but obscurely satisfied by this revelation. He was across the road and halfway back down Fleet Street before it occurred to him that they had been staring at him like that because they thought he was trying to push in at the head of the queue.

He went into an espresso bar and drank some coffee. No one turned round to look at him. He was a failure, certainly. Failure, it occurred to him, was the secular equivalent of sin. Modern secular man was born into a world whose moral framework was composed not of laws and duties but of tests and comparisons. There were no absolute outside standards, so standards had to generate themselves from within, rela- tivistically. One's natural sense of inadequacy could be kept at bay only by pious acts of repeated successfulness. And failure was more terrifying than sin. Sin could be repented of by an act of volition; failure could not be disposed of so easily. Sin could be avoided by everyone, if he chose, but failure could not. For there to be any who succeeded, there had to be some who failed; there was no better without worse. The worse had their function. Without himself, thought Dyson, or at any rate the possibility of himself, Norman Ward Westerman would be unadmired, unloved, and unrewarded.

'Seen you somewhere before, haven't I, squire?' said a weary young man in a coffee-stained white jacket who was clearing the tables, without any great interest.

'Possibly,' said Dyson, feeling himself flushing at once with apprehension and pleasure.

The young man sank slowly into the seat opposite him, and got out a cigarette. 'Yes, I seen you somewhere all right,' he said. 'Not in here.'

'No, I haven't been in here before.'

'Where was it, then, captain? Up the Oasis, was it?'

'No, I don't think so.'

'Down the club, was it?'

Dyson discovered that he wanted the young man to know where it was more than he wanted him not to know. 'I do a certain amount of television,' he said offhandedly, with a slight disclaiming smile.

The young man went on staring at him; the idea that he had seen Dyson on television seemed to be too far-fetched even to penetrate his consciousness. 'No, I seen you somewhere, captain,' he said.

Dyson's slight disclaiming smile vanished. 'Yes,' he said rather irritably. 'On *television*.'

The young man rose slowly to his feet, and took Dyson's empty coffee-cup back to the counter. He gazed mournfully out of the window into Fleet Street for some minutes. 'Up the Streatham ice-rink, was it?' he suggested.

Not to have achieved recognition as a failure, felt Dyson, was almost worse than the failing itself. It made him feel that he had failed even at failing.

When Dyson got back to the office old Eddy Moulton had subsided into sleep again.

'Thank God,' muttered Dyson to Bob intensely. 'I don't think I could have stood any more of *that* this morning.'

94

He sat down and plunged himself into his work. The item uppermost on his desk was a note in his own handwriting which said: 'Straker hol – chck Daw 1st 2 pts Pellings chchiness.' What the hell was that supposed to mean? He looked up, frowning, and saw that Bob was gazing at him apprehensively.

'I've been walking up and down Fleet Street, if you want to know,' he said, 'to see whether I could still show my face in public. Did somebody get some copy out of Morley?'

'It's promised for tomorrow,' said Bob.

'I'm sick of Morley. He's not a real professional.'

'He's a canon, John.'

'He's a stupid little prick. I'm not going to use him any more. That's final.'

He scrabbled angrily among the papers and galleys on his desk until he found the copy pad, and wrote on it: 'Morley stpd lttle prck. Rmmbr n to use.'

Where had he been, when Bob had interrupted him? Oh, yes, looking at this note about Straker. 'Pelling's chchiness'? What in the name of God could that be? Well, he hadn't time to mess around unriddling Pelling's tomfooleries. He screwed the note up and threw it in the general direction of the wastepaper basket. Bob was still looking at him.

'How about a bite of lunch, John?' Bob asked anxiously.

'I don't want any bloody lunch,' said Dyson, thinking of the usual crowd standing round in the Gates. It didn't matter if you made a fool of yourself in front of strangers – he saw that now. It probably didn't matter much if you did it in front of your friends. The shameful thing was doing it in front of strangers, and being seen by your friends in the process.

He turned to the next item on his desk, a note on top of a copy-pad which said: 'Morley stpd lttle prck. Rmmbr n to use.' What drivel was this? He tore it off and threw it at the wastepaper basket. The next thing was a memorandum from Bill Waddy, the News Editor, which said: 'Your department's turn, I think.' Clipped to the back was a letter headed 'Magic Carpet

Travel Limited. Specialist consultants in all forms of travel management.'

'Dear Sir,' said the letter. 'Magic Carpet Travel announce with pride the opening of an entirely new sunshine holiday area – the Trucial Riviera. The exotic shores of Trucial Oman, washed by the warm sparkling waters of the Persian Gulf, and rich in all the Arabian Nights romance of the Middle East, offer something unique in holiday experience to the get-away-from-it-all holiday-maker . . .

'To celebrate this remarkable new breakthrough in British holiday technology, we are inviting the press to join us on a special round trip to Sharjah, the Pearl of the Trucial Riviera, next month . . .'

Whose turn was it for a facilities trip? Bob had had the Bulgarian State Non-Ferrous Metals Trust jamboree the previous month, and he'd had the Cosmosair inaugural to Saarbrucken himself. It was old Eddy's turn.

'Eddy,' he said, 'would you like a little jaunt to Trucial Oman? Eddy?'

No reply. Well, to hell with him. If he chose to be asleep when the lollipops were handed round, that was his lookout. Dyson couldn't be expected to wet-nurse his staff – he'd far too much on his hands already. In fact, he'd do the trip himself. He desperately needed a holiday. The Saarbrucken trip had been a disaster; it had rained continuously. In fact, it had just added to his burdens. He was ill with overwork. He really was. He was suffering from insomnia and hypertension. And now his tlvsn apprnce (his mind sheered off identifying it more fully even to himself) had finally set the seal on it all. His health was breaking down.

'I couldn't eat any lunch if you paid me,' he said.

'We could go to the Mucky Duck for a change,' said Bob.

Dyson sat hypertensely clenching and unclenching his fingers, trying to think of a headline with no more than ten characters for a piece about the dangers of the exaggeratedly indifferentist liturgical tendencies inherent in ecumenicalism.

He could remember a time when he had fallen asleep as soon as his head touched the pillow, and when he had always had a healthy appetite. By half-past twelve each day he had had a hunger pain. He had a pain in his stomach now, ironically enough, which felt almost exactly like a hunger pain. He knew what it was. It was the irritation of overstrained nerves. The stomach acid, with no food to work on, was quietly starting to digest and ulcerate the stomach lining.

'Perhaps I ought to try and eat something,' he said, 'to give the stomach acid something to work on.' He jumped up hypertensely.

'The Mucky Duck?' said Bob, getting to his feet too.

Dyson shook his head impatiently. 'The Gates, the Gates, the Gates,' he said. 'Let's get it over with.'

But no one in the Gates had seen him.

'I didn't know you were on, John,' said Ralph Absalom. 'I didn't know he was on. Did you, Lucy?'

'I knew he was on,' said Gareth Holmroyd. 'But I thought he said it was tonight.'

'Anyway,' said Mike Sparrow finally, 'how did it go, John?'

'Terrible,' said Dyson.

'He was very good,' said Bill Waddy, arriving with more drinks for people. 'He was very good indeed.'

'You saw him, did you, Bill?' said Andy Royle.

'No, I missed him, unfortunately,' said Bill Waddy. 'Old Harry Stearns told me.'

'John was very good,' said Bob, who had told old Harry Stearns that he was very good in the first place.

'You saw him, did you, Bob?' said Ted Hurwitz.

'Yes. He was very good.'

'Yes,' said Bill Waddy, 'old Harry Stearns said he was very good.'

'Yes, he was,' said Bob. 'Very good.'

'I was terrible,' said Dyson.

'You were very good, John,' said Bill Waddy. 'Old Harry Stearns told me.'

'Good for you, John,' said Pat Selig.

'What was the programme about?' asked Gareth Holmroyd.

'The colour problem,' said Dyson.

'Well, anyway,' said Gareth Holmroyd, 'I'm glad you made a good job of it.'

It rained on and off most of the afternoon. Dyson sat back in his chair watching it, yawning, his hands behind his head. He was in a rather more agreeable mood. Jannie, Bob, old Harry Stearns, Bill Waddy, Gareth Holmroyd – they could scarcely *all* be wrong. In fact, if one tried to think about it objectively, they were likely to have been able to make a more accurate assessment of his performance than he could himself. One couldn't help being over-critical of one's own performance. One knew just how much labour and effort had gone into it. One knew exactly where there had been difficulties and compromises behind the scenes. But Jannie and Bob and old Harry Stearns and Bill Waddy and Gareth Holmroyd saw only what was put before them, which was in fact all that counted. And of course he had been extremely relaxed and natural, he could see that. He had been very fluent and articulate.

'Do you believe in success and failure, Bob?' he asked, yawning.

'I suppose so,' said Bob, not looking up from his work.

'Do you think competitiveness is just an aspect of the society we live in, Bob?' said Dyson. 'Or do you think it's absolutely endemic in man?'

'I don't know, John.'

Dyson yawned. 'I think I'm really competitive by nature,' he said. 'I have a tremendous fundamental urge to get out and make my way in the world. Do you feel that, Bob?'

'No.'

'Well, of course, you're a writer. It's different for you. I'm merely an administrator, an organizer. It's natural for me to be more aggressive and pushing. I make no apology for it.'

He yawned again, uncontrollably. 'God, I'm really going to make a resolution about no beer for lunch,' he said. One fought and struggled, he thought. Sometimes one had terrible doubts about how one was doing. But one tried to put a good face on it and keep them to oneself. One could not afford to admit to weaknesses, the competition was so ruthless. Once one had slipped, no helping hands would be extended. Well, he liked it like that. He welcomed it.

And what happened if you failed to make the grade? You ended up like poor old Eddy Moulton, put out to pasture in some quiet department where nobody bothered to talk to you, doing small unworthy chores and dozing the day away. Dyson looked at old Eddy, head down behind the dusty newspaper files, nothing visible of him but his tousled white hair. Who knew now, or cared, what old Eddy had done in his prime? What stories he had beaten the great Stanford Roberts on, or even whether Stanford Roberts had been great after all? Well, thought Dyson suddenly, *he* cared. Old Eddy meant something to *him*. He would take him to the Gates that evening and get him talking. He would ask him about Stanford Roberts. About Walter Cunningham and Sidney Naylor. Just get him talking, and then listen, really listen, while old Eddy disinterred one man's life from the dust of time, and put it together again before his eyes.

There was something about old Eddy's appearance which had been worrying Dyson subconsciously for some minutes, and he suddenly realized what it was.

'Eddy,' he said sharply, leaning forwards and bringing the front legs of his chair down onto the floor with a crash, so that Bob looked up startled.

'Eddy!' said Dyson, scrambling to his feet and going across to Eddy's desk. '*Eddy!*'

He hesitated, frightened of making an embarrassing mistake, then felt the wrinkled white hand lying on Eddy's desk top.

'Fetch someone, Bob!' said Dyson. 'I think Eddy's ill!'

From the scared tone of Dyson's voice, Bob knew that what he meant was that he thought Eddy was dead.

People kept phoning up, after the body had been removed, and Dyson and Bob were rushing to catch up and finish preparing the copy that had to be set overnight.

'I hear you were on the box last night,' said small, cheerful voices in Dyson's ear. 'I'm told you were rather good.'

'Very kind of you to say so,' Dyson would reply, not knowing what else to do, but turning his back for shame on Bob and poor old Eddy's empty desk. 'I'm glad your wife enjoyed it. . . . Yes, I enjoyed doing it . . . Well, I thought it went off quite well, but one never knows with these things . . .'

Events were devoured by events, thought Dyson, states of affairs were overtaken by states of affairs . . . He cut five lines from the Country Day by Day proof, then restored them, realizing that he had misread the layout sheet. He felt very shaky. How long had Eddy been dead before they noticed him? Already the phone was ringing again.

'Hello, David . . . Yes, I wanted to talk to you about your Country copy. You've written, "I saw a pair of golden plover . . ." What? Oh, it's very kind of you to say so . . . Well, I thought it didn't go off too badly . . .'

They went to the Gates afterwards to have a glass of whisky. It was late; they were both very tired and shaken. And Dyson felt that something ought to be said. But what? They sat in the private bar at the Gates looking down into their glasses, trying to think what it should be. Dyson tried over inside his head: 'It's funny to think that only this morning poor old Eddy was talking about Stanley Cunningham's funeral . . .' 'It's funny to think that only this morning we were trying to persuade poor old Eddy to go off and enjoy himself on a facilities trip to the Persian Gulf . . .' 'It's funny to think that just this afternoon I had the idea of getting poor old Eddy to come over to the Gates and tell me something about himself . . .' But the funniest thing of all, really, was that until just a few hours ago Eddy had been, and now he was not. That, thought Dyson, really was the funniest thing about death; that's what really took some getting used to.

He looked up and caught Bob's eye.

'God strikes again,' said Bob thoughtfully.

7

Tessa got out of the train at Paddington already painfully
sensitive to the erotic implications of the city. Between
Newbury and Reading a middle-aged man had pressed his
knee against hers, and she had had to change compartments,
doing her best to look unconcerned about it, as if she often
heaved her suitcase down from the rack halfway between
stations to try the view farther down the train. In the corridor
she had passed compartments full of young men playing cards,
who looked up and appraised her face and figure with impersonal interest, and when she found another seat it was in a
compartment with three other women travelling up to London
on their own, all with suitcases and trim suits and carefully
made-up faces. The train hastened through the flat Thames
Valley fields and flat Western suburbs with single-minded
impatience; Tessa felt that everyone aboard, like herself, must
be on the way to some metropolitan sexual encounter.

And Paddington had changed. Whenever she had arrived
before, with her mother, or on her way to stay with relatives
and school friends, it had been full of innocent bustle presaging
lunch at Marshall and Snelgroves and tea at Fortnums. Now
its innocence had vanished, and it was thronged with worldly-
wise urban people intent upon sophisticated urban undertakings. It was half-past four. Self-contained men in well-cut
dark overcoats strode across the concourse with the air of
being on their way from spending the afternoon in small
Bayswater hotels with other men's wives. Girls with white
faces and heavily kohled eyes hurried out towards Praed
Street, as if hastening to appointments with abortionists in

seedy consulting-rooms behind the Edgeware Road. The taxi-drivers waiting on the rank looked knowingly at the racing pages of evening papers folded into quarters, ready to suggest to uncertain fares the addresses of drinking clubs and prostitutes.

Tessa did not take a taxi. She had been brought up to be thrifty and careful. She did not take taxis if she could walk. She did not throw clothes away if she could mend them or alter them to make them more fashionable. She did not go up to London to see her lover without first drawing fifteen pounds out of her bank account, and thinking up a convincing story to tell her parents, and packing a good book to read on the train (it was *U.S.A.* by John dos Passos, and she had read four and a half pages of it before she had been interrupted by her neighbour's knee), and looking up her lover's address in the *A to Z.*

She walked briskly out of the station, and set off in the direction of Bayswater, stopping every hundred yards or so to put down her dark blue Revelation suitcase (a Christmas present from her parents) and change hands. She did not like to stop and rest her arm for too long. She was afraid that one of the men who hung around the London termini waiting for girls arriving from the provinces would come up and offer to carry the case for her. She would not be taken in, of course; but it might be difficult to refuse politely.

She hated herself for being impressed and frightened by London, but she was impressed and frightened all the same. The long terraces of stuccoed houses – how self-sufficient and unattainable and urban they seemed! The traffic was somehow specially London-like, too. On and on it flowed past her, indifferent to her and her suitcase. Ford Cortinas, Minis, Volkswagen vans, Rovers – they all looked strange in these grey London streets, navigating with an inscrutable sense of their own direction and destiny. Even the grey, slightly misty afternoon light seemed impersonal and uniquely metropolitan. And the most impressive and frightening and metropolitan thing of all about London was that it was where Bob lived. At the thought of Bob, unpredictable and darkly smiling, her mouth went dry and her stomach felt liquid with impatience and nervousness.

She passed women with blonde hair and ski-caps, walking their dogs, and olive-skinned girls in belted raincoats, carrying portfolios or violin-cases. She knew they were more attractive than her. At every moment she caught sight of some slight figure with twinkling knees, slim golden calves, and massed, luxuriant hair. She felt uneasy; she did not fit in here at all. Her raincoat was not belted – her skirt was too long – her brown hair hung down her back with a pale blue kerchief tied over the top of it to keep it clean on the train. It was all hopeless! She felt like a peasant. Well, of course, she could get her hair cut and buy new clothes. But she was the wrong shape altogether. She was tall and big-boned, with strong, thick legs, and big breasts that jounced up and down as she walked. She didn't know what to do about her breasts. If she strapped them up they stuck out like a shelf, and ached. If she strapped them down to make herself look boyish they just stuck out a foot farther down, and ached. And really her wrong shape was only a symptom. She was the wrong sort of person, that was the basic trouble. She was awkward, and naïve, and thrifty, and ill-read, and genteel. She had a great square face, with a large jaw, and cheeks that were permanently red. She had no right to Bob. She had no right to *anyone*, in a world so full of slight creatures with delicate bones and neat boyish faces. She wasn't a girl at all, in any sense that the fashion magazines would recognize. She was just a young female human being, fit only to be somebody's cousin or aunt.

It took her much longer to get to Leominster Gardens, where Bob lived, than she had expected. Streets which had looked short on the map seemed endless when one had to walk them with a suitcase. She lost her way; new flats had been built across roads marked in the *A to Z*, and it was difficult to find anyone who had heard of Leominster Gardens. The light became greyer and smokier. Small corner shops shut as she approached them.

But when she did find the street, it seemed curiously familiar. Bob had never described it to her; it just seemed right for him. The cream stucco on the houses – the imposing pillared porches with their black-and-white tiled steps; she felt as if she had seen it all before in a dream. Through the ground-floor window of one house she saw a room lined with dusty books. A man with his back to her bent over a large table covered with papers, his silver hair catching the light from an overhead lamp. She knew that if he turned round she would recognize his face. At other windows she could see tables with folded paper napkins and nickel-plated cruets. They were small private hotels. She knew exactly how the dining-rooms smelt inside, and how they would look at seven o'clock, when the weak lights in their brown parchment shades were turned on, and large, ungainly old men with sticks stumped to their tables.

As she drew near to number 86, her mouth went dry again, and her heart beat painfully. She stopped and put her case down for a moment to try and collect herself; her hands were trembling uncontrollably from the weight. It was stupid to be like this. It was silly to have come at all if she was going to feel so shaky and helpless. Anyway, Bob probably wouldn't be home yet. Her plan was really just to find the place, then go away and have tea somewhere while she waited for him.

She tucked stray wisps of hair back under her kerchief, then picked up her case and walked up the steps on to the porch. 'Flat 4,' it said on the board, 'R. Bell.' His name! Somehow it was a terrible shock to see it. Her cheeks were blazing red, she knew. The bell-pushes on the board were all empty, so she tried the door and it opened. Inside was a hall with a dingy maroon carpet, and a massive veneered dining-table covered with old election pamphlets, soap coupons, and handbills from firms purchasing second-hand jewellery. She tiptoed up the stairs, wondering what she would say to anyone who saw her.

One of the stairs cracked sharply beneath her foot; she heard the front door of one of the ground-floor flats open behind her, and as she turned the corner of the staircase she caught a glimpse of a single eye and a draggle of grey hair at the crack.

There were no windows on the first-floor landing, and in the dark it was difficult to make out the numbers on the doors. She crept about, grasping the suitcase, putting her eye very close to each of the two bell-pushes in turn. Absurd anxieties fled across her mind. Had she posted her letter telling Bob she was coming? Had she put a stamp on it? As she hesitated outside Bob's door she heard a muffled metallic thump from within, as of a saucepan being put down on a gas-stove, then the sound of a tap being turned on. He was in! She quickly rang the bell, not knowing what to think or to feel. There was a silence, and then the sound of quick, light steps coming towards the door. He was running! Oh, Bob, she thought. Oh, *Bob*!

The door opened.

'Oh, Bob!' she said helplessly.

'Come on in, darling,' said the sharp little woman who was holding the door, screwing up her eyes shrewdly against the cigarette-smoke she was blowing out in order to speak. 'I'm just making the great man's supper. We can have a little heart-to-heart while we wait for him.'

'Throw all those bedclothes off the chair and sit down, darling,' said Mrs. Mounce, peeling potatoes at the sink.

'I'm all right, thank you,' said Tessa, standing with her hands behind her back, pretending she was examining Bob's pictures.

'Lovey, he may not be back till eleven! Go on, sit down. I was airing his sheets, you see, darling. They never get aired properly if I don't do it myself. Go and pour yourself a drink, love – you look whacked. Do you know where it is? It's over on the bookcase.'

'No, thank you.'

'I'll make us some tea, then.'

Poor kid, thought Mrs. Mounce, she really did look whacked. For a moment after she'd come in her face had gone all stiff, as if she were trying not to cry. Bob was a stinker. He could have been at home to meet her.

'He could have been here,' she said. 'It wouldn't have killed him to be here for once.'

'I expect he's busy.'

'I expect he's boozing.'

Tessa looked disapproving. 'Do you cook and clean for Mr. Bell?' she asked.

'Oh yes, darling!' said Mrs. Mounce, turning her head upwards and sideways, so the smoke from the cigarette in the corner of her mouth missed her eyes. 'I'm just the skivvy round here! Cook the din-dins, put the cat out, clear up the junk on the great man's desk, and hope my lord throws me a kind word from time to time. That's me, sweetheart!'

And when he came in at eleven o'clock breathing beer and curry fumes, try to fight off his hot little hands. Oh, she knew what was going through his head all right, and how careful she had to be not to say or do anything he might misinterpret. And now she was expected to entertain his lady-friends until such time as he chose to remember they were there! Well, she knew who this lady-friend was, anyway. This was the famous Tessa, who wrote Bob twelve-page letters which he left lying around open on top of his desk. This was the famous lady-friend who went round wearing Bob's letters down her blouse. Frankly, she looked as if she'd got a few bundles of twelve-page letters stuffed up her woolly even now. Either that or she'd got two woollies on. Honestly, people talked about the kids today as though they were all Dior models, but they still had spots and puppy-fat just like kids always had, and always would have. Poor kid, she looked so pathetic sitting there on the edge of the chair, all stiff and upright like some tragedy queen, thinking Woe is me, my precious Bob has fallen into the hands of this designing woman. Well, making his room fit

107

to live in was just possibly a better way to go about it than writing him twelve-page letters, as dearest Tessa might in time come to realize.

'The water's almost boiling,' she said. 'Incidentally, I know what you're thinking, and I'm not.'

Tessa's face went red all over, from neck to temples.

'I wasn't . . .' she said. 'I didn't . . .'

'I'm just a good fairy, darling. That's all. I live downstairs, you see. I just pop up from time to time to see if Bob's all right.'

'Well, of course . . . that's very kind of you.'

'Just keeping him in good condition for you, darling.'

'Thank you.'

Poor kid – she *was* out of her depth.

'Did you manage to get anything to eat on the way?'

'I had a sandwich at Taunton.'

'*Sweetest*! You must be *fam*ished! We'll get Bob's old birthday cake out! Though I must admit, I only have a bite at lunchtime myself. I have to think of my figure.'

'Your figure's very pretty,' said Tessa politely.

'Do you think so?' said Mrs. Mounce. She swivelled round on her heel, and struck a pose with her left hip thrown sideways, and her cigarette hand extended in a rather classical way She could have been a model, people always said so. She could have been a dancer if she'd taken lessons.

'Like a model,' said Tessa. 'Perhaps you are one?'

'I could have been. But you know how it is, with one thing and another. Of course, I have to keep slim for my hubby. He'd go mad if I started putting on weight. I put on five pounds at Torremolinos one year and he went on and on about it. Was I sure I wasn't pregnant? You know.'

'Well, I wish I looked like you.'

'You're absolutely lovely as you are, darling.'

And really, thought Mrs. Mounce, she wasn't such a bad-looking kid. A little of the old black-coffee-and-orange-juice, and a good roll-on, and she really wouldn't look too awful.

'Are you an undergrad or something, darling?' she asked.

108

'I'm at a college of citizenship in Bath.'

'*Darling*! That sounds terribly brainy.'

'It's not, really.'

'Do you study economics and all that kind of thing?'

'A bit. We do History of Ideas.'

'Lovely.'

'And we have a course in World Literature. Last term it was Russia. Next term it's India, China, and Japan.'

'How super, darling.'

'Well, I'm not sure. One never seems to catch up.'

'I know, sweets – once you start swotting there's no end to it. That's what put me off studying, really. Do you do ordinary things like Domestic Science?'

'Well, we do Nutrition. And Contemporary Culture Appreciation, and Social Situation Training.'

'Super.'

'We all think it's terribly draggy. There's a terribly draggy lot of people teaching us.'

Mrs. Mounce made the tea.

'I should be helping you,' said Tessa. 'How rude of me!'

'All right, sweets. Make the bed – then you can lie down and take the weight off your feet while we talk. But tuck it in properly, darling. Make proper hospital corners, or one of you will be falling out in the middle of the night.'

Tessa's face went red all over again. Mrs. Mounce watched her with discreet curiosity. She'd never seen such a champion blusher. Kids weren't getting tougher these days at all – they were getting *soppier*. Well, she'd learn, she'd learn. She just needed someone to take an interest in her, someone to draw her out and tell her what time of day it was.

Mrs. Mounce kicked off her beaded moccasins, curled up in the armchair with her cup of tea, and began to tell Tessa about her hubby and his job, about Dotty and the work they were having done in the house, and about their friends. Tessa first of all sat down on the edge of the bed, with her knees together, her feet crossed and slightly to one side, her back straight, and her cup and saucer at chest height, as she had learnt in Social Situation Training. By the time she had fetched her second cup of tea, Mrs. Mounce was on to their relations with their bank manager, and Tessa kicked off her shoes and tucked her legs up beneath her to be companionable. Her third cup of tea she balanced on her stomach, lying full length on the bed and pointing her stockinged toes into the air, sighting various objects over them with one eye closed. 'How frightful,' she murmured from time to time, as Mrs. Mounce catalogued another misfortune, another misunderstanding. 'How absolutely frightful.'

'Because there I was,' Mrs. Mounce ran on, as the blue haze of cigarette smoke thickened in the dusk, 'honestly, darling, without a stitch on, and this lunatic hammering on the door and shouting he'd wake the whole hotel if I didn't open up . . .' 'Anyway, I told Dotty, 'Dotty darling,' I said, 'this terrible possessiveness of yours about the house is definitely something sick, something absolutely psychological.' I mean, I had to be frank with her. "Dotty, precious," I said, "this is the sort of thing they lock people away in mental asylums for . . ." ' 'Well, I went to clinics, I went to specialists, they poked and they peered and they prodded, they took X-rays, they did tests, I don't know what they didn't do, and they all said the same thing. "Mrs. Mounce," they said, "there's absolutely nothing wrong with you." Well, lovely, I knew there *was*, you see . . .'

It was half-past eight when the key turned in the lock and Bob came in. Tessa had turned on the little light on the bedside table, but otherwise the room was in darkness, and for some moments Bob stood by the door, twisting his head backwards and forwards, trying to take the situation in.

'It's a pity you bothered to come home at all, darling,' said Mrs. Mounce. 'We were having a very cosy little chat here.'

'Oh, it's you,' said Bob. He came over to the bed, holding up his hand to shade his eyes from the bedside light, and peering almost comically close, so that Tessa could smell the whisky on his breath.

'Who's this?' he said.

'It's me, Bob,' said Tessa in a small voice.

'Oh God,' said Bob. 'Tessa! What on earth are you doing here?'

'Didn't you get my letter, Bob?'

'Your letter? Oh, yes. Yes, yes, I did.'

'What did I tell you?' said Mrs. Mounce. 'He'd clean forgotten about it.'

'No, I got held up at the office.'

'You are a stinker, sweetie,' said Mrs. Mounce. 'You really are. If I hadn't let her in she'd have had to sit on her suitcase in the hall for three hours.'

'I'm sorry, I got held up at the office.'

He went over and kissed Tessa, who was half sitting up, not knowing quite what to do with herself.

'Anyway,' he said, 'it's marvellous to see you.'

She hugged him roughly. 'You've been boozing,' she said.

'Of course he's been boozing,' said Mrs. Mounce.

'I had to stop for a quick drink on the way home with John Dyson,' he said. 'I couldn't really get out of it.'

He straightened up. Tessa would have liked to hide her face in the covers and cry.

'Well, well,' said Bob. 'Where are you staying, Tessa?'

'Bob!' cried Mrs. Mounce. 'You absolute skunk!'

'No, it's just slipped my mind for a moment . . .' said Bob.

'She's staying here, for heaven's sake! Where do you think she's staying?'

'Well, don't get excited – that's all I wanted to know.'

'I'm going to find a hotel,' said Tessa.

'You really *are* a stinker, you know, sweetie!'

'Look, she's perfectly welcome to stay here – I just didn't know exactly what her plans were.'

Mrs. Mounce jumped out of the armchair and twinkled away to the door. 'Well,' she said, 'I'll leave you to it. There's din-dins for two in the uvvy. Tessa sweetie, be firm with him. And if you get depressed at all, come downstairs and have a chat.'

Tessa couldn't think of anything to say after Mrs. Mounce had gone. She sat on the edge of the bed, looked down into her lap, and felt great tears run out of her eyes. They ran down her red cheeks, and splashed like huge summer raindrops onto her hands.

'Oh, *Tess!*' said Bob, sitting down on the bed and putting his arm round her shoulders. 'Don't cry, Tess. I'm terribly sorry everything got so buggered up. I must have misread your letter somehow.'

'I don't think you read it at all.'

'Yes, I did, Tess. Honestly I did. Only everything's been so buggered up today in general . . .'

'Anyway, it doesn't matter. I'm sorry to cry like this. It's just that everything's so different from how I imagined it. I kept imagining coming up to London to see you. And now I've come . . .' She sobbed. 'And everything's just not quite how I expected it. I mean, arriving here and finding Mrs. Mounce . . .'

'I'm terribly sorry you got stuck with her,' said Bob. 'She's a dreadful woman.'

'No, she was very sweet to me. I thought she was dreadful at first. I suppose she is rather dreadful. But, Bob, she's had such a sad life!' She wept again. 'I just suddenly thought,' she said, 'everyone's life is very sad really.'

Bob got up and began to put the things on the table for dinner. Tessa stopped crying and sighed a deep, uncontrollable sigh like a yawn. She got up, and seized Bob as he moved between table and oven, putting her face down on his shoulder and hugging him fiercely. She would have liked to dissolve into him and become part of him, so that she could never be subject to his indifference, or even be looked at by him in any objective way.

'Sometimes you're not at all good to me, Bob,' she said.

'I'm sorry, Tess,' said Bob. He kissed the top of her head, and moved on to get a saucepan out of the oven. She caught him again on the way back between oven and table, and sank herself into him once more, but after a moment became conscious that he was having to make a considerable effort to hold the hot saucepan away from her at arm's length.

When they sat down at table she couldn't manage to eat anything. She held Bob's left hand in both of hers under the corner of the table and gazed at him.

'Oh, Bob!' she said.

'Oh, Tessa!' said Bob, taking a forkful of stew with his disengaged hand.

The doorbell rang. It was Mrs. Mounce.

'Sorry to disturb, darling,' she said to Bob, 'but I've brought you a bottle of Sauternes to wash the stew down with, so you can celebrate. I don't suppose you thought of bringing any booze home yourself.'

After Bob had closed the door he poured out two tumblers of the wine.

'To us, Tess,' he said.

She took his hand again. 'To you, Bob. Whatever happens to us, I hope things always go right for you.'

Bob put his glass down. 'Tess,' he said, 'I'm honestly not worthy of you.'

'That's a silly thing to say, Bob.'

'It's true, Tess. You're generous and selfless in a way I could never be.' He picked up his fork, prodded ineffectually at his stew for some moments, and then withdrew his left hand from hers. 'I just want to cut up this piece of meat, Tess,' he said.

'I love you, Bob. I've never really loved anyone before.'

The doorbell rang again.

'Bob, sweetie,' said Mrs. Mounce, 'I've just remembered you haven't got any salt. I thought I'd pop up with some. Don't worry, I'll leave you in peace after this. How's the stew?'

'Oh, Bob!' said Tessa, as Bob sat down again.

'Oh, Tess!' said Bob.

* * *

Bob lay in bed gazing vaguely up at the ceiling, which was glowing red in the light from the gas-fire, not entirely sure whether he was awake or asleep. There was a dull pain in his left biceps – Tessa's head was pillowed on it. He cautiously pulled his arm free. He couldn't think whether they had been in bed for an hour, or four hours.

'Poor Mrs. Mounce,' said Tessa.

'Mm,' said Bob.

'I'm glad she's not your mistress, Bob.'

'What?'

'I didn't really think she was, of course. I thought she was the cleaning woman first of all.'

'I don't know what she is.'

'I think I'd understand if you wanted to sleep with other women, Bob. I know it's different for men. All the same, I suppose I'm glad it's not Mrs. Mounce. She's so tied up with unhappiness. She'd pull you down into it.'

'Yes.'

'Poor Mrs. Mounce.'

Bob dozed.

'. . . into Taunton yesterday,' he became conscious of Tessa saying some time later, 'to get some special new anti-biotic for Jester. Did I write and tell you about Jester falling?'

'Mm.'

'Poor old Jester . . .'

Bob felt himself swooping down again into the great soft darkness of sleep. Somewhere down there he stubbed himself against an ill-defined but hard mass of fact, and brought it up to the surface to examine it.

'John Dyson was on television last night,' he said. 'Did you see him?'

'Is that the Giant Dyson?'

'What?'

'Who subdued the Tyrant Cox?'

114

'Search me,' said Bob, sinking slowly away into the depths again.

'. . . frightened when I arrived in London today,' he heard Tessa saying at some stage. Time was no longer sequential; it was mere isolated incidents unrelated by before and after. '. . . a stupid thing to feel, I know . . . on the train . . . cars in the streets . . . like a child . . .'

Tessa turned over, unwinding the bedclothes off him as she went. He turned over himself, to wind them back on. There was scarcely room enough to turn; it was surprising how obstinately single a single bed was.

'I'm right on the edge,' he said. 'Are you sure you couldn't move over an inch or two?'

There was no reply; now that he was fully awake, she was fully asleep. He tried cautiously to shove her over by main force, but she was too heavy. He lay on his side, holding the covers over him by their edges, gazing at some of his copies of *Vogue*, which Tessa had been looking through and left lying on the carpet in front of the fire, where they glowed pink and red. He thought about models' bottoms, feeling Tessa's bulking large against the small of his back. Funny how he never seemed to meet girls . . . Just not attractive to women in some way . . . The copies of *Vogue* slipped slowly sideways and upwards, and disappeared into darkness . . .

'. . . told me,' said Tessa's voice hours or minutes later, 'that they've borrowed a lot of money from the bank to do some conversion work in their flat.'

'Um?' mumbled Bob. 'Whosiss?'

'Mrs. Mounce and her husband. Her husband's impotent. Did you know that?'

'No.'

'But terribly jealous. She has affairs with other men and he finds out and flicks her.'

'Does what?'

'Flicks her. With the back of his fingers somehow. She says it hurts terribly.'

Bob felt suddenly wide awake. For some reason he had just remembered poor old Eddy Moulton.

'A man in the office died this afternoon,' he said, then immediately doubted his own words. Had it really been that afternoon? 'A man' – 'died' – could poor old Eddy, leaning drunkenly across the desk with his hand shading his eyes, really be fitted into those abstract, impersonal formulae? It seemed like some event described in a legend, remote and formal.

'Someone you knew well?' asked Tessa.

'He was a very old man who worked in the same room as John Dyson and myself.'

'Is that why you were late back this evening?'

Bob considered. 'I suppose it was,' he said.

'Why didn't you tell me?'

Bob tried to remember why he hadn't told her. It was probably because the blue fug of cigarette smoke in the flat when he had come in, and the light, and the voices, and the terrible feeling of guilt, and Mrs. Mounce shouting, and Tessa weeping, had all swept poor old Eddy's death right out of his mind. But he couldn't really remember the reason. It was already lost – part of the jetsam of discarded immemorabilia which disappeared astern all the time. From hour to hour one's life slipped away from one into the haze, before one had really looked at any of it properly.

'I suppose I didn't think of it,' he said.

'You are a gink, Bob.'

Bob said nothing. The word gink seemed a good ten years too young to bear thinking about.

Tessa turned carefully over towards him, rolling the under-sheet away from beneath his legs. 'I can stay for three weeks, if you'd like me to,' she said. 'Oh, Bob! Three weeks together – on our own!'

'Marvellous,' said Bob.

'Everything's always so much more complicated and awkward than one bargains for,' she said. She settled her head on his left biceps again and closed her eyes. 'I shall always love you, Bob, whatever happens to us.'

'I love you, too, Tessa.'

The doorbell rang.

'God in heaven!' said Bob, wide-awake, and casting about for his dressing-gown. 'God in holy heaven! Still at it, at this hour! This is the fifth time she's been up! I swear I'm going to throw her downstairs and break her neck!'

It was indeed Mrs. Mounce yet again, and in her frilly nightwear, but Bob did not throw her downstairs and break her neck.

'Hello,' he said politely.

'Oh, you've gone to bed already,' she said, trying to peer past Bob into the room to see.

'Yes.'

'Oh, sweetie, I'm sorry! I just thought – Reg is away tonight, so why don't you and Tessa sleep in our double bed downstairs? There's a single bed in one of the upstairs flats I could sleep in. You'd be much more comfy – you don't have to tell me what it's like sleeping two in a single bed, darling.'

'We're very comfortable here, thanks.'

'Well, it was just a thought.'

'Yes. Thanks.'

Bob shut the door.

'Poor old Mrs. Mounce,' said Tessa.

'But at four o'clock in the morning!' said Bob.

He looked at his watch in the firelight. It was quarter to twelve. Well, it felt like four. And four and a quarter hours later, when it actually was four, and the bedclothes both above and below were a mere conglomerate heap, and Tessa's strapping behind had pushed right across the bed, and Bob was cold and stiff from head to foot, and had been neither asleep nor awake for a moment, it felt as though the solar system had finally run down and stopped, and closed off the ever-renewing spring of pure, fresh time for good and all.

* * *

8

God knows I'm a failure, an insignificant speck of human nothingness trampled on indifferently by every casual passer-by, thought Dyson as he followed his wife out of the kitchen into the living-room, with his fists clenched in his trouser pockets and his face set in an unyielding frown, but there is one thing in this world that I'm not going to stand for, and that's being nagged by my wife. I'm not reduced to *that*.

God knows, he thought, I shouldn't say anything about it if she nagged me in any halfway reasonable manner. I'm used to being treated like dirt – I'm not proud. It's this nagging by saying nothing that I can't stand. It's this terrible pseudo-rational nagging by just carrying on normally, as if she weren't nagging me at all. It's this stupid leaving me to guess what I'm being nagged about. Well, I'm honestly not going to spend the whole of Saturday morning putting up with this sort of thing. I'll just go out of the house without a word, and stay at my club for a few days. Or I would if I had a club.

'Look, Jannie,' he said reasonably, following her back to the kitchen, 'just *tell* me what it is you're going on about. That's all I ask.'

'I'm not going on about anything, John,' said Jannie.

'Yes, you are, Jannie.'

'No, I'm not, John.'

'Look, we both know we're having an argument! Let's not have another argument about whether we're having an argument or not!'

Jannie gazed into the food cupboard, picking up cereal packets and shaking them to see if they needed replacing.

'There's some coffee in the pot, if you'd like to light the gas,' she said.

Dyson lit the gas absently. It was self-defeating, this sort of nagging, he thought. That's what I really object to. If I haven't the slightest idea what the hell I'm being nagged about, how the hell can I possibly do anything about it?

'Put some milk on, too, will you, John?'

He put some milk on, sighing. I mean, he thought, I know what she's *up* to, all right. I'm not a complete fool. This was the classic method of brainwashing, after all, used by interrogators, priests, and psychoanalysts alike. 'I think you have something you want to tell me' – that's what their technique was. Then they simply waited for you to accuse yourself.

Jannie sat down at one corner of the great kitchen table and began to write a shopping list.

Dyson stood by the stove, gazing down at her with serious ferocity. 'Jannie . . .' he began.

'Yes, John?'

Dyson stopped, frowning harder. 'Why do you call me John in that tone of voice?' he demanded.

'Don't you like me calling you John?' asked Jannie, not looking up from her shopping list.

'You don't normally go round calling me John all the time.'

She didn't answer. Good God, he thought, I should like to do something that would really make her jump out of her skin for once. He pictured himself smashing both fists down in the middle of the kitchen table, or taking a china jug off the shelf and hurling it across the room. It was absurd that Norman Ward Westerman and Lord Boddy should listen with real deference to his views on Halifax, while at home he couldn't even get a hearing from his own wife. Scribble, scribble, scribble, she went. Eggs, butter, tea, coffee – oh God, the *smallness* of things! The endless petty demands of life! They rained down like small coal from a sack, filling the air with choking dust which settled grimly over everything and made the whole world smell grey.

'It's that patch of mould on the ceiling in the boys' room, isn't it?' he said. 'That's what you're going on about, isn't it, Jannie?'

Rice Krispies, navy thread, tuna fish, wrote Jannie.

'Well, I can't do anything about it today,' he said. 'And that's final.'

One bottle Thawpit, wrote Jannie, cigs, birthday present for John's sister-in-law.

'Look, be reasonable, Jannie,' said Dyson. 'I'm going to be absolutely up to my eyebrows in work this week-end. I've got a piece to write for the Overseas Service. I've got an obit of poor old Eddy Moulton to do for the *Journalist*. How can I possibly make a career for myself when you keep on, nag, nag, nag, about patches of mould on the ceiling?'

Jannie looked out of the window, chewing the end of her pencil thoughtfully. 'The milk's boiled over,' she said.

'Oh, *God*!' cried Dyson, springing away from the stove, then springing back to turn the gas out. 'This is exclusively your responsibility! You realize that, don't you, Jannie?'

'The cloth's in the sink, John.'

'I don't see any reason on earth why *I* should clear this up. Where's the cloth? Why the hell is there never a cloth to hand when it's wanted?'

Oven-cleaner, wrote Jannie on her list. 'The phone's ringing,' she said.

Let it ring – what do I care? thought Dyson, as he hurled himself out into the hall to catch it before it stopped ringing. God really was seeping in this morning from every direction, and chiefly through the condition of marriage itself. That was what was holy about holy matrimony, he realized suddenly; it was just another divine instrument for increasing entropy, like damp and coronary thrombosis and woodworm.

'Hello; Dyson,' he snapped.

'Bob!' he said cheerfully a fraction of a second later, smiling warmly into the microphone. 'How nice to hear from you! . . . No, no – not an inconvenient moment at all . . . *Who's* with you?

. . . Tessa? Is that your lady-friend from Somerset? Well, give her our regards, Bob . . . Can you do what? . . . Oh, I see . . . Yes, by all means . . . By all means, Bob . . .'

Dyson walked back to the kitchen grinning. Ah, bachelor-hood! The idea of being a bachelor, and having bachelor affairs, suddenly seemed almost unbearably sweet. A girl coming to stay in one's flat . . . He envisaged a slight girl with a tender face and dark, tumbling hair, wearing a pair of borrowed pyjamas which came down over her hands and feet . . .

'Bob's got his girl-friend staying with him,' he said to Jannie, still grinning, as he sat down at the kitchen table and sipped absently at the cup of coffee which had appeared there. 'She's called Tessa. Apparently her parents think she's staying with friends – Bob wanted to know if she could send them our phone number and say she was staying here. I said we'd be delighted. If anyone rings and asks for her, we're to say she's out, then pass the message on to Bob so that she can ring back.'

Dyson went on grinning to himself. The slight girl with the tumbling hair, he was thinking, would take a shower (bachelor flats had showers), putting her head back and letting the water cascade down between her breasts . . . In the afternoon they would make love, with the great windows open to the sky, and a hot, heavy summer rain falling, crushing the flowers and filling the air with the scent of roses . . .

'Did you invite them round?' asked Jannie.

'No. Should I have done? Wouldn't they rather just get on with it in peace?'

Jannie returned to her shopping-list in silence.

'Do you think we should?' said Dyson. 'If you'd like to, you go ahead.'

Leg of lamb for 6, wrote Jannie.

Dyson remembered, at the sight of her silently writing, that she had been nagging him. 'Look, Jannie,' he said, his good humour abruptly vanishing, 'I'm not going to ring them. It's the wife's job to send out invitations and manage a couple's social life, not the husband's.'

Paper napkins, flowers, wrote Jannie.

'Good God, Jannie,' said Dyson. 'It was your idea, not mine. If you want to satisfy your curiosity about Bob's girl-friend, you ring him yourself. I'm far too busy to mess about with this sort of thing today. And that really *is* final . . .'

'That was John Dyson again,' said Bob, as he put the phone down. 'He was inviting us for Sunday lunch tomorrow. I said yes – I hope that was all right. Their kids are quite sweet, as a matter of fact.'

Tessa watched him, completely absorbed in him, as he sat wearily down at the table again, located the brown sugar among the remains of the breakfast things, and dug a spoonful out to lick at. She was sitting curled up in the armchair like Mrs. Mounce, nursing a final cup of cold Nescafé.

'You're very fond of the Dysons, aren't you?' she said.

'I suppose so,' he replied. He thought about the Dysons' solid, regular married life, and it filled him with nostalgia. The Dysons didn't have to exhaust themselves wondering if they loved each other, and what they should do about it if they didn't. They weren't overwhelmed by the sheer mechanics of daily life. Happily married couples, he thought, stood not face to face, absorbed in each other, but back to back, looking outwards upon the world. He gazed despairingly about the room. The breakfast things were still on the table; the bed-clothes lay tangled on the floor; Tessa's clothes straggled across the carpet from her open suitcase. Tessa wasn't even dressed – she was wearing his old tweed overcoat over her pyjamas. By the time they had got the room cleared up and were ready to go out it would be getting on for twelve. By the time they had done the shopping and got back and Tessa had cooked the lunch (as she insisted on doing in her eagerness to keep house for him) it would almost certainly be something like three o'clock. A world of muddle seemed to enclose Bob like a jungle. He rubbed his eyes and yawned.

'Didn't you get to sleep at all?' asked Tessa.

'I think I must have dozed off about six.'

'Poor old Bob!'

He took another spoonful of sugar. It hadn't been a *night* they had lived through; it had been the Dark Ages – all seven centuries of them, with wars and oppressions, visions and turbulences. The worst moment of all, he thought, had been at a quarter to nine that morning, when he had been roused from the bottom depths of heavy, dream-tangled sleep by the door bell, and when, having stumbled across the room, still not knowing where he was or what was happening, he had found Mrs. Mounce at the door, asking if she could do any shopping for them.

Tessa came over and kissed him. He opened his eyes quickly, unaware until then that they had fallen shut.

'I'm going to have a bath,' said Tessa. 'Where's the bathroom?'

'Well, it's a bit awkward,' said Bob. 'There's only one in the house, on the landing halfway downstairs. Are you sure you want a bath?'

'Not if it would be embarrassing for you, Bob.'

'Oh, I don't mind. I was thinking about you, Tess.'

'*I* don't mind. I've burned my boats now.'

'I suppose so.'

He took her down to the bathroom, and turned on the geyser for her.

'Are you going to come in the bath with me, Bob?' she asked, reddening.

'Well, I think I'd better wash up the breakfast things, if you don't mind. Otherwise we shan't be getting lunch till teatime.'

'Oh, yes. I'd forgotten about the breakfast things.'

Bob had almost finished the washing up when the doorbell rang. He threw down the washing-up mop and stood stock-still for a moment, gripping the edge of the sink. He thought very carefully what he was going to say. 'Mrs. Mounce,' he thought he might put it, in a calm, almost pleasant voice, 'if you ring this bell once more I will call the police and have you charged with causing a nuisance . . .' No – '. . . will instruct my solicitor to proceed against you for trespass . . .' No, no. The bell rang again. He strode across to the door. The words '. . . unless I receive an assurance that you will seek immediate psychiatric advice . . .' flashed into his mind with horrible pleasingness.

But it was not Mrs. Mounce – it was Mrs. Hennessy, the cleaning woman. Bob stared at her with his mouth open. 'Forgotten I was coming, had you, love?' she said agreeably, rolling hugely past Bob into the room, from one swollen carpet-slippered foot to the other, trailing brooms, brushes and vacuum-cleaner behind her. She dumped all her equipment down, breathing heavily.

'You could leave it today, if you liked . . .' said Bob uneasily, stepping on Tessa's suspender-belt, and kicking one of her shoes backwards under the armchair.

'Don't worry about me, love,' said Mrs. Hennessy. 'It'll only take me ten minutes . . . What have you been doing with your bed, love? Been having nightmares, have you?'

'Oh, yes,' said Bob. 'Yes, I did have rather a bad night.'

Mrs. Hennessy looked at the open suitcase. 'Going away for the week-end, are you, love?' she said.

'No,' said Bob, following the direction of her gaze only slowly. 'I mean, yes, I am.'

'Have a lovely time.'

'Yes, I will.'

Mrs. Hennessy bent down and began to pick up the bed-clothes. Bob bent down, too, and moved discreetly about picking up the more obviously feminine articles of clothing around the floor. He wished he didn't mind about it, but he did. He wished his first instinct had not been to conceal the traces of Tessa's existence, but it had been. It was not because *he* would be embarrassed if Mrs. Hennessy knew he had a girl staying there, he told himself. It was not even because Tessa would be embarrassed. They were both a little too adult to care what other people thought. It was Mrs. Hennessy he was trying to protect. It was she who would be embarrassed if she knew, or at any rate, if she knew that he knew that she knew.

'That's right, love,' shouted Mrs. Hennessy over the noise, as she switched on the vacuum-cleaner. 'If you just clear your little bits and pieces off the floor I can get round with the vacuum.'

Bob pushed everything into the suitcase and crammed the lid shut, ignoring the various shoulder-straps and corners of translucent nylon which stuck out. He was just looking round for some quiet corner to put the case when faintly above the noise in the room he heard the doorbell ring. God, it was Tessa coming back from the bathroom! He hurried across to the door, still grasping the case.

'Bye bye, love,' shouted Mrs. Hennessy. 'Have a lovely time.'

'Oh. Yes. Thanks,' shouted Bob.

He opened the door. It was not Tessa outside – it was Mrs. Mounce.

'Bob, darling!' she whispered dramatically, taking his hand and leading him out on to the landing out of Mrs. Hennessy's earshot. 'I meant to tell Mrs. Hennessy not to disturb you. Shall I get rid of her for you?'

'No,' said Bob. 'That's fine.'

'I just thought I'd offer, sweetie.'

'Everything's fine. Don't worry about us.'

Mrs. Mounce looked down at the suitcase. 'You off somewhere, darling?' she asked.

'No, no. Well, you know, we might go somewhere.'

'Well, don't forget I'm downstairs if you want me.'

'I shan't forget.'

He shut the door and carried the suitcase back into the room. Mrs. Hennessy looked at him in surprise and switched the vacuum-cleaner off.

'I thought you'd gone, love,' she said.

'Well, not quite.'

'What's the matter? Forgotten your pyjamas? Here they are, love – I was just going to put them under the pillow.'

'Oh, thanks,' said Bob. He opened the suitcase and crammed the pyjamas inside.

'Got everything else, have you?' asked Mrs. Hennessy. 'Got your shaving kit? No, I can see it over by the sink.'

She rolled effortlully across to the draining-board and fetched it for him.

'Thanks,' said Bob, stuffing it into the case.

'You'll forget your own head one of these days,' said Mrs. Hennessy. 'What else haven't you got? Slippers? Look, they're on the floor here all the time!'

'I don't really want slippers, thanks.'

'Course you want slippers! Catch your death on some of these cold floors. Come on, love, put them in. What about your dressing-gown? Your dressing-gown's hanging up behind the door! There you are, then. Now, are you sure you've got a change of socks?'

'Yes, yes.'

'And plenty of warm woollies?'

'Yes, yes, yes.'

Reluctantly, Mrs. Hennessy bent down and switched on the vacuum-cleaner again. Almost at once the doorbell rang. Bob hurried to answer it, trying to force the lid of the overloaded case shut as he went.

'You off then, love?' shouted Mrs. Hennessy. 'Ta-ta. Have a lovely time.'

'Oh, thanks,' said Bob. 'Yes, I will.'

This time it was Tessa, holding her pyjamas in her hand and wearing nothing but the tweed overcoat pulled tightly around her.

'Oh, Tess,' whispered Bob, pushing her back on to the landing and pulling the door to behind them. 'It's a bit awkward at the moment. Mrs. Hennessy's here.'

Tessa gazed at Bob seriously.

'Who's Mrs. Hennessy, Bob?' she asked.

'She's the cleaning woman, Tess.'

'*Another* woman who does your cleaning, Bob?'

'Oh, Mrs. Hennessy's just, you know, the char. Look, I've put all your things in the suitcase. Take it back to the bathroom and get dressed there, Tess.'

Tessa gazed at Bob sadly in the half-darkness of the landing, and shivered slightly. 'I don't think you ought to be embarrassed about me now I'm here,' she said.

'I'm not embarrassed, Tess.'

'Well, *I'm* not, Bob.'

'I know. It's Mrs. Hennessy I'm thinking of. I don't think we ought to embarrass her, you see. Look, all your clothes are in the case. I'll come and call you when things are a bit less hectic.'

He watched Tessa start reluctantly down the stairs, cradling the open suitcase in her arms, then went back into the flat, wishing it were the middle of the night once more.

'Back again?' said Mrs. Hennessy, turning off the vacuum-cleaner. 'What have you forgotten this time, love?'

'Oh, you know, I thought perhaps I'd just check through things and make sure.'

He began vaguely opening drawers and cupboards, trying to see out of the corner of his eye whether there were any more of Tessa's belongings lying about the floor. For a moment they caught each other's eye. Bob looked away hurriedly, and Mrs. Hennessy bent down and switched on the vacuum-cleaner.

The doorbell rang.

'Off again, are you?' said Mrs. Hennessy, watching him run. 'Ta-ta then.'

'Bob, I'll *have* to come in,' whispered Tessa. 'Mrs. Mounce is in the bathroom.'

Bob pushed her back onto the landing once again, and again pulled the door to behind him. 'We can wait out here for a bit, can't we?' he asked. 'Mrs. Hennessy won't be a moment, Tess. Let me carry the case for you, anyway.'

They stood, not looking at each other, with Bob holding the case. Tessa started to shiver.

'George God strikes again,' whispered Bob.

'What?'

'George God – he's getting at us.'

'Who's George God?' asked Tessa. Her teeth were chattering.

'I know,' whispered Bob suddenly. 'Mr. Mounce is away, so if Mrs. Mounce is in the bath their flat must be empty, and she's probably left the door open. Go and dress down there.'

Bob watched her all the way down the stairs, agonized on her behalf; still more agonized when it occurred to him, just as she went out of sight, that he should have gone down with her and carried the case.

'Hello,' said Mrs. Hennessy, turning off the vacuum-cleaner once again as he came into the room. 'You remind me of radishes, the way you keep returning. I know what it is this time, though, love.'

'Oh?' said Bob. 'What is it?'

'You've left your money on the bedside table.'

'Oh, so I have.'

'Can't get far without money, you know.'

'No, you can't.'

Mrs. Hennessy collected up her equipment.

'Well, I'll say ta-ta, love,' she said. 'Don't forget anything else, now, will you? Got your ticket?'

'Yes.'

'That's right. Have a lovely time, then.'

She rolled across to the door, trailing sticks and poles. Bob hastened across and then flung the door open for her. There on the threshold, barring her progress, stood Tessa, still wearing nothing but the tweed overcoat and still nursing the over-stuffed open suitcase. She looked desperately from Bob to Mrs. Hennessy and back again.

'I'm sorry, Bob,' she said wretchedly, 'but Mrs. Mounce's husband's home now.'

'You get something on before you catch your death, love,'

said Mrs. Hennessy to Tessa reproachfully. 'If you're looking for your undies, I've folded them up and put them on top of the TV for you. Ta-ta, loves. Have a lovely time.'

It was Damian, the Dysons' younger son, who first brought up the subject of marriage.

He stood up on his chair all the way through lunch, with the gravy running down his great red face on to his bib and flying off the spoon he was waving on to other people's clothes; and in his loud, pharyngitic voice he kept up a perpetual background noise of questions and comments. His brother Gawain ignored him, gazing at the salt cellar or the window for minutes at a time and stolidly chewing. So did Dyson, intent upon pushing a heavy agenda through committee – roast lamb, the state of the newspaper industry, the beauties of Tessa's native Somerset, second helpings of lamb, the shortcomings of primary education, the exact age of poor old Eddy Moulton, apple crumble, and how funny it was that only the morning that poor old Eddy had died, etc. He seemed unaware of the noise Damian was making. Bob's head ached and filled with fog at the effort of filtering the adult conversation out from it.

'Are Bob and Tessa married, Mummy?' he became aware that Damian was asking, over and over again. 'Are Bob and Tessa married, Daddy? Are Bob and Tessa married, Mummy?'

'No, we're not, Day,' he said, to halt the noise.

'Why aren't you married?' asked Damian.

'We're just not,' said Tessa. 'Not everyone's married.'

Damian thought about this, scratching his private parts thoughtfully with his spoon. 'Mummy and Daddy did be married,' he said.

'Sit down and eat up your lunch, Day,' said Jannie.

'Jack did be married,' said Damian.

'Oh, not Jack, *please*, Damian!' said Dyson.

'Who's Jack?' asked Tessa.

'That's impossible to explain,' said Bob. 'Who did Jack marry, Day?'

'Jack did marry his Mummy,' said Damian. He looked surprised when everyone laughed, then joined in himself, with very hoarse, loud laughter which made everyone start laughing all over again.

'Jack did marry his Mummy,' he said, as soon as the laughter had subsided, and laughed again himself, which made Bob and Tessa start again, too.

'For God's sake don't encourage him,' said Dyson irritably. 'He'll go on for hours.'

'Jack did marry his Mummy,' repeated Damian, beaming around the table with the confidence of a man who knows he has a fully pilot-surveyed and market-researched product to offer.

'That's enough, Day,' said Dyson sharply.

'Did you know,' said Damian to Bob in a specially humorous voice, and with a *risqué* expression on his great round face, 'Jack did marry his Mummy?'

'Day!' said Jannie.

'Did you know . . .' began Damian to Tessa.

'*Damian*!' shouted Dyson.

'Did you know,' said Damian, leaning humorously across the table towards Gawain, who was gazing transfixed at the top button of Bob's coat, 'Jack did marry his Mummy?'

Gawain roused himself from his daze. 'Don't repeat your jokes, Damian,' he said coldly.

Damian sat down slowly in his place, completely silenced by the rebuke, staring at Gawain as if he were trying to understand the thought-processes which had led up to it.

'Marriage is something which I must say I'm strongly in favour of,' said Dyson with comfortable good humour, cutting himself another sliver of meat off the joint. 'I think everybody should marry. Marry anybody. No nonsense about waiting for your one and only soul-mate to show up. It's the state of marriage that counts.'

'Not peating my jokes,' said Damian softly, gazing at his brother.

'That's a stupid thing to say to anyone, John,' said Jannie. 'A bad marriage is much worse than no marriage at all.'

'Not peating my jokes,' said Damian, slightly more loudly.

'Adaptation to the idea of marriage,' said Dyson. 'That's the only thing that counts.'

'Yes, you are,' said Gawain to Damian. 'You're repeating your jokes.'

'*Not* peating my jokes!'

'You've only got to look around you at the marriages of people we know,' said Jannie, 'to see that's not true.'

'Damian's repeating his jokes again.'

'*Not* peating my jokes!'

'Good God, Jannie, think about it *statistically*! How many marriageable girls does a man meet? Or vice versa? Twenty? Fifty? A hundred? All right, say a hundred . . .'

'Damian *is* repeating his jokes, isn't he, Daddy?'

'. . . of whom we think in our romantic way that one and only one is the ideal mate. All right. Now the population of the world is three thousand million. Divide by two for members of the opposite sex – fifteen hundred million . . .'

'You know this is preposterous, John. You're just being deliberately irritating.'

'Not peating my jokes, am I, Mummy?'

'. . . so *pro rata*, even by our own romantic criteria for singling out just one girl from the hundred we meet, there must be at least fifteen million members of the opposite sex in the world who would make an ideal mate! . . . What the *hell* is it, Gawain?'

'Damian's repeating his jokes, Daddy.'

'John, you're just trying to be shocking,' said Jannie. 'What do you think, Tessa?'

'I beg your pardon?'

'Day's repeating his jo-okes!'

'*Not* peating!'

'. . . about marriage . . .?'

'Day's repeating his jo-okes!'

'Not peating! Not peating! Not peating!'

'. . . Oh . . . very much like to . . .'

'Like to what?' shouted Dyson. 'Shut up, Damian.'

'Daddy, Damian can't say "repeat," can he?'

'. . . get married . . .'

'Are you? Shut *up*, Damian – I mean, Gawain! Well, congratulations!'

'I *can* say peat!'

'. . . thoroughly recommend it . . .' shouted Dyson.

'Damian's going to cry-y!'

'. . . haven't had children . . . really lived . . . do you think, Bob?'

'Look, Daddy, Damian's crying!'

When everyone moved out of the kitchen into the living-room after lunch, leaving Jannie to put the coffee on, Bob lingered behind with her, savouring the sudden calm. He felt something like battle-fatigue – a great desire to lie down on the ground with his hands over his ears and take no further part in the war. He remembered now; he always felt the same by this stage of every visit he made to the Dysons' house in the daytime, while the children were about. Between visits nature obliterated the memory of them, in the same way that it expunged the dread of battle and the pain of childbirth, so that war and childbirth and social visits to the Dysons could continue.

'I like Tessa very much indeed, Bob,' said Jannie, lighting the gas and stacking plates.

'Do you?' said Bob, too worn down to think of any intelligent reply. 'Good, good.'

'You are serious about her, aren't you?'

'Oh, yes. Jannie, could I possibly borrow a couple of aspirins? I've got rather a headache coming on.'

'I think the aspirins are in the cupboard with the spice jars. She's very much in love with you, Bob. You know that, don't you?'

'Yes. Yes, I do. This cupboard?'

'That's right – at the back. It would be terrible to hurt her in any way. Wouldn't it, Bob?'

'I suppose it would.'

'You *suppose* it would?'

'I mean, of course it would. May I take four, Jannie?'

Tessa had subdued the two boys, Bob discovered with relief and admiration when he went out to the living-room. She was telling them a story, and they were sitting on either side of her on the sofa with their mouths hanging slightly open, Gawain meditatively fingering a lock of her long, dark hair, Damian staring at her and absently scratching his balls. Every now and then one of them would stand up on the sofa and trample restlessly round like a dog resettling itself into its sleeping place. Bob sank into the scrunching springs of an old armchair, put a hand over his eyes, and watched them through his fingers. He was touched by the sight, and felt suddenly tender towards Tessa. If that feeling wasn't love, what was? He had felt sour ever since her arrival – he could admit it to himself now – but simply because it had all happened so unexpectedly and confusedly. He liked life to be predictable and orderly. He liked to have time to think what he was going to feel about something before it happened.

When Tessa went out of the room to see if she could help Jannie the boys turned on Bob at once with all their usual wildness, jumping up and down in his lap, punching him in the chest, and trying to pull off his shoes.

'Ouch! Ouf! You would, would you?' said Bob with as much avuncular bonhomie as he could force out of himself, feinting punches back at them, turning them upside down, and trying not to scream and double up when Damian trod on his genitals.

'Just chuck them off if they're a nuisance,' said Dyson, stretched out in the least broken armchair with the *Observer* and the *Sunday Times*.

'Oh, I don't mind them,' said Bob, wedging his head against the back of the chair, so that the colossal thumping going on inside his skull wouldn't shake it loose from its mountings. 'Do I, men?'

'Punch, punch, punch!' cried Damian, finding Bob's nose.

'Do you read Brooks, Bob?' asked Dyson.

'You mean the estate agent? No – should I?'

'I suppose you'll be reading him now. The thing is, Bob, if I may give you some advice based on long and hard experience, not to start off by renting somewhere, if you can possibly avoid it.'

'I suppose you're right.'

'Punch punch punch!' said Damian.

'You're just wasting valuable years, renting. Buy something and get on the escalator. Then at least you're not slipping behind the field as prices go up.'

'I suppose not.'

'Bash bash!'

'And do be practical, Bob. So many people start off with some hazy idea of finding a little Georgian house in W.I. for five thousand pounds. The thing to do, Bob, is to face up to the fact right from the beginning that it's going to be something Victorian or Edwardian, and that it's going to be in some slightly less fashionable postal district.'

'I suppose so. Ugh! Gawain, that really hurt.'

'I don't know whether you know this area at all, Bob?'

'Well, you know . . .'

'Pinch pinch pinch!'

'It's got quite a lot to be said for it, Bob. For a start it's got a village atmosphere which I must say we find rather agreeable. Well, you know, there are little corner shops which still have some sense of individuality about them. There's a certain sense of community that you wouldn't find somewhere like Chelsea or South Kensington. You've met our neighbours, Ecosse and Princess St. George?'

'Yes.'

'Then again, it's on the Tube, or almost on the Tube. And, Bob, it's an area that's bound to go up.'

'Bite bite.'

'Definitely no biting, Damian! Yes, I remember your saying, John.'

'Bound to. *Must* do, you see. Big, roomy houses – just right for expanding middle-class families. People have got to go somewhere. It absolutely *must* go up.'

'I suppose it must.'

'Snip snip – I'm a hairdresser!'

'Do fling them off if they're getting obstreperous, Bob. Anyway, I'll get Jannie to look in the local agents and keep her ears open.'

'Well – No, Gawain, let go! – thanks, John.'

Bob lit the gas-fire and sank down on his bed without even taking his overcoat off. 'You were very good with those children, Tess,' he said, with his hand over his eyes.

'It's just a matter of being sensible,' said Tessa, lighting the gas-stove and filling the kettle, without taking her overcoat off either. 'Will scrambled eggs be all right tonight, Bob? They're quite nice boys, but those silly people just let them run wild.'

'I don't think they really notice the noise themselves,' said Bob, slightly irritated that she should presume to call them silly when they were after all his friends. 'They're hardened to it.'

'I'm hardened to the noise that D and Baby make at home, but I don't let them get away with it while I'm around.'

'Perhaps it's a bit more difficult with children of your own.'

'Well, I shouldn't let them get away with it like that, all the same.'

Bob reflected in silence for some moments.

'Jannie likes you very much,' he said finally. 'She told me so.'

Tessa broke three eggs into a bowl, frowning. 'I'm not sure I like *her* all that much, Bob,' she said. 'I thought she was trying to marry you off.'

'Don't be silly, Tess. That was just some silly misunderstanding at lunch.'

'Was it?'

'Of course it was. Anyway, we've got wills of our own. There's no need to let ourselves be rushed into anything, just because other people think it would be a good thing. It's up to us, what we do, not anybody else. Isn't that right, Tess?'

Tessa said nothing. She beat up the eggs, splashed a drop or two on the lapel of her overcoat, and wiped it off carefully with her finger. 'Well,' she said finally, 'I thought your friend Mrs. Dyson was a little bit in love with you, to tell you the truth.'

Bob sat up on the bed and gazed at her in astonishment. 'She wants to marry me off to you,' he said, 'and she's in love with me? What on earth are you talking about, Tess?'

Tessa banged saucepans about irritably. 'She thinks I wouldn't be too much competition for her,' she said, 'because she thinks you're not very much in love with me.'

'She told you this?'

'Of course not. It's just what I think.'

Bob picked up one of his bedside *Vogues* and withdrew into the world of the advertisements. One of them showed a pair of slim, naked legs, cut off a fraction of a millimetre below the groin, running through a meadow full of dewy grass and pale blue cornflowers. They advertised depilatory cream. He yearned for them, in all their innocence and simplicity, as if they were childhood.

'What was all this about a house?' asked Tessa.

'Search me,' said Bob.

He slipped a peppermint into his mouth and curled up, gazing at the legs. If only he were attractive to women!

9

Dyson was invited to appear on television again. He and Bob were rushing to get a whole day's work done before lunchtime, in order to get away for poor old Eddy's funeral in the afternoon, when a woman called Samantha Lightbody rang from the BBC. She said she was terribly sorry to disturb him. She wasn't disturbing him at all, said Dyson, swinging round in his chair and resting his elbow comfortably on the stacks of unsubbed copy and uncorrected proofs. She said she was sure she had rung at the worst possible moment – she always rang important people at the worst possible moment. The moment couldn't have been better, said Dyson, taking another armful of stuff from the messenger.

'The point is,' said Samantha Lightbody, 'I'm researching a programme about – well, it's about race relations, I'm afraid. I know – yet another. Groan, groan, and all the rest of it. I hardly dare tell anyone.'

'It sounds absolutely fascinating,' said Dyson.

'Well, we thought it could be quite fun if we got one or two really interesting new people like yourself to come along and take an entirely fresh look at the subject. I know you appear in programmes about race relations from time to time, but you're not one of the usual old gang of faces that everyone's sick of. Do you know what I mean? Anyway, could we *possibly* persuade you?'

'Well,' said Dyson luxuriantly, pressing the point of his pencil through the surface of a copy-pad, 'I am rather heavily committed, of course. When is it?'

'Friday the eighteenth, at seven o'clock, if that doesn't seem too hopeless. It's in a series called *New Perspectives*.'

Dyson slowly turned over the empty pages of his diary. 'I shall be away in the Persian Gulf that week,' he said.

'Oh dear . . .'

'It's a terrible bore, but something has cropped up out there. I don't think I can really get out of it.'

'So you can't possibly do the programme?'

'Oh, yes, I think so. I mean, I shall be back from the Middle East on the seventeenth. It won't affect us at all for the eighteenth. I just thought I should mention it.'

'Oh, marvellous. That really is awfully kind of you. I know everyone here will be tremendously thrilled. I'll get our contracts department to ring you about a fee.'

Dyson sat back in his chair expansively. 'You know the man you ought to get for this sort of programme?' he suggested. 'Lord Boddy.'

'Oh, we have!'

'*Have* you?'

'He's one of the team. You know him, do you?'

'Oh, I know Frank Boddy very well. *Very* well.'

'I suppose it's another of these tight little worlds, is it, the racial experts?'

'Oh, pretty tight. Yes, pretty tight.'

There was one small question nagging him which he asked just as Samantha Lightbody was ringing off.

'Did you, as a matter of interest, happen to see me on *The Human Angle* last week?'

'It's an awful thing to have to admit,' replied Samantha Lightbody, 'but I'm afraid I missed it.'

'Did anyone there see it?'

'I'm not sure that they did. I'm terribly sorry.'

'That's all right,' said Dyson. 'That's quite all right.'

Dyson scarcely had time to stride up and down the office that morning, lecturing Bob on the importance of television, but he was in great form all the same. Bob was too busy to notice, but

Tessa was in the office, trying to keep out of everyone's way and write a letter to her parents, and Dyson directed his surplus good humour at her. 'It is rather naughty, you know, my lord,' he would say into the phone; 'I shall be coming after you with a big stick if the copy's not here by tomorrow.' And he would catch Tessa's eye and make a humorous grimace, to show what he really thought about bishops. Tessa blushed at the sight.

Bob would catch her eye in his turn as he telephoned. But each time he looked quickly away. He was embarrassed, she knew, because she was sitting at old Eddy Moulton's desk, upon the top of which poor old Eddy had so recently laid down his head and died. She was sitting there because Dyson had invited her to, and Dyson had invited her to because there wasn't anywhere else to sit. But at the sight of Bob's expression she got up, blushing again, and walked about the room as if she were looking for something. She stood by the window for some minutes, looking down into Hand and Ball Court, where an old tramp was feeling his way round the walls and trying not to catch people's eyes. She sympathized with his efforts. When she felt she could not naturally stand by the window any longer she went and inspected the gritty old review copies of books which had somehow collected over the years on the office shelves – *Take Your Car to North Africa! Think Your Way to Good Health and Dynamic Living! The ABC of Practical Woodworking. National Debt or National Death? – The Bankers' Plot Exposed.* She took one or two of them down and turned the pages over, trying to persuade herself she was reading them. But the meanings of the words seemed to dart away from her like a shoal of minnows as she advanced upon them, and she felt more uneasy still. She would never catch up with the enormous range of reading which seemed to be taken for granted by Bob and his friends, never.

'Tessa, Tessa, Tessa!' said Dyson cheerfully, pressing his receiver rest down and then dialling another number. 'Sit down and make yourself comfortable. I can't bear people who walk up and down the room all the time.'

'Sorry,' said Tessa. She blushed and went back to the chair in which old Eddy had died.

'Are you happy, Tess?' asked Bob, between calls.

'Yes,' said Tessa. 'I'm going in a moment, anyway.'

'Are you? Oh, all right.'

'I just want to know whether you want me to go to Mr. Moulton's funeral with you.'

Bob's face went blank.

'Hello,' he said into the phone. 'Canon Morley? . . . It's Mr. Dyson's office here. Look, this copy you phoned in; when you say, "I know only that I have a deeply satisfying face which shines with a radiance beyond the brightness of this world . . ." – should that be "faith"? And what about ". . . justifying God's wheeze to man . . ."?'

'Bob,' said Tessa, when he had put the phone down again, 'do you want me to come to the funeral or not?'

'It's up to you, Tess,' said Bob. They were both speaking very quietly, so as not to disturb Dyson, who was still on the phone.

'I'll come if you want me to.'

'O.K.'

'Do you think I'm dressed all right for it? This is the darkest outfit I've got with me.'

Bob ran a hand through his hair.

'You want to come, do you?' he said doubtfully.

'Only if you want me to. I didn't even know Mr. Moulton.'

'I shouldn't come if you'd prefer not to.'

'But, Bob, what do *you* want me to do?'

Bob's phone rang, and while he was talking Dyson, who was sitting back in his chair and waiting for someone at the other end of the line, covered up the mouthpiece of his phone and said, 'Are you coming to the funeral, Tess?'

'I was just asking Bob if he thought I should.'

'Why don't you? Funerals are quite fun, you know. Well, perhaps "fun" isn't the right word. But the sheer language of the service is *marvellous*! "Man that is born of a woman has but a short time to live, and is full of misery . . ." Hello? Hello – Sir William?'

Bob put his phone down. 'The only thing is,' he said uncertainly, 'if everybody started turning up with their girl-friends . . .'

'I certainly don't want to embarrass you, Bob.'

'It's not that. But if everybody suddenly started turning up with their girl-friends . . .'

'All right, Bob, I won't come.'

'I mean, you're welcome to come as far as I'm concerned. But I somehow feel that it's not a sort of social occasion . . .'

Tessa folded up her half-written letter and put it in her handbag.

'If ever you don't want me to come with you somewhere, Bob, you've only got to say. I honestly don't mind. I wouldn't have come to the office in the first place if you hadn't asked me.'

'No, I was very pleased you came . . . You're not going now?'

'I thought I might go shopping, or visit St. Paul's.'

'Well, if you want to. But don't feel in any way . . .'

Bob's phone rang. Dyson, putting his own down a moment later, as Tessa looked around for her gloves, said, 'I know what, Tessa. You look rather at a loose end over there. Would you like to become a journalist for an hour or so, and copy out one or two "In Years Gone By" columns for us from the files? It would help us out of a most tremendous hole if you would.'

Tessa was already turning the tatter-edged yellow pages over, trying to find the right date, when Bob put his phone down.

'I thought you said you were going?' he said.

'John asked me to do a job for him first.'

'I see.'

'Is that all right, Bob?'

'Of course it's all right. Why should I mind? It's nothing to do with me what you do.'

Dyson had brought his car into town specially, and everyone in the Gates at lunch wanted a lift to the funeral in it. With six large journalists aboard, all well filled with beer and sandwiches, there was scarcely room for Dyson to turn the wheel or change gear without jamming his elbow into Ted Hurwitz's stomach.

'Perhaps it's just as well Tessa didn't come, Bob,' said Bill Waddy.

'She could have sat in my lap,' said Gareth Holmroyd.

'Ay, ay!' said Ted Hurwitz.

'I thought she was a very nice girl, Bob,' said Gareth Holmroyd.

'Ay, ay, ay!' said Ted Hurwitz.

Laurence Evenden belched behind his hand. 'I *beg* your pardon,' he said.

'The point is,' said Dyson, thumping the car down into second to slow up at the traffic lights, 'a journalist ought to be specializing by the time he's forty. That's really why I'm rather pleased about this BBC thing. I do seem to be accepted as part of the regular television establishment. Do you know what I mean?'

'The light's green, John,' said Ted Hurwitz.

Dyson let the clutch in with a belated jerk, which brought some hard and heavy object tumbling down from the dashboard to hit Bill Waddy on the knee and roll away out of sight beneath the front seats.

'God Almighty,' said Bill Waddy, rubbing his knee. 'What was that?'

'The point is,' said Dyson, 'I don't feel one can go on just doing the general odds and sods indefinitely without more or less destroying oneself. Do you see what I'm driving at?'

'It looks like the other side of the road to me,' murmured Bill Waddy.

Dyson swung the wheel to the left, then swung it sharply to the right again to avoid a lorry which was overtaking him on the inside.

'My God,' said Dyson, 'the lunatics you meet on the roads these days! I'm sorry to go on about this BBC thing, but it does seem important to me.'

Laurence Evenden belched. 'I *beg* your pardon,' he said.

It was like a holiday, driving out through the suburbs on a weekday afternoon. Every now and then the sun came out, lighting up women out walking with prams and push-chairs.

'There's the Royal Oak,' said Bill Waddy. 'Do you remember the Siege of the Royal Oak in 1947, Gareth? When the old publican went off his head and shut himself up in the snug with an ex-War Department Verey pistol, and shot distress signals through the serving hatch at anyone who came near?'

'That's right,' said Gareth Holmroyd. 'You were on the *Mail* then, weren't you, Bill? There was you and I there, and old Freddie Samuelson of the *Express*, and Walter Edgworth of the *Mirror* . . .'

'Old Walter's dead now, you know.'

'No! Is he? Poor old Walter!'

'He went out to a paper in East Africa. Got some disease out there.'

'What will you do now that poor old Eddy's gone, John?' asked Laurence Evenden. 'Will you get someone else, do you think?'

'I'll have to have someone, Laurence. I was absolutely run into the ground as it was. And now it looks as though I'm going to be tied up with television work pretty regularly.'

'You know Harry Stearns wants you to take over "Lighting-Up Time" and "Phases of the Moon," John?' said Gareth Holmroyd.

'I know. I can't possibly do it. Not without more staff. I've told the Editor.'

'Charles Baker's trying to get rid of "Shipping Move-

143

ments," ' said Ted Hurwitz. 'I bet he manages to land them on poor old John in the end.'

'He won't,' said Dyson. 'He can't. I can't do it.'

'He tried to unload it on me,' said Gareth Holmroyd. 'I told him I thought John Dyson was the man.'

'Well, I'm not,' said Dyson.

'Old John'll manage somehow,' said Bill Waddy. 'Why don't you change down, John? We've almost stopped.'

Bob, who had sat in silence from the beginning of the journey, crushed between Gareth Holmroyd and Laurence Evenden in the back, sighed meditatively. 'It's funny to think we're on our way to poor old Eddy's funeral,' he said.

'Look, Dancy Street,' said Bill Waddy. 'Wasn't that where some bakery foreman dressed himself up in a turban, said he was an Eastern potentate, and persuaded half a dozen women to move in with him as his harem? Nineteen-forty-nine, I think it was.'

'Nineteen-fifty-one,' said Gareth Holmroyd. 'The old king died next day and killed the story stone dead. There's Holt's Depository – remember that? Where the kids shot the sky-rocket through the fan-light and set fire to all the furniture? You know who was on that story? Old Jimmy Mulholland of the *Guardian*. He's a P.R.O. with the Coal Board now.'

'He's not, you know,' said Ted Hurwitz. 'He's dead.'

'No!'

'Died of lung cancer last summer. I saw his brother in the Cock a couple of months ago.'

'Well, who'd have thought it! A great big, strapping man he was. Poor old Jimmy!'

'I can't help feeling, to revert for a moment,' said Dyson, 'that television is rather more my *métier*. I do think that one can put one's ideas over rather more forcefully and precisely when one's present in the flesh, with all one's conversational resources to hand.'

'Poor old Jimmy!' said Gareth Holmroyd.

'It's a funny thing,' said Bob, emerging from his silence

again. 'I was just thinking about poor old Eddy. He'd have enjoyed being on this trip with us today, you know.'

'He wouldn't have enjoyed going to his own funeral, Bob,' said Laurence Evenden. 'He wasn't *morbid*.'

'I didn't mean that . . .'

'Do you remember Basil Merriman's funeral, Gareth?' said Bill Waddy. 'It was snowing a blizzard, and we got lost in the middle of nowhere out beyond Aylesbury?'

Dyson swerved to avoid a hole in the road, hit it dead in the middle, and brought Bill Waddy's window down with a crash.

'Don't worry,' said Dyson. 'That's always happening. Just jam it with that wedge of paper.'

Laurence Evenden belched. 'I *beg* your pardon,' he said.

Tessa sat at Bob's desk in the empty department all afternoon, newspaper files stacked in front of her, trying intermittently to finish the job that Dyson had given her. She didn't find it easy; she wasn't a great reader. Between whiles she got up and looked out of the window, watching the pale sunshine come and go on the elaborate mouldings and cornices of the offices on the opposite side of Hand and Ball Court, until she realized she was being watched from a window of the floor above by two young men in shirt-sleeves. They smiled and waved at her, and she hurried back to the desk, blushing.

It was quiet and calm in the empty room. From time to time one of the phones rang, and she stared at it and held her breath till it stopped. Now and then messengers would come in, look in the empty out-baskets, and go out again without a word; or put proofs on the desk beside her – rolled galleys and damp, folded pages. 'Thank you,' she said, not daring to look them in the face. But most of the time the only reminders of the outside world were remote sounds which merely emphasized the quiet of the room itself – the murmur of traffic away in Fleet Street, a typewriter clicking somewhere, some girls giggling, milk bottles falling over, a boy whistling.

She looked through the drawers of Bob's desk, curious to

explore even the most unconsidered corners of his life. She found a paper bag with two toffees in it; a book on Burma with a page of Bob's notes inside; yellowing, dusty copy paper, crumpled carbons, expired typewriter ribbons; a briar pipe, grey with age, left over perhaps from some previous occupant; a dusty brown shoe with a hole in it; three rusty razor-blades; an ancient copy of *Queen* magazine; a letter from herself . . .

She opened the letter and began to read it. 'My dearest, darlingest Bob,' it began. 'Masses of hugs and kisses from your silly adoring Tessa, because the sun's shining, and I *know* there'll be a letter from you tomorrow, and because anyway all I want to do is to send you masses of hugs and kisses . . .'

She put her hand over her eyes, too embarrassed to read on. How could she have written such stuff? How *could* she? It was like coming across an embarrassing old photograph of herself. The letter was dated four weeks before. It could have been four years. She felt that she had changed entirely since it was written, and chiefly during the three days since she had been in London.

How would she write to Bob now? She leaned on the files, making her sleeves grey with dust, looking up at the pale blue patches appearing and disappearing above the rooftops outside the window. 'Darling Bob,' she would start – nothing more elaborate, nothing more gushing. No, not even that. Just 'Bob.' 'Bob, I understand now that nothing in life is as easy as it at first seems, and that being in love is a condition which can cause one a great deal of pain. Of course, I knew that before. But I supposed that it was only the sweet pain of yearning, the sweet uncertainty of what-may-perhaps-be. But now I see that the sweetness goes, and that the pain which remains is just the ordinary, unilluminating misery of humiliation, embarrassment, and inadequacy. You have hurt me a lot in the past three days, Bob, and I think you will hurt me a great deal more in the days to come. You don't love me very much. Perhaps you don't love me at all. But why should you? I can see how hopelessly unsuitable I am for you; all I ever do is misunderstand what you say, and weep. But you'll never have the strength to send me away – you're so *weak*, Bob, that it embarrasses me – and in the end the job will fall to me; I shall have to send myself away. What a miserable responsibility to be loaded with! I put it off from day to day out of pity for myself. For in spite of everything, you are present in all my waking thoughts. Whichever way I turn – you. I revolve about you, dazed and unhappy, with my eyes fixed on you helplessly. Look how I write you this letter! I keep it inside my head, so that you'll never see it, or anything like it . . .'

Tears brimmed out of her eyes, and ran down her cheeks. She walked about the room, hating herself for pitying herself. She looked out the window, carefully read the titles of all the books on the shelf, from *Take Your Car to North Africa!* to *National Debt or National Death? – The Bankers' Plot Exposed*, and stopped crying. She sat down and set to work on the files. The phone continued to ring from time to time; messengers continued to call. Once or twice people put their heads round the door and asked her if the Meditation proof was up yet, or whether she knew that she had four inches less than usual on page twelve. 'I'm sorry,' she told these heads, keeping her red eyes turned away from them, 'Mr. Dyson and Mr. Bell are at the funeral. I don't work here myself.' 'I see,' they said, not seeing, and withdrew uncertainly.

The only caller who stayed for any length of time said nothing at all. Tessa became conscious of a mottled red face gazing at her, and the right half of a short, bulky body wedged in the jamb of the door with one shabby braces strap visible. When she looked up, the man smiled shyly and nodded at her. She told him where Dyson and Bob were, and he nodded and smiled again, as if he had known already. Then he gazed absently at the window for some minutes, blinking.

'Can I help you at all?' asked Tessa, increasingly nervous at this silent presence. 'I mean, I don't work here myself. Well, I'm working here *now*. But I don't actually *work* here.'

The man nodded and smiled.

'I'm really just waiting for Bob,' said Tessa. 'I'm his – his fiancée.'

She blushed to say such a thing. But some sort of concrete explanation had to be offered.

The man nodded and smiled all over again – rather encouragingly, this time – and then, smiling in a somewhat more valedictory sort of way, edged slowly back out through the door. Tessa could hear him breathing on the threshold outside for several minutes more, as if he were trying to summon up the courage to return and say something.

Many people had worked on the paper for twenty years, and never once come face to face with the Editor.

Dyson fixed his gaze upon the east window of the crematorium chapel, screwing up his eyes, trying to fill his head with the radiating rods of light and a steady contemplation of death. Light; flowers; brass fittings; solemn intonation; and in that box the already decomposing remains of the man who had occupied the corner desk in Dyson's office each day since he had taken the department over. Then poor old Eddy had been a jungle of faint electric circuits connected to make thoughts and memories and aches and sleepiness, like a blackboard of chalk dust patterned to form the binomial theorem or the history of the Fourth Crusade. Now those slight differences of electrical potential had disappeared, like the chalk dust at the end of the lesson. Old Eddy had been wiped clean. Dyson tried to fix his mind upon the tiny grains of chalk fleeing before the duster, filling the air, and settling upon shiny surfaces, totally and eternally discharged of theorem and crusade, or any lingering imprint of them.

There were a dozen mourners from the family in the front pews – women with grey curls and mild glasses, an old man bent over a stick, his head projecting forwards from the unoccupied collar of his overcoat like a tortoise's; a schoolboy in a neat navy-blue trenchcoat, holding a maroon cap. Women in tweed overcoats, men in dark melton overcoats – they seemed more overcoats than people; the sort of people whose personalities are not large enough to dominate their outdoor clothes. Two of the ladies' overcoats were sniffling, and with infinite discretion blowing their noses. I have a lump in my throat, thought Dyson. I definitely have a lump in my throat. I am pervaded by a deep and solemn sadness. Yes, yes, I am awed by a cognition of mortality. A *cognition*? Why not 'a sense'? God, one's thoughts need subbing at times! All the same, a cognition is what it feels like, set among these flowers, these stabbing rods of light, these solemn sacerdotal periods, this indisputable lump in the throat. The lesson was from Corinthians. 'If after the manner of men I have fought with beasts at Ephesus, what advantageth it me, if the dead rise not?' Such words! Such sonorous words, breaking like a dark, silver-shot ocean upon this unpromising overcoated shore!

'For this corruptible must put on incorruption, and this mortal must put on immortality. So when this corruptible shall have put on incorruption, and this mortal shall have put on immortality, then shall be brought to pass the saying that is written, Death is swallowed up in victory.' Yes, thought Dyson, at that I can feel a pricking behind the lids of my eyes! At that I am almost ready to break down and weep! And yet . . . do I in any sense believe that poor old Eddy shall put on immortality? Isn't it rather terrible that what brings the pricking behind my eyelids is not old Eddy's death, or even the thought of human mortality in general, but certain strokes of rhetoric – certain alliterations, repetitions, and verbal sonorities which don't hold any literal meaning for me? I'm more moved by literature than by what it describes!

The lump in the throat – where has it gone? Oh God, have I forgotten how poor old Eddy sat at his desk in Hand and Ball Court on the last day of his life, talking about those past times which were most important to him, and how nobody took any notice? Have I forgotten how nobody really cared, how nobody really knew him? Doesn't that bring the lump back to the throat, if one really dwells on it? Well, doesn't it? And isn't it a little moving to think of all these various people being moved by poor old Eddy's death? Moved enough, anyway, to abandon their day's work and come here to be told that the trumpet would sound, and poor old Eddy be raised incorruptible? There was anguish in thinking of the anguish felt within the overcoats; and in the hearts of people from the office with some substance and standing, like Gareth Holmroyd and Laurence Evenden; and in the heart of one whose face would be well-known to anyone in the front pews from their television screens, if they happened to turn round . . .

But I *did* feel something. In that horrible moment when I looked across the room and realized that poor old Eddy was dead I certainly felt something. I felt frightened, physically frightened. What else? I felt disbelief, and some sense of outrage that this should happen to me. Yes, I certainly felt *something*.

And when the priest came to commit poor old Eddy's body to the flames, Dyson felt something else. For slowly, propelled by some unseen force, the coffin began to jerk sideways, until it reached the wall of the chapel, when a trapdoor opened, and in a series of irregular jerks, man that was born of woman disappeared into the wings. Dyson was stunned by the vulgarity of it. That poor old Eddy should come to this! That he should last be seen being dragged jerkily offstage by theatrical machinery, like the cardboard ship in *Dick Whittington*! Dyson half expected him to come jerking back for a reprise of the First Collect. It would have been different if the trapdoor had been the actual door of the furnace; or if the coffin had been dragged by visible human operatives; or if it had gone smoothly, as by the hand of God or the power of irresistible mechanical principles. But as it was . . . As it was, Dyson had experienced a genuine spasm. And another, secondary spasm, when he thought about the first one, and realized that he was more appalled by vulgarity than he was by death.

With great discretion, the overcoats in the front pews blew

their noses. With great discretion, Laurence Evenden released the excess gas pressure in his duodenum. With great discretion, Dyson yawned, straining his muscles to keep his mouth shut at the same time. He yawned again, uncontrollably, concealing it behind his service-card. God, he thought, I really must give the beer at lunch a miss.

Reg Mounce marched into Dyson's department, kicking the door open in front of him.

'Oh, it's you,' he said to Tessa, looking sourly round the room. 'Both at the wake, are they?'

He hesitated, frowning at a sheet of paper he was holding.

'It was one or the other of your bright boy-friends who sent me this, was it?' he demanded, tossing the paper down in front of her. She picked it up and read it.

> Editor to R. Mounce. PRIVATE AND CONFIDENTIAL
>
> I cannot trace any acknowledgment from you of the memorandum I sent you on the twelfth of this month, regarding your talents and the scope for them in this office. Since the matter is important, I wonder if you would take the trouble to write to me again, indicating particularly whether such other arrangements as you will be making are likely to commence at an earlier date than one might otherwise suppose. Certain other arrangements which I must make naturally turn upon this.
>
> I trust that your own other arrangements are proceeding satisfactorily.

'Some sort of joke, is it?' demanded Mounce bitterly.

'I'm afraid I don't know. It looks as if it's from the Editor.'

'Oh, it *looks* as if it's from the Editor,' said Mounce ironically.

'It says it's from the Editor.'

'Oh, it *says* it's from the Editor. The last one *said* it was from the Editor. But it wasn't. It was just a load of crap that some joker had sent. All this crap about 'other arrangements'! It's just crap.'

'Is it?' said Tessa, wondering if perhaps it was. She tried to focus her mind on the words. 'Other arrangements' – well, other arrangements were alternative dispositions. And alternative dispositions were – well, they were other arrangements. But somehow, she felt, the words had passed right through her mind without leaving any deposit of meaning behind.

'Well, isn't it?' said Mounce. 'People aren't asked to make other arrangements on this paper, are they? Have you ever heard of anyone in this office being asked to make other arrangements?'

'Well, no . . .'

'So it's obviously a load of crap. Everyone saw that. This isn't the *Express*, after all.' He took the note out of Tessa's hands and began to read it through again, rubbing his chin uneasily. 'I mean,' he said, 'you don't think this *is* from the Editor, do you?'

'I've honestly no idea.'

'I mean, this is just the sort of shit the Editor would write. "Other arrangements" – that's just the sort of stinking thing he'd say.'

'I thought,' said Tessa timidly, 'that you said people weren't asked to make other arrangements on this paper?'

'No, but what I mean is, if they *were* asked to make other arrangements, making other arrangements is just what the stinking Editor would call it.'

Mounce held the note up to the light, as if looking for a watermark. 'I wonder,' he said gloomily. 'Now you've put doubts in my mind.'

'I suppose you could ring the Editor's secretary and check . . .' suggested Tessa hesitantly.

Mounce stared at her absently, pushing his lower lip up.

'I suppose I could,' he said. He read through the note again, frowning. Then he went over to the window, and gazed down into Hand and Ball Court for several minutes, frowning and pushing his lower lip up alternately.

'I suppose that would be one way of tackling it,' he said. He took another look at the note, putting a finger into his mouth and trying to dislodge some irritating morsel of lunch from between his back teeth. Slowly, still rereading the note and still working on his teeth, he wandered out of the room.

'I'll bear it in mind,' he said gloomily, without turning his head, as he went through the door.

'Hello,' said Bob, coming back into the office and holding out a bag of sweets to Tessa. 'Have a peppermint. How were things in the office, Tessa?'

'All right. How was the funeral?'

'Fine.'

He picked up the mail and messages on his desk, and at once sorted out a small brown envelope addressed 'R. Bell Esqre.'

'Oh God,' he said, 'something from the Editor.'

He ripped it open. It said:

Editor to R. Bell. PRIVATE AND CONFIDENTIAL.
Congratulations.

'What does it say?' asked Dyson. 'You look as white as a sheet.'

Bob shook his head blankly. 'It just says "congratulations". But what on, for God's sake?'

Dyson thought for an instant, and then laughed. 'Bob!' he said reproachfully. 'On your *engagement*!'

10

Bob, arriving at the office before Dyson one morning, found a man he had never seen before working at poor old Eddy's desk. He appeared on the whole to be middle-aged. His face was middle-aged – unnaturally neat and pale, with spare flesh padding the line of the jaw, and lifeless sandy hair brushed inertly to the shape of the head. But his clothes were young men's clothes – a very dark jacket buttoned on four buttons, revealing a triangle of dark tan shirt with a strip of black suede tie, and an inch and a half of tan cuff at each wrist. He looked up at Bob; his eyes were ageless and neutral.

'Hello,' he said, and returned to his work.

'Hello,' said Bob. He took off his overcoat and sat down at his desk, staring at the man. He felt he ought to query his presence – particularly his use of poor old Eddy's desk – but everything about him suggested that his right to be in the room was firmly established – perhaps more firmly even than Bob's. Besides, Bob felt diffident about challenging an older man. Without taking his eyes off him, he opened the drawer of his desk and felt about inside it until he had located a toffee. The man continued to work. He was writing something in long-hand, the paper turned sideways, the pen flying along the lines away from him at great speed. His left hand rested on the desk, a silver ring set with a large brown stone on the little finger, and between the first and second fingers a cigarette with a thin blue tape of smoke rising steadily from it. The finger-ends were pale amber, the rest of the hand marble-white, and slightly fleshy. As Bob looked at it, the hand performed a sudden evolution like a conjuring-trick, turning over and producing from nowhere a pack of American cigarettes, with one of the cigarettes extended towards Bob. The right hand continued to write. The blue tape of smoke from the left hand snaggled for a moment, then the snaggle slid up the tape and disappeared, leaving the smoke rising as steadily as before from the underside of the hand.

'Cigarette?' said the man.

'No thanks,' said Bob.

'My name's Erskine Morris,' said the man, vanishing the cigarettes as deftly as he had produced them, and continuing to write as he spoke. It looked like some sort of play he was writing, so far as Bob could see. There were names down the margin, each followed by a colon and a short sentence ending in a row of dots. 'I'm Moulton's replacement.'

'Oh, I see,' said Bob. 'Well, welcome to the department. My name's Bob Bell.'

'Hi, Bob,' said Morris expressionlessly. Bob wondered if he was an Englishman who affected American usages, or an American with an English accent. Was he a young American with middle-aged English characteristics? Or a middle-aged Englishman with middle-aged American mannerisms? Or . . . Another thought struck Bob.

'Does Dyson know you're joining us?'

'You tell me, Bob.'

'He hasn't said anything to me about it.'

Morris wrote on in silence.

'I don't think I've seen you round the office before,' said Bob finally.

'No,' said Morris.

'You've just joined the paper?'

'Sure.'

'Who were you with before?'

'I was at university before.'

Bob stared at Morris – mainly at the back of his head, since it was turned slightly away from him to follow the speeding journeys of his pen across the paper.

155

'You mean, you've just come down?' said Bob, trying out of politeness not to sound incredulous.

'Sure.'

'You mean, *straight* down?'

'Last year.'

'Forgive me asking, but how old are you?'

'Twenty-two.'

Morris's left hand stretched out from its one-and-a-half-inch cuff and stubbed out its half-smoked cigarette in the ashtray. Then, while the right hand wrote on, it conjured up the pack of cigarettes once again, conjured one out, and conjured a flame out of a butane lighter it suddenly turned out to be holding. Bob followed each movement with his eyes.

'Which university were you at?' he asked.

'Cambridge.'

'Cambridge? I was at Cambridge.'

'Sure.'

'John Dyson was at Cambridge.'

'Sure, sure.'

Morris administered his sures and sure sures in a soothing tone, like pats on the head for an importunate child. Bob felt rather like a child, talking to Morris. He went over to the window and gazed down into Hand and Ball Court. Reassuringly familiar, homely figures like Gareth Holmroyd and Pat Selig were arriving for work, pacing out the well-worn diagonal trail across the court from the end of Hand and Ball Passage to the main door of the office. They seemed almost embarrassingly innocent and unsophisticated, compared with Morris.

'Are you on the paper's graduate trainee scheme?' he asked.

'Sure.'

'I joined the paper as a graduate trainee.'

'Oh?'

Bob tried to imagine Morris completing the trainee scheme, joining the pensions fund, and going on to groove out the diagonal of Hand and Ball Court morning and night for twenty or thirty years. It was somehow not a very plausible picture.

Erskine Morris . . .

'That's a coincidence,' said Bob. 'You've got the same initials as poor old Eddy Moulton.'

'Sure.'

'I'll help you move poor old Eddy's junk out of the desk, if you like, so you can move your own stuff in.'

'Thank you, Bob – I've done it already.'

Going back to his desk, Bob looked discreetly over Morris's shoulder. The only page he could see of Morris's manuscript started off:

BENNY: If Patrick says you're going to get done, you're going to get done, sunshine. Inne, Patrick?

OLD MAN: No! *No!*

PATRICK: He's going to get *done* all right . . .

BENNY: You see, sunshine? You're going to get done. Patrick says so . . .

[*The camera holds* OLD MAN *in M.C.U., tightens on his terrified eyes, then whip-pans to C.U. of knife in* PATRICK'S *hand.*]

'What did you do with poor old Eddy's stuff?' asked Bob.

'I put it in the wastepaper basket,' said Morris.

Dyson got off on the wrong foot with Morris from the very beginning, even though Morris politely stopped writing while Bob introduced them, and sat back in his chair to look at Dyson.

'Hi, John,' he said, with some slight suggestion of benevolence in his voice, as if he were taking Dyson on his staff in spite of a prison record.

'Erskine's just joined the paper as a graduate trainee, John,' said Bob. 'He's apparently coming to us as a replacement for poor old Eddy.'

Dyson was visibly irritated. 'I haven't heard anything about this,' he said. 'I think there must be some mistake here. Are you certain you were told to come to this office?'

'Sure,' said Morris.

'Well, I haven't heard anything about it. I'm certainly expecting *someone*. God knows, I *need* someone. But someone *experienced*! A trainee is no earthly use in here at all.'

Dyson took off his overcoat and went to his desk, frowning heavily. Morris said nothing. He put his cigarette to his lips, drew in smoke, sat silent and impassive for some moments, then blew the smoke out of his nose in two impassive grey plumes.

'You can sit here for the moment,' said Dyson, opening the mail from his in-tray, 'while we get this sorted out. You can watch us at work. I haven't got time to start showing you how to do anything. But you might pick up a thing or two just by looking. I suppose it's all experience. Has Morley produced yet, Bob?'

Bob shook his head.

'Oh *God*!' said Dyson, clenching his fists. 'Oh God, oh God, oh *God*!' He looked across at Morris. 'It's a madhouse in here,' he said. 'Which university were you at?'

'Cambridge,' said Morris. When he was not writing or smoking, Bob noticed, he sat absolutely still, so still that the ribbon of smoke from his cigarette hung almost undisturbed for two or three feet above his hand.

'Which college?'

'King's.'

Dyson was impressed. 'I was at Sidney,' he said in a different voice. 'Well, well. As a matter of fact, I started on this paper as a graduate trainee myself. It's not a bad office. Of course, it's not *typical*. But then I doubt whether such a thing as a typical newspaper office exists. It's a very funny business, the newspaper business.'

'Sure,' said Morris.

'You get quite a good general introduction to the industry as a graduate trainee, you know. You'll probably do six months in the news room first, then six months in the subs, then maybe six months in the commercial room . . .'

Dyson broke off in mid-explanation, frowning at a piece of copy-paper he had taken out of a little brown envelope marked 'J. Dyson Esqre.'

'That's funny,' he said irritably. 'You *are* supposed to be here. The Editor's sent you.'

'Sure,' said Morris.

'I don't know why I wasn't told about this before,' complained Dyson. 'I think I should have been consulted. The Editor knew what the situation was in here.'

'Sure, sure,' said Morris soothingly, conjuring up the cigarette pack again. 'Have a cigarette, John, and tell me what I'm supposed to be doing.'

Dyson set Morris to work copying out the extracts for the 'In Years Gone By' column. But Dyson's opinion of him, which had risen noticeably on hearing that he had been at King's, had fallen back to zero again; his having been at King's was cancelled out by his having been right about his instructions to join Dyson's department.

A slight difficulty arose about whether he might type the extracts.

'Eddy always used to write them out in longhand,' said Dyson.

'I'd prefer to type them.'

'Yes . . . well . . . I suppose you could. There's only one typewriter in here, I'm afraid.'

'I'll use that for now. I'll get another one sent in later.'

'I'm afraid you won't be able to get another one,' said Dyson. 'We have to make do with one in here, sharing it. Poor old Eddy didn't type, you see.'

Morris typed throughout the morning, driving the carriage of the department's battered portable along with his two hammering fingers just about as fast as it would go. He worked with scarcely a break to search out a new passage in the files, or to pick up the half-smoked end of his last cigarette from the ashtray, stub it out, light a new one, and put it down in its place. The noise of the typewriter and the gathering haze of cigarette smoke in the room both seemed to disturb Dyson. He kept glancing across at either the typewriter or the cigarette in the ashtray, and frowning. Morris's presence also put him off his stroke on the phone. 'Good morning, Sir William, I hope I'm not intruding,' he would say, smiling self-deprecatingly at the distant Sir William. Then he would remember he was being watched by Morris, and he would frown, and stuff his finger into his left ear to keep out the noise of the typewriter. 'What was that, Sir William? You were just doing what, Sir William?' Then he would realize he was smiling again for Sir William's benefit, and swing round in his chair so that Morris couldn't see the smile.

But when Morris stopped typing, just before lunchtime, and sat back in his chair looking through his handiwork, the silence disturbed Dyson even more. He stared at Morris disapprovingly, as if Morris had spent the whole morning in idleness.

'How are you getting on?' he asked.

'I've done a week's supply, John.'

'Of hundreds or fifties?'

'The lot.'

'Twenty-fives and tens as well?'

'Sure, sure.'

'Let me have a look.'

Morris clipped the papers together and tossed them across onto Dyson's desk. Dyson had for some reason assumed that Morris would bring them over and stand beside him while he went through them. He went through them none the less, frowning. He had spent most of the morning frowning, except when he had been talking to Sir William Paice and others. Morris lit another cigarette.

'This is all right,' said Dyson, taking pains to ink in one or two faint characters and slipped capitals, in lieu of anything else to correct. 'This is quite good. Quite good work.'

'What next, John?' asked Morris.

Dyson gazed at the sheets of copy, shuffling them about in his hand, trying to think. 'You'd better do another week's supply,' he said. Morris accompanied Bob and Dyson to the Gates for lunch. Bob invited him; Dyson frowned all the way there, and abandoned the other two as soon as they were inside.

'Every newspaper office has its own particular pub,' explained Bob. 'The Gates happens to be ours.'

'Sure,' said Morris, looking round the bar with his noncommittal eyes.

'Well, some people go off to El Vino's or the Falstaff. But a certain set on the paper come here pretty regularly. You can usually count on finding old Bill Waddy sitting up at the bar here, and old Gareth Holmroyd hovering about somewhere.'

'Sure, sure,' said Morris. Bob introduced him to some of the usual crowd, and Morris asked Bill Waddy, who was buying, for a Pernod. They all stared at him over their halves of bitter. Morris appeared not to notice.

'Who's the joker up the end?' he asked Bob quietly. 'Is he one of your team?'

'The one leaning on the bar? That's Reg Mounce, the Pictures Editor.'

'He's high.'

'A bit, possibly. It's quite funny, actually. You see that dog-eared piece of paper he's showing Gareth and Mike? That's a note he got from the Editor the other day, giving him the sack.'

'What's he flashing it around for, then?'

'Well, he's surprised by it, you see. The point is, people don't get the sack on this paper. It's that sort of paper. So he keeps going round asking everyone what they think he should do.'

Morris stared at Bob expressionlessly. 'And?' he said.

'Well, everyone thinks he should just ignore it. Pretend he never got it. People don't think the Editor would have the nerve to challenge him about it.'

'A popular man, is he, Reg?'

161

'Oh God no. Everyone thinks he's an absolute tit. It's just a matter of solidarity.'

'Oh. That.'

'It's that sort of office.'

'Sure.'

'It's really not at all a bad sort of office to be in.'

'Sure,' said Morris, conjuring another long cigarette out of the air. 'Oh, sure, sure.'

Relations between Dyson and Morris deteriorated still further after lunch. Morris left the Gates as soon as he had finished his Pernod. When Dyson and Bob got back to the office, he was at his desk already, typing. It was not the department's battered old machine he was typing on; it was a brand-new electric portable. Dyson stopped in his tracks, gazing at it. He was almost too angry to speak.

'Look,' he said, 'I'm not standing for this. Year in, year out, Bob and I have had to make do with one rotten reconditioned typewriter between us. And the first day you arrive you contrive to get hold of this! Well, I'm not having it.' Dyson wrenched off his overcoat, dragging the lining out of the right sleeve. He sat down at his desk, not looking at Morris, his face rigid with anger. Morris watched him expressionlessly.

'You can borrow it if you like,' he said.

'I can borrow it?' cried Dyson, flaring up at once. 'Did you say I can *borrow* it?'

'Sure. Whenever you like.'

Bob slipped a peppermint into his mouth, not daring to look at either of them until Dyson had found words to speak.

'That typewriter's going back at once,' he said inadequately.

Morris inhaled smoke, held it for some minutes, and then let it out down his nose. 'John,' he said impassively, 'this isn't an office machine.'

'What?' snapped Dyson. 'What is it, then?'

'It's my own.'

'Yours? Where did you get it from?'

162

'I bought it.'

Bob averted his eyes again. It was as embarrassing to see a friend under the influence of adrenalin when one had not lost one's own temper as it was to see him under the influence of alcohol when one was sober.

'*Bought* it?' queried Dyson, as if the word were some rare form of Sanskrit preterite.

'Sure.'

'In a shop?'

'Sure.'

'In the lunch-hour?'

'Sure.'

'An *electric typewriter*?'

'Sure, sure.'

Dyson continued to gaze at Morris for some moments, his mouth very slightly open. Then, abruptly, without a word, he turned away, picked up a piece of copy, and began to correct it with short, violent strokes and swirls of his pen. Morris turned his head slightly and caught Bob's eye. Bob at once stopped moving the peppermint about in his mouth.

'If you pay Schedule D,' said Morris, 'it's tax-deductible.'

Bob made a point of taking a benevolent interest in Morris over the next few days, to balance out Dyson's hostility. He got him an office towel for the washroom. He told him to whom to apply for union membership. He showed him how to make out his expenses chits, filling in 'Office duties, 5s. 6d.' for each day of the week, as laid down in the house agreement between union and management. Bob could remember his own loneliness and isolation when he had first come down and started work on the paper. Morris didn't *seem* lonely or isolated himself, but a hard shell was usually a sign of vulnerability underneath.

People were also taking a benevolent interest in Bob. Gareth Holmroyd, Ted Hurwitz, Mike Sparrow, Ralph Absalom – they were all keeping their eyes open for a house for him. Each day they brought him cyclostyled sheets from their local agents, and the telephone numbers of friends' relatives whose relatives' friends had seen a board up somewhere. Bob felt obliged to go and look at a certain number of these places out of politeness. He took mornings off from work to inspect houses of character in Ealing, imposing residences in Hendon, and important properties in select residential districts just thirty minutes from Waterloo. With unseeing eyes he gazed at usual offices, charming patios, 'Ideal' boilers, and mature fruit-trees. He asked the young men from the agents who showed him round if the pipes were lagged and whether the soil was chalk or clay; he couldn't think of any other questions. Almost the only thing he could think of coherently as he peered at the Dutch tiles and crazy paving was that according to his last statement of account he had £67 12s. 9d. in the bank. He dwelt on the figure gratefully. Whatever happened, however far he was driven by forces outside his control, there was surely no way in which a man with only £67 12s. 9d. could find himself acquiring a delightful property or superior detached residence. In the last analysis the £67 12s. 9d. would stand revealed; the pen would be taken out of his fingers just before he signed across the excise stamp; gentle hands would conduct him back to the comfortable shabby gloom of Flat 4, 86 Leominster Gardens.

Jannie was taking a benevolent interest, too, inviting not Bob but Tessa out to look at houses she had found for them in s.w.23. The houses Jannie found did not have charming patios or mature rose-gardens. Most of them were noticeably short even on usual offices, and it did not occur even to the agents to describe them as imposing or delightful. Still, they had something; they had potentialities. And sitting tenants.

'It's just a matter of agreeing compensation with them,' said Jannie, leading Tessa in and out of rooms impregnated with such poverty and squalor as she had never dreamt existed. 'Everyone does it. The present owner would probably arrange it for you, if you feel awkward about it.'

'Yes,' said Tessa, trying not to breathe the sweet-sour air into her lungs.

'You could knock this wall down, and make one large room through from front to back.'

'Yes.'

'Or make the flat at the back into the kitchen, and rent the basement out as a bed-sitter . . .'

For Bob and Tessa's house Jannie projected all the reconstruction and improvement which she and John had never found either money or energy enough to carry out in their own. As she took Tessa over a house, the West Indian family in the second floor back dissolved in her mind into an *au pair* girl, the brass taps and greasy gas-rings in the ground-floor scullery into a row of shining white domestic machinery. She had never had an *au pair* girl or a laundry room herself. Her visualization was as generous to Bob and Tessa as it was careless of the existing occupiers. All Tessa could do was blush. She felt she was blushing all the time on these trips, at the conditions of life they were intruding upon, at Jannie's plans to turn it to their advantage, at Jannie's evident affection for her. Jannie really seemed to like her, in her oblique, distracted way. Perhaps just because she was Bob's fiancée – but Tessa felt that it was for herself as well. She wished she could like Jannie more in return. She could see her qualities; she could see why Bob liked her. All the same, when Jannie spoke in that curious Oxford-and-Cambridge accent she had, she seemed to Tessa immeasurably remote and eccentric – a woman of some quite different generation. Then again, she was in love with Bob, and embarrassingly old to be. It was as if one's aunt were competing against one.

'It would be so nice if you did come and live near us when you're married,' said Jannie wistfully. 'One does feel a bit cut off out here.'

The whole business was ridiculous, of course. They would never get married – it should have been obvious to everyone. They *couldn't* get married. Bob wasn't in love with her. You

165

didn't get married to people who weren't in love with you. But if Jannie couldn't see this for herself, how could she explain it to her – *now*, after they had trailed round looking at all those houses? How could Bob suddenly start explaining it to John, to Gareth Holmroyd, to the Editor? How could she and Bob even put it in words to each other?

'I mean,' said Jannie, 'it's very central here. It's just that one sometimes feels rather – oh, I don't know. You and Bob could get a mortgage all right, couldn't you?'

'Oh, I should think so,' said Tessa, blushing yet again. She didn't know whether they could get a mortgage or not. She had no clear idea of what a mortgage *was*. And she resisted finding out, in the way that other girls she had known kept themselves in deliberate ignorance of such things as impregnation, in the unarticulated hope that if they didn't know what it was it couldn't happen to them.

Mrs. Mounce busied herself with being kind to Tessa, too. But this she found easier to bear, partly because Mrs. Mounce had so many troubles herself that she was able to be kind back to her, and partly because Mrs. Mounce's world and Mrs. Mounce's advice seemed even more remote and unreal than Jannie's.

'Honestly, sweetest,' said Mrs. Mounce, 'don't go lumbering yourselves with a house and a mortgage right at the beginning. Rent a nice little flat somewhere where you know exactly what your outgoings are – where you know you're not responsible for anything. You can always do a little bit here and a little bit there to brighten it up.'

Tessa liked her, in a dreary sort of way – the sort of way one liked picking one's nails or staying in bed all morning. They sat for hours drinking tea in Mrs. Mounce's flat downstairs, while Mrs. Mounce talked about her affairs with moustached men in export-import, and Tessa looked at the little bit here and the little bit there which Mrs. Mounce had done herself to brighten her own place up. Most of the little bits seemed to be made of cream-painted hardboard and enamelled black wrought iron. She imagined showing her parents round a home of her own decorated in the same way. 'And this is the cocktail bar, Daddy. Bob and I made it out of hardboard and Formica. . . . Do you like the individual wrought-iron bottle stands at the back? Bob screwed them on the mirror himself . . .'

The thought made her smile to herself, for what she recognized were basically snobbish reasons. She was pleased to find she was still able to smile, even snobbishly. She had the impression that she hadn't smiled for several months.

Steadily, quietly, electrically, Erskine Morris typed the 'In Years Gone By' column several weeks into the future. There had never been so much 'In Years Gone By' copy set, or so much waiting to be set. From day to day the dark shades of his shirts, ties, and high-buttoning suits subtly changed. But the pallid face above them remained impassive, and the waiting cigarette continued to smoke ritually in the ashtray, like a joss-stick before some inscrutable joss. And Morris's presence continued to cramp Dyson's style. He was if anything more irritated by the quiet drumming of the electric typewriter than by the clatter of the old mechanical one. It was harder to notice exactly when it stopped, and Dyson liked to know. Round about four o'clock in the afternoon he would sometimes forget Morris and sprawl back in his chair with his hands behind his head, yawning and looking at the ceiling, just as he had before Morris's arrival. Then he would suddenly realize that the typing had ceased. Fearing that Morris had stopped to watch him yawning, he would at once return to his work, and try to conceal his yawns behind his hand. At other times, he would sit back in a thoughtful, philosophical mood and ask Bob whether he felt one ought to have one's name printed at the head of one's private writing-paper. Morris's typewriter would stop at once. 'Oh, forget it, Bob,' Dyson would mutter. A great deal of work was done by all three of them.

Dyson became quite unlike himself in his dealings with

Morris. Every time Morris got a telephone call which sounded from his laconic replies as if it were private business, Dyson frowned at him warningly. He also prowled about the room from time to time, passing as if accidentally behind Morris's chair and looking over Morris's shoulder out of the corner of his eye. It was in this way that he discovered that not all Morris's application with the typewriter was devoted to 'In Years Gone By.'

'What's this?' he demanded one day. ' "Terry had been on tea for four years before he first began using horse." What the hell's this?'

Morris helped himself to a couple of lungfuls of cigarette smoke. 'It's an article on junk,' he said.

'Junk?'

'Drugs. It's for the features department.'

'They asked you to do it?'

'Sure.'

Dyson walked round the room like a patrolling school-master. 'Have you written anything else for other departments?' he asked.

'Oh, a couple of leaders. Some diary pars.'

Dyson patrolled on. 'If you want to write anything for anyone else again,' he said roughly, 'do it in your own time, not in mine.'

'O.K., John,' said Morris.

Dyson knew he was behaving stupidly, which made him more graceless still. Bob tried to talk him out of it when they were on their own, at the sandwich bar in the Gates.

'You'll have to find him something else to do, John,' he said. 'He's five weeks ahead on "Years Gone By" already.'

'But what else *can* I give him to do?' wailed Dyson. 'He's just a trainee – he doesn't know how to do anything.'

'He can learn, John, just like you and I did.'

'Bob, I can't let him sub, because I haven't got time to go through it all again and check it. And can you honestly imagine him ringing up Sir William Paice? Or the Bishop? Or even Canon Morley?'

'Well . . .'

'He's just not the type, is he, Bob? Anyway, poor old Eddy did "In Years Gone By" for over ten years. I don't see why Mr. Morris shouldn't stick at it for a week or two.'

'Morris isn't the same sort of man as poor old Eddy, John.'

'Don't tell me! Honestly, Bob, that office was a happy place until Morris came. To me he seems to cast a blight over the whole day.'

'You do overdramatize things a bit, you know, John. He's a bit shy, that's all.'

'Do you know what Bill Waddy calls him, Bob? Erskine Absinthe. Fancy coming in here and demanding a Pernod on his very first day at the office! And he didn't even buy a round himself! He just swilled down his Pernod and walked out!'

'He's a bit on the defensive, John.'

'He never bought a round! And all this classless business he tries to put across. Honestly, Bob, he went to Rugby! Did you know that? I asked the personnel director. You and I went to ordinary grammar schools, Bob – but we don't go round pretending to be classless. And he went to Rugby! Well, for God's sake, Bob! For God's sake!'

Remembering all the dinners he had eaten at the Dysons' when he had been living on his own, Bob invited Morris back to his flat one evening so that Tessa could cook dinner for him in his turn. Tessa was nervous about it; she had never entertained anyone in the flat before, apart from Mrs. Mounce. She became worried about the appearance of the place, about her cooking, and about her anomalous position in the household. But Morris turned out to be completely uninterested in all three. When he arrived he put his cold, white hand in hers for a moment and said, 'Hello, Tessa,' as if he had always been aware of her as part of the background furnishings. Then he ignored her for the rest of the evening. He produced a full bottle of whisky from his briefcase, poured out three tumbler-fuls, and asked if he could have the television on. 'There's something coming up that I have an interest in,' he said, fiddling expertly with the controls of the set.

'Something you wrote?' asked Bob, remembering the dialogue he had seen on Morris's desk.

'Sure.'

'A play?'

'A song.'

'What sort of song, Erskine? A pop song?'

'Sure, sure. I'd just like to see how it goes.'

There was a whole programme of pop songs on. Morris sprawled back in the one armchair with his whisky, watching them all impassively. As each new number came up Bob looked at him and asked, 'This one?' Morris shook his head without interest. Bob began to get nervous on his behalf.

'You're very casual about it, Erskine,' he said.

'What is there to get excited about?' said Morris easily, the flesh beneath his chin folding over the top of his collar as he leaned back into the cushions. 'It's just a song.'

'But to get it on television! Or have you done it before?'

'I've had a few numbers on.'

Bob stared at him. 'What a strange man you are, Erskine!' he said. The corner of Morris's mouth twitched up into his cheek and fell back. Bob became embarrassed at his own effusiveness, and turned back to the screen, tapping out the rhythm with his fingers on the side of his glass. 'What's this number of yours called?' he asked.

Morris blew smoke down his nose. ' "I Can't Stop Crying," ' he said.

A girl with dark-rimmed eyes and long straight blonde hair appeared on the screen, picking her way through a number of abstract decorative shapes at the back of the studio.

'I can't stop crying,' she sang in a plaintive voice. 'All through the night, I can't stop crying. Know it's not right, but can't stop crying. I can't stop crying, 'cause I am crying for you.'

'Is this yours?' asked Bob.

'Sure.'

'I can't stop crying,' sang the girl. 'Though I'm a fool, I go on sighing. Know I'm a fool, not even trying. It can't be right to cry through the night. I can't stop crying for you.'

'Very good,' said Bob, when she had finished. 'I liked the tune.'

'I did the words,' said Morris. 'Someone else did the music.'

'The words were very good, too.'

Morris shrugged. 'It's what the children like,' he said. 'They don't like anything new or strange. Children are very conservative.'

They left the television on while they had dinner, because Morris wanted to watch a Western. Thinking that he wanted to watch it because he thought it was funny, Bob made a few humorous remarks at the expense of the characters on the screen. But Morris didn't smile. He watched silently and impassively, chewing his overdone steak, and retrieving his cigarette from the ashtray between courses. Bob took the point; Morris didn't think the Western was funny.

When the Western was finished they watched the hospital serial. And when the hospital serial finished they carried their coffee across to the set and watched the courtroom serial. Bob and Tessa sat on the floor, their arms round each other. Morris sprawled in the armchair, dispensing whisky. Mrs. Mounce rang the bell and was invited in. 'Hello, Glenda,' said Morris when Bob introduced them. She curled up on the floor and leaned against the arm of Morris's chair. He poured her a tumbler of whisky.

'*Sweetest*!' she cried flirtatiously. 'You're trying to get me tight!'

'Sure, sure,' said Morris absently, his attention on the screen.

And so they sat. The telephone rang three times; each time

it was for Morris. 'Sure . . .' they heard him murmuring into the mouthpiece, between the noise of gunshot and the scream of tyres. 'I could be interested . . . I should want to use him in a completely different context, of course . . . Sure, sure . . .'

After the third call Morris said to Bob, 'I asked some people to step round.'

'Fine,' said Bob. 'They're welcome.'

But when they arrived, Morris didn't seem particularly interested in them – not, anyway, enough to stop watching the television. 'Lake, Brian, Andy,' he explained, scarcely looking up from the screen. 'Tessa, Glenda, Bob. Pour out the rest of the whisky, Brian.'

Brian and Andy lounged against the edge of the dining-table at the back of the group, half watching the television, half talking to each other. Lake perched on the arm of Morris's chair and stared at the screen. She was a girl; she was the girl who had sung 'I Can't Stop Crying.' Bob gazed at her, drinking her in. She shone in the half-darkness of the room. Her long bleached hair shone; her polished white raincoat shone; her white boots and her unstockinged knees shone.

'How did it look?' she asked Morris, not taking her eyes off the screen.

'Great,' said Morris, not taking his eyes off the screen either. He slipped a noncommittal hand round her waist, so that the smoke from his cigarette rose past her left ear.

Bob couldn't stop staring at her, even though he had his arm round Tessa. He rubbed his chin absently on the top of Tessa's head, so that he could look over it at the girl. Tessa and Mrs. Mounce, he knew, were watching her out of the corner of their eyes too, as silent and overawed as he was himself. He knew without even thinking about it consciously that she had no bottom worth worrying about. God almighty! A girl in show business, with white boots and no bottom – in his flat!

'It looked all right, did it?' she asked Morris again, perhaps forgetting that she had asked him once already.

'Great, great. Have you eaten?'

'We're going to get something at Nick's. You coming?'

'O.K.,' said Morris. He stood up and put his cigarettes in his pocket. 'Thanks, Tessa. Thanks, Bob. I enjoyed that. Bye, Glenda. Bye!'

They had gone, all four of them, almost before Bob realized they were going.

'Darling!' said Mrs. Mounce admiringly. 'I never knew you had such smart friends!'

Bob drew the curtain to one side and looked out of the window. The four of them were just climbing into a long red two-seater sports car standing double-parked almost in the middle of the roadway. Its headlights came on full beam, and it accelerated away with a rising roar which brought heads to windows all along the street.'

Silently, Tessa switched the television off and began to clear the table.

11

Dyson wandered about the Final Departure Lounge at London Airport in a curious state of elation. The Magic Carpet Travel plane was late leaving; Dyson and the rest of the press party should have taken off for the Trucial Riviera ten minutes before. But he didn't mind at all. He loved airports. He would have liked to feel blasé about them, but he didn't have the opportunity to use them often enough. As soon as he got inside one he became elated. He seemed to have a heightened sense of reality. Moving staircases, rubber plants, low black leather armchairs; 'Flight BE 4029 for Copenhagen and Stockholm is departing now . . . This is the last call for passengers travelling on Flight LH 291 for Düsseldorf and Berlin . . .' He bought *Oggi* and *Neue Illustrierte* at the bookstall, even though he could scarcely read a word of either Italian or German, because being inside an airport made him feel that he could. The Final Departure Lounge, sealed off from gross particular Britain by passport and customs barriers, was a bright nowhere land, sterilized of nationality and all the other ties and limitations of everyday life. Here Dyson felt like International Airport Man – neat, sophisticated, compact; a wearer of lightweight suits and silky blue showercoats; moving over the surface of the earth like some free-floating spirit – from Karachi to Athens to Hong Kong, from Honolulu to Tangier to New York – unimpeded by the traffic problems of Karachi or the housing situation in Honolulu, not deflected from New York by any emotional attachment in Athens, or kept from Hong Kong by business entanglements in New York. Airports and television studios – this was the way of life Dyson felt he was intended for.

He could pick out some of the other journalists in the Magic Carpet group sitting about the lounge; they were all, like himself, carrying the folder of publicity material Magic Carpet had issued them with. There was a photographer who had checked in just ahead of him. He seemed to have brought a couple of models with him – badly dressed girls with pained expressions and tragically thin legs. And the tall, cavernous man with the dark blazer and the ex-officer's moustache – wasn't he from the *Telegraph*? The red-faced young man with the thin hair falling all over the place was a humorous writer for somebody – Dyson had seen him on television. There was a man in a blue pinstripe suit, with elegantly grey curls, who freelanced food and wine, and an anxious young woman with dark eyes and three strings of beads to chew who did Travel for one of the glossies; Dyson had seen them both on facilities trips before. Oh God, he thought, facilities trips! How awful they were! He could picture the holiday development at Sharjah already – new concrete hotels built too quickly, no amenities, the squalor of the local population beyond the new concrete reserves. It was only the travelling there and back which made them worthwhile at all. They could be hours late leaving for all he cared; he was quite happy to sit at London Airport all day and watch the aircraft coming and going.

Ah, the aircraft! He gazed at them through the windows of the lounge. They stood ranked on the apron, shimmering in the morning sunlight. The tangled confusion of ground equipment which surrounded them – the lorries, steps, and generators, the ordinary shoddy private cars in which the aircrew drove themselves out, the temporary sheds and stacks of building materials – only emphasized their remote and fragile perfection. They stood like swans standing – on unlikely legs, in tangled nests. Like swans they would fold their legs and beat up into the uncluttered, abstract sky. One of them moved off the stand as Dyson watched, its engines whining, the blast of air behind it crinkling the standing rainwater on the apron into a million fleeing furrows ... And there, away across the grass a mile beyond it, one of the big jets was just starting its take-off run. Slowly, very slowly, the great bulk gathered speed, as if the Bank of England or the National Gallery had started to walk and were trying to run. It drew level with the airport buildings, the colossal baggage of noise it trailed swelling and fading in the breeze. It went away to the west, travelling at great speed now, but still heavy on the ground and never in a million years capable of leaving it – a great beast charging head down at central Middlesex. Then, suddenly, it lifted its head above the runway, looked round and sniffed the air for a moment – and went straight up into the sky like spring-heeled Jack, levelled off, and vanished against the shifting clouds. Four lines of brown exhaust, rounded off at the top, hung faintly in the air where it had leapt.

Dyson turned round, moved by the performance – and there behind him, about three feet away, picking absently at a morsel of food between his front teeth and twitching his nose from time to time to ease some hidden blockage in his nasal passages, was Reg Mounce. The supraterrestrial perfection of the Final Departure Lounge faded a little.

'Well, well, well!' said Mounce, taking his finger out of his mouth, as surprised as Dyson.

'Hello,' said Dyson unwelcomingly.

'What are you doing here?'

'I'm going out to the Persian Gulf,' said Dyson coldly. 'For the paper.'

'The Magic Carpet beano?'

'Yes.'

'Well, snap! Stinking snap!'

The Final Departure Lounge seemed to Dyson suddenly no more isolated from the imperfections of life than the saloon bar of the Gates of Jerusalem, and the great silver aircraft no rarer or lovelier than red London buses.

'I'm doing it for a load of crap called *Leisure and Pleasure* magazine,' said Mounce. 'They don't pay much, but what the hell? It's a week off from the stinking office, with nothing to do but collect a few pix from the firm, slap some sort of crap together from the handout, and get some serious drinking done.'

'I see,' said Dyson.

'Charge some exes up, of course. Charge a few more up to the paper. It all adds up.'

'Yes.'

'To tell you the truth,' said Mounce confidentially, 'I can do with a few days in the sun just at the moment. All this business about Other Arrangements – it's been rather getting me down. I thought it might be clever to shove off for a few days and let it all blow over.'

Dyson said nothing. He was swearing a solemn oath to himself that he would be absolutely ruthless about Mounce on this trip. When they went aboard the plane he would firmly find himself a seat next to the wine-and-food man, or the girl with the beads, and ignore Mounce's existence until they were back in London.

'I think it'll all just simmer down, won't it?' said Mounce.

'What?'

'All this Other Arrangements business. It'll blow over. In a month's time we'll be laughing about it. Don't you think so?'

'For God's sake – *I* don't know.'

Mounce fell silent, thoughtfully trying to remove the last traces of breakfast from his teeth with his tongue. Dyson took the opportunity to move away and sit down on the other side of the lounge. He found that Mounce had followed him across the room and had sat down in the seat beside him.

'We're twenty-five minutes late,' said Mounce.

'Yes.'

'These stinking trips are always late.'

A small man with an archaic toothbrush moustache and a wild tangle of stand-up hair above a domed forehead came hurrying across the lounge. About half his height seemed to be forehead. He had thick spectacles, behind which his eyes darted keenly about like goldfish searching for a way out from their bowls. He had introduced himself to the party earlier, at the air terminal, as Starfield, Magic Carpet's Air Transportation Director.

'Magic Carpet group!' he cried to the room, pressing his palms together as if about to sing a tenor aria. 'This is an announcement concerning the Magic Carpet party travelling to Sharjah. There is a slight delay, boys and girls, caused by the fact that the aircraft which will be taking us has burst a tyre on touchdown from Amsterdam, and there will be a slight delay on account of this cause while this fact is rectified. While we are waiting. I have arranged for drinks to be served at the bar, compliments of Magic Carpet Travel, and I would ask you to rest assured, believe me, that everything humanly possible is being done to facilitate our getting away at the earliest possible moment. Thank you.'

Mounce let his breath slowly out between his teeth. 'Here we go again,' he said. 'Bang on stinking form, as stinking usual.'

Morris's electric typewriter drummed steadily on. Bob sat with his chin in his hands, sucking a liquorice and watching him.

'I'm afraid John's taken against you for some reason,' he said.

Morris typed on, saying nothing.

'I don't know what's got into him,' said Bob. 'He's always been very good to me. You've rubbed him up the wrong way somehow.'

He leaned back in his chair and gazed at the people working in the offices on the other side of Hand and Ball Court. He felt disinclined for work. With Dyson away and the sun shining there was a certain sense of holiday in the air which made leaning forward over the desk somehow physically difficult. He swallowed the remains of his liquorice and took another

178

one. 'It's not getting you down at all, is it, Erskine?' he asked.

'What's that, Bob?' said Morris, without looking up from his typewriter.

'John's attitude. It's not getting you down at all?'

Morris stopped typing, picked up his cigarette from the ashtray, and masticated smoke for some moments while he read through what he had typed. 'No,' he said. He started typing again.

After a while Bob picked up a piece of 'Country Day' copy about stoats and weasels, and tossed it across onto Morris's desk.

Morris glanced at it inquiringly as he worked.

'I thought you might like to have a go at subbing while John's away,' said Bob casually. 'Make a break for you.'

Expressionlessly, Morris picked the copy up and tossed it back. 'You do it, Bob,' said. 'I'll look it over when you've finished it.'

Bob felt a little hurt. He had had a vague idea that he might try to teach Morris the rudiments of subbing and ordering copy while Dyson was away, so that Dyson would no longer have any excuse for refusing to let Morris do anything.

'Look, Erskine,' he said, 'you can take a rest from "Years Gone By" for the next day or two. I'll take full responsibility if John raises any question.'

Morris rested his pale, neutral eyes on Bob for an instant. 'This isn't "Years Gone By," Bob,' he said. 'This is a memo to the Editor about the new pre-teen page.'

Bob stared. 'What new pre-teen page, Erskine?' he said. 'I haven't heard anything about a pre-teen page.'

'You will, Bob, once the Editor's read this.'

Bob went on staring at him.

'There's a lot of advertising in pre-teen A/Bs,' said Morris.

Bob subbed all the copy that had come in by the morning post. Later, when Morris had finished his memo and put it in the out-basket, he came over to Bob's desk and helped himself to some of the subbed copy to study.

'There's nothing to it, really,' said Bob modestly. 'It's just a matter of checking the facts and the spelling, crossing out the first sentence, and removing any attempts at jokes.'

'Sure,' said Morris. He bent down and wrote something on one of the sheets.

'What are you doing?' asked Bob, rather sharply.

' "Exhilarating" with an "a," Bob.'

'Oh . . . yes . . .'

Morris looked through another page, and made another correction.

'Now what?' demanded Bob.

'The territory of the Canaanites was west of Samaria, not east.'

'Oh, was it?'

Morris began marking something on a number of pages.

'What's this, Erskine?'

'I've had an idea, Bob. I'm marking all next week's "Meditations" to be set in italic.'

'You're what?'

'I'm marking them for italic.'

'We can't do that, I'm afraid, Erskine, because . . .'

'I think it'll look quite good, Bob. We'll put a heavy rule round it, set the head in forty-two-point Old English, and put a single flower from the print-books next to it.'

'I think it would look very pretty, Erskine, but it's not for us to . . .'

'It'll look rather Giles Gilbert Scott – rather Guildford Cathedral. The G. G. Scott mood. It's the next one out from platform one, Bob.'

'Look, Erskine, this is Dyson's department. We can't make any decisions as major as this while he's away.'

'Sure, sure,' said Morris, putting the copy in one of the special envelopes with COMPOSING ROOM printed on them. 'Don't worry, Bob. I'll take responsibility if Dyson questions it. I see Morley's copy's not in yet, incidentally. Get on to him, will you, Bob, and find out where it is?'

The Magic Carpet party got airborne eventually.

'Two hours late.' said Mounce bitterly, several times as their second-hand turbo-prop climbed through ragged cloud into the world of shining snowfields above.

'For God's sake shut up, Reg,' said Dyson, gazing out of the window at the stark absolutes of white and blue.

'Yes, but two hours late! I could have mended the stinking puncture myself in that time.'

They were not flying to Sharjah direct. Dyson realized he must have misread the invitation slightly. They were going to Paris first to pick up another party of journalists which had assembled there from the rest of Europe. The Continental contingent was waiting in the departure lounge at Le Bourget when the London party arrived, and had of course been waiting there for over two hours, consuming drinks supplied with the compliments of Magic Carpet. There were about thirty of them, some carrying complicated camera kits; some, as Dyson noted with approval, wearing silky blue showercoats; all of them carrying folders of Magic Carpet handout material. There were two models among the group, even worse dressed and more pained than the English pair; they looked as if they were already preparing themselves spiritually for posing in the middle of some Arab village or Bedouin encampment wearing nothing but see-through bathing costumes and gauze yashmaks. The Paris party stared coldly at the London party, associating them with the plane's puncture and its lateness. The London party stared back no less coldly, feeling that they would be halfway to Sharjah by now but for the selfish insistence of the Paris party on being fetched along too.

Mounce, however, began to cheer up slightly. He looked round the departure lounge with some interest and sniffed the air. 'Ah, the smell of France,' he said. 'Smell it the moment you arrive. Have you ever noticed that, John?'

'Yes,' said Dyson. But the sight and smell of the departure lounge at Le Bourget had the opposite effect on him. The pleasure he got from airports, it occurred to him sadly, was subject to the law of diminishing returns.

'Do you think the bar'll take sterling?' said Mounce. 'Let's have a quick one before they shove us back on that snotty little plane.'

'I don't think there's time. We'll be leaving again directly.'

But, it turned out, they were not leaving again directly. No announcement was made about rejoining the aircraft, and Starfield seemed to have disappeared. Gradually the London party subsided into seats. A certain amount of muttering commenced within the various linguistic groups. Someone overheard, deduced, or invented the information that the Scandinavian party, which was flying down from Copenhagen to join the expedition, had landed at Orly instead of Le Bourget. Slowly the word crossed the various linguistic barriers, until even Dyson and Mounce had heard.

'Trust the Swedes,' said Mounce bitterly. 'Trust the Swedes to get the whole stinking thing screwed up.'

'But are they *still* at Orly?' cried Dyson to the wine-and-food man.

'I expect so,' said the wine-and-food man, sipping a lightly chilled Chambéry vermouth. 'I expect they're waiting for us.'

'*Où sont-ils?*' shouted Dyson boldly at one of the men in silky blue showercoats.

The man shrugged his shoulders in a typically French way. 'Who knows?' he said, with a German accent.

'Trust the stinking Swedes,' said Mounce.

Starfield came hurrying anxiously into the lounge. 'Boys and girls!' he cried, pressing his palms together. 'I regret to have to inform you of the fact that we have a slight snag on our hands, owing to the fact that our Scandinavian friends are unfortunately not yet with us, the fact being that they were booked in error on to a flight arriving at Orly. As soon as they arrive we shall be departing as planned, though of course a little later than scheduled. In the meantime, there are drinks and a sandwich lunch available at the bar, compliments of Magic Carpet Travel. Thank you.'

But not much more than three-quarters of an hour later, just as everyone was moving on from the free aperitifs to the free champagne with the free sandwiches, Starfield came hurrying back.

'Sorry, folks!' he said, pressing his palms together once again. 'Sorry, boys and girls! There's been a bit of a misunderstanding over the phone. It seems that our Scandinavian friends are still at Orly, waiting for *us*, as a result of which I feel it would facilitate things best if we went on without them, leaving them to proceed independently by separate means of transportation and join us at the other end. Will you therefore proceed at once to the departure gate for immediate embarkation? Thank you.'

Grumbling, the party picked up its folders of publicity material and shuffled towards the gate, hastily draining glasses and gnawing at ham sandwiches as it went. The language barriers began to break down slightly under the common bond of mutual discontent. 'It is bad,' said a Dutch photographer to Dyson, shaking his head and pursing his lips. '*Ja*,' agreed Dyson emphatically. '*Ja, ja, ja.*'

As the plane rushed past the airport buildings on its take-off run, Dyson thought he could see a number of people jumping about and waving their arms in front of the departure gate. They looked to Dyson remarkably like Scandinavian journalists. Still, they had perhaps not missed very much, because as soon as the plane was airborne Starfield came hurrying up to the front of the cabin, pressing his palms together for yet another aria.

'Our next port of call, boys and girls,' he announced, 'is Amsterdam.'

A noise of multilingual outrage and complaint arose from the body of the plane.

'Amsterdam!' cried Dyson, unable to believe his ears. 'But that's in the opposite direction to the Middle East!'

'What do you expect, John,' said Mounce comfortably, from

183

the middle of a benevolent haze of alcohol, 'with a load of crap like this?'

Starfield seemed astonished at the feelings his announcement had aroused. His eyebrows climbed out from behind the shelter of his glasses and attempted the ascent of his great forehead. Dislodged by the upward progress of the eyebrows, his glasses came landsliding down his nose. He pushed them back.

'Boys and girls!' he protested. 'If we want to get to Sharjah we have to go to Amsterdam first, owing to the simple fact that the plane which is taking us to Sharjah is waiting for us at Amsterdam!'

The noise of complaint continued.

'There'll be drinks at Amsterdam,' appealed Starfield. 'I'm radioing Schiphol Airport now to lay on full bar facilities, compliments of Magic Carpet Travel. Thank you.'

He disappeared hurriedly in the direction of the flight-deck.

'Oh *God*!' said Dyson.

'Try and be philosophical about it, John,' said Mounce. 'Think of the drinks. The booze is always the only good part of these spotty jaunts. The rest's always just a lot of crap, one way or another.'

He was still looking on the bright side when they all filed into the transit lounge at Schiphol.

'I've always wanted to go to Amsterdam,' he said, looking round with interest. 'Do you know John the girls sit in shop-windows here, just waiting for you to go along and take your pick. How about that? They sit in stinking shop-windows, John – doing their stinking knitting!'

Schiphol, coming after Heathrow and Le Bourget, did not make Dyson feel like International Airport Man, free-floating in a medium entirely isolated from the world's troubles. It made him feel like a traveller on the District Line, forced by the tiresome vicissitudes of the Underground to change at Earl's Court as well as South Kensington.

The terrible claustrophobia of travel began to descend on

him. He was trapped in the channels of communication, suffocating in the nothingness of neither-here-nor-there.

Bob had been going to take Tessa out that evening for a meal in some small Indian restaurant, so that they could tell each other their latest house-hunting experiences over the biriani and enjoy a quiet laugh together about the situation they'd got themselves into. At least they could still enjoy a joke together sometimes, thought Bob; or at any rate they could provided he avoided any literary allusions, and explained all references to the newspaper industry, well-known personalities, and politics. But Morris insisted that they both come out to dinner with him instead. Tessa wouldn't be pleased, Bob knew. She didn't like Morris – she didn't like any of Bob's friends very much, except Mrs. Mounce and just possibly John Dyson. But there was nothing much she could do about it when Morris arrived with Bob at their rendezvous. 'Hello, Tessa,' said Morris, with no more and no less familiarity than he had at their first meeting. He didn't rest his hand in hers this time, however; he put it round behind her back and laid it inertly on her farther hip for a moment or two, like a pound of plasticine, in some notional representation of an embrace. After which he ignored her for the rest of the evening.

He took them first for a drink at the Ritz. He didn't much like the Ritz, he explained, as Bob and Tessa gazed covertly about at the furnishings, but they were meeting Lake, who was coming on from making a personal appearance at a convention of canning machinery manufacturers in the Westbury, just up the road. And when Lake arrived, her long silver hair breaking and spraying over her glossy black dress as she walked, like some unbelievable moonlit sea on wet rock, Morris laid his brief tribute of plasticine on her hip, and took them all on to what appeared to be a private restaurant, in what looked like a private Georgian house just behind Park Lane.

Bob could not remember ever being inside a more visibly expensive eating-place. It had deep pile carpet and stripped

pine panelling everywhere, as he imagined high-class gamb-
ling clubs had. And it had a great deal of space left between
the tables. At current Mayfair land prices they would be
paying about three-halfpence a mouthful for the surplus floor
area alone. Looking at the distant tables round about, Bob
thought he recognized some of the other diners who were
shouldering a share of the rating assessment. He had seen them
in films and plays, reading the eccentric will in Act One, or
covering up for the hero as chairman of the Stalag Luft escape
committee in reel six.

'Isn't this place rather expensive?' he whispered.

Morris looked round without interest. 'About the same as
other places,' he said. 'It's handy to have it. I hate trying to
think where to eat.'

The sight of the prices on the menu confirmed Bob's expect-
ations, and brought on in him the symptoms of mild nervous
indigestion. They ordered and ate their way through what
might as well have been, from its cost and for all Bob could
enjoy of it, portions of grilled, stewed, and marinated bank-
notes, and drank two bottles of a wine apparently fermented
from the juice of sun-kissed golden sovereigns. When the
dessert-trolley was brought round, and Lake asked for a helping of out-of-season wild strawberries, Morris commandeered
the whole bowlful to share between them. Bob refused his
portion queasily, too occupied with praying that he was right
in assuming that Morris would insist on paying the bill. He
slipped his hand into his back pocket and tried to feel how
much money he had on him. It felt like four pounds, unless
one of the notes had got folded over and counted twice.

Lake was the only one who talked much during the meal.
'Do you have trouble with your feet?' she asked Tessa. 'I've
got rotten feet. They get so tender I can hardly walk on them.
Sometimes I get a terrible sort of itch underneath the front part,
just behind the toes. Know where I mean? Do you get that at
all?'

'No,' said Tessa.

'Sometimes I get a sort of terrible tickle between the toes. I just want to kick my shoes off – doesn't matter where I am – and scratch, scratch, scratch. I've got really rotten feet.'

Morris seemed uninterested in conversation. But he was clearly well-known in the restaurant, and several people greeted him on their way in or out. A girl wearing what looked like backless striped pyjamas came over and held out her cheek to be kissed. Morris obliged without getting up. 'Hi,' he said, unenthusiastically. A couple of men came over to the table to talk business with Morris. One seemed to be arranging for him to organize an exhibition of somebody's paintings, the other for him to come in on a complex deal which involved selling share capital in a group of fashion photographers.

'You seem to have fingers in a number of pies,' said Bob admiringly, as Morris paid the bill.

'You've got ten fingers,' said Morris. 'Why not stick them in ten pies?'

Bob supposed that the evening's entertainment was over. But without a word Morris hailed a taxi and took them off to a pub in the Isle of Dogs to hear a new kid singing in whom he thought he might just possibly be interested. The taxi ride took over half an hour and cost twenty-five shillings; the extravagance of travelling to the East End by taxi made Bob almost as nervous as he had been in the restaurant. By the time they got to the pub the kid had sung her songs and departed. Bob tried to persuade Morris to stay and watch the female impersonator. 'Aren't they rather fashionable now?' he suggested, partly in order to justify the expense of time and money in getting there, and partly in the hope of making a business suggestion which Morris would find useful. But Morris shook his head without interest. 'They're finished,' he said. They took another taxi back to some sort of older children's night-club in the King's Road, at a similar outlay of time and money all over again.

'I thought night-clubs were finished?' said Bob, trying to get ahead of the game.

Morris shook his head. 'Not yet,' he said.

It was far too noisy to talk in the night-club, which Bob found rather agreeable, since they had nothing to say to each other. He and Morris drank a lot of whisky, which made Morris more and more impassive, if that were possible, and himself more and more conscious of the girls' knees that came dancing by, and of Lake, with her moon-white bleached hair and her night-black artificial eyelashes. He invited her to dance, taking hold of her with the utmost precaution, like some rare and fragile artifact. But even this delicate touch seemed to surprise her. She backed away from him as if he had made an indecent assault upon her.

'What's all this?' she demanded suspiciously.

'What's what, Lake?'

'What you're up to.'

'It's the foxtrot, isn't it?' replied Bob uncertainly.

'The what?'

They moved about vaguely at arm's length, looking at each other with incomprehension.

'The foxtrot.'

'You're joking!'

He couldn't understand what point she was trying to make.

'Isn't it a foxtrot?' he said. 'Slow, slow, quick, quick, slow . . . No . . . Slow, slow, quick, slow . . . No, no . . .'

She stared at him.

'How old are you, anyway?' she demanded.

'Twenty-nine.'

'Oh. They used to do the foxtrot when you were young, did they?'

Poor Tessa's head kept sinking with boredom. Yet later they found themselves in Morris's flat, gazing impassively into space and sipping more whisky. It was a furnished flat in a pre-war block just off the King's Road. The furnishings suggested period, without tying themselves down to any one period rather than any other, and bore no imprint of Morris's inscrutable personality whatsoever.

Lake kicked off her shoes, rolled down her stockings, and rubbed her feet. 'I had terrible corns, even as a child,' she said companionably to Tessa. 'Did you? I had a rotten childhood altogether. Spots and boils, the lot. I had ringworm once. Did you ever have ringworm?'

'What I can't for the life of me understand,' said Bob to Morris suddenly, 'is what made you become a graduate trainee on a newspaper at fifteen pounds a week, when you've obviously got so many other more profitable lines of business.'

Morris took in a mouthful of smoke and worked it over in his mouth for some time. 'I'm interested in newspapers, Bob. I think they still have a big future in front of them. I want to learn the business.'

'You really see yourself working on a paper for the rest of your life, Erskine?'

'I see myself owning one, Bob.'

Bob, lying back in his armchair gazing up into the air, turned his head to stare at Morris.

'Sure,' said Morris. 'Why not? Someone's got to own them. Go into it through magazines. Buy up derelict properties like *Leisure and Pleasure* and tailor them for the right markets. Lot of markets still untapped, Bob. Take the fifties age-group. Maximum earning-power; children off their hands; ten years to go before retirement. Lot of money there, Bob. Sell them sports cars, jock-straps, buckskin boots – young men's kit. They've got the money to be young at that age.'

Hazed by the whisky, Bob felt himself becoming rather emotional. 'You could do it, too,' he said.

'Sure.'

'You could do it, Erskine.'

'Sure, sure.'

'All you'd need is the money.'

'The money's never any difficulty, Bob. All I need is a look at the industry from inside, and a nucleus of really smart young toreros. Interested?'

'Me, Erskine?'

'Sure, Bob.'

'I'm not a smart young torero, Erskine.'

'I could use you somewhere. One of the anchor-men. You're good with copy. You're slow and solid.'

'Yes, but . . .'

'You don't work too hard, Bob. That's what I like about you. Get some high-pressure team of kids working to build something up and they all work too hard. They work themselves dry – they start to make mistakes. I've seen it happen, Bob.'

'I don't know what to say, Erskine. I mean, in many ways I admire you more than anyone I've ever . . .'

'Sure. I just mention it to keep in mind. Nothing will be moving for a year or so yet.'

When Bob woke Tessa up to take her home he remembered that he had spent almost his last shilling in insisting on paying the bill at the night-club. He asked Morris if he could borrow some money for the cab fare. Morris, still leaning impassively back in his armchair, tossed him a fiver.

'An advance against salary, Bob,' he said.

There was one particular travel poster on the wall of the lounge at Schiphol Airport which became imprinted on Dyson's memory as the evening wore on. It was of a girl in a swimming-costume, frozen in the very moment of stepping off the side of a swimming-pool. It irritated Dyson. She had already stepped right out into unsupported space, and was looking down at the water beneath her with a slightly anxious smile of anticipation on her face. And there, in mid-air, she remained suspended. She was there at six, when it was still generally believed that the Scandinavian party they were all waiting for was somewhere *en route* between Paris and Amsterdam. She was there at seven, when the French journalists, who were beginning to emerge as the leaders of opinion in the expedition, put the story about that the Scandinavians had by an error been flown not to Amsterdam but back to Copenhagen. At eight o'clock, when the French announced that the

Scandinavians' plane had crashed, the poor girl had still not got so much as a toe into the water. The anticipation in her anxious smile was as keen as ever at nine, when the French declared that the Scandinavians had landed at Brussels and were coming on by train. It had still not faded at ten, when all the various nationalities present abandoned interest in their Scandinavian colleagues, and instead rose and mobbed Starfield as he hurried anxiously between telephone and cable office, and threatened to petition their respective governments for the revocation of all Magic Carpet's licences and landing rights if he did not immediately arrange everyone hotels in Amsterdam for the night.

They took off soon after ten o'clock the following morning, without the Scandinavians, in another turbo-jet, larger and even more visibly second-hand than the first one. A small panel fell out of the internal trim in front of Mounce and Dyson just after take-off, and swung back and forth on the end of a piece of wire. Mounce, who had subsided into an early-morning liverish bitterness again, watched it sourly.

'This stinking plane's never going to get to the Middle East,' he snarled. 'It looks about a hundred years old.'

'Oh, for God's sake!' snarled Dyson, who was also a little hung-over. 'It's a jet!'

'It's got stinking straight wings, John!'

'All right – it's got straight wings! What's wrong with straight wings, for God's sake?'

'Because they mean it's just a cartload of old scrap-iron! It's obsolete!'

'Obsolete? How can it be obsolete when it's jet-propelled?'

'For God's sake, John – stinking jets have been around for a hundred stinking years! They were new when you were a kid – but that's a long stinking time ago now.'

Dyson was right, though; the old plane did not break down. The loose panel swung and danced on the end of its wire, but the plane whined on across Europe unaffected.

'Anyway,' said Dyson, 'I don't know what you've got to

worry about. I should be doing the worrying – I've got to be back in London on Friday for a television programme, on which I may say my whole future career depends.'

Mid-morning drinks were brought round; then pre-lunch drinks; then a sandwich lunch with lunch drinks, followed by after-lunch drinks. Everyone began to cheer up – even Starfield, who came working his way down the cabin, cheerfully saying a word here and a word there. 'All right, folks? Everyone happy, boys and girls?'

'We do still reckon on getting back to London by Thursday night, do we?' Dyson asked him.

'There's a lad here worried about getting back already!' cried Starfield jovially to everyone around. He turned back to Dyson and patted his shoulder reassuringly. 'Don't worry, boy,' he said. 'We'll get you back on time, never you fear.'

After the fifth lot of drinks Mounce began to take some sort of interest in the scenery. 'Rome,' he said, gazing vaguely earthwards out of the window. 'I'd like to take a look at Rome. Did you see *Dolce Vita*, John? Lot of crap, really. One or two quite juicy bits, though . . .'

Dyson tried to look out of the window over Mounce's shoulder, to see if they were in fact passing over Rome. But Mounce seemed to be reviewing the European scene at large. 'I wouldn't mind taking a gander at Hamburg, for that matter,' he said dreamily. 'See some of those old judies wrestling in mud . . . Or Beirut. Old Jimmy Knowles on the *Express* was telling me about Beirut. He said it was fantastic. "You like leetle girl, sahib? I breenga you leetle seester for one half-dollar." All that kind of crap.'

There was a gap between after-lunch drinks and mid-afternoon drinks, however, during which Mounce began to subside a little into melancholy.

'I didn't know this stinking flight was going to take as long as this,' he complained. 'What time are we supposed to be getting there?'

'I don't know,' said Dyson.

'It's nearly half past two already! I thought we were supposed to be travelling in a proper plane, not some snotty old wreck out of the Science Museum with straight wings. Is that the Persian Gulf down there now?'

Dyson craned over and looked out of the window. They were flying over a deep blue sea studded with islands.

'I don't think there are that many islands in the Persian Gulf,' said Dyson doubtfully. 'I think that must be the Aegean.'

'The Aegean?' said Mounce indignantly. 'The one next to Greece? Don't talk crap, John! We've been flying for hours. This is a plane, not a horse-and-cart.'

More drinks were served, and more again. Just after four o'clock they began to descend. Starfield appeared at the front of the cabin, and pressed his palms together. 'In just ten minutes time, boys and girls,' he began, 'we shall be landing to refuel at Beirut.'

He paused, as if expecting the same sort of reaction as the announcement about Amsterdam had caused. None came; everyone took the news in silence. Dyson wondered if everyone but himself and Mounce had known already that they were only just over halfway, or whether, like himself, they were too stunned to speak, or whether, like Mounce, they were too boozed to take it in. Starfield himself seemed to be slightly taken aback by the lack of response. The glasses slipped down his nose disbelievingly. 'Anyway,' he said, pushing them back nervously, 'drinks will be served in the transit lounge, compliments of Magic Carpet. Thank you.'

Jannie hated it when John was away. He was away so rarely that she always forgot what it was like, and looked forward to it, thinking that she would be somehow free and able to get things done. She had a vague picture of herself, absolved from the necessity to cook proper dinners and to sit late over them talking about what Gareth Holmroyd had said to Harry Stearns and what latest outrage Reg Mounce or Erskine Morris had committed, reading good books instead, making clothes for the children, putting up the hems of her dresses, re-arranging the living-room furniture, and thinking how she could earn some money to clear off their overdraft. But in fact she did none of these things. There was much less extra time created than she had imagined. And what there was she wasted. She couldn't settle to anything when she was alone in the house for the evening. In the end she turned on the television, to watch it for half an hour and settle her mind, and sat in front of it all evening with a growing sense of waste and guilt which seemed to make it not easier but more difficult from one moment to the next to get up and switch it off, until at last the BBC took the decision for her by closing down for the night. She didn't even manage to get to bed early. After the television had stopped she sat about glancing at the daily papers, half-reading items which had already been made out-of-date by the news programmes she had seen on television that evening. She trailed dismally to bed at a quarter to one, leaden tired, and hating herself for her feebleness. She had been going to wash her hair; she hadn't even done that! In bed she couldn't get to sleep. She kept turning towards the side on which John usually lay to put her arm round him for comfort. It was not only the bed that was empty. The whole room – the whole house – seemed filled with an unnatural quietness. In the morning she got up tired, shouted at the boys, and subsided before the television in the evening feeling even worse.

She thought with amazement about women whose husbands went away for weeks at a time on business trips – or for years at a time, on war service or to prison. How could the prospect of such separation be borne? The idea occurred to her while she was washing up, and came to her with such force that she stopped and gazed helplessly out of the window for some minutes, the mop and a plate trailing motionless in her hands. One forgot for years at a time, living in a round of only small anxieties and only small resentments, what ranges of human suffering there were – suffering beyond one's experience, beyond even one's imagination. Was this how her mother had felt when Father died? This frightening bleakness, as of unfamiliar country when the light began to go on a winter's afternoon? This grey filter coming down over one's senses, draining the colour and the savour out of things? This sudden awareness of oneself? When one was happy, one scarcely knew one was there. One was just a mathematical point at which rays of light from the rest of the universe converged. And then the balance of things was disturbed, and suddenly one became aware of the complex spiritual machinery which kept one going. It was like noticing one's heartbeats. The fragility of the whole mechanism became painfully apparent.

A grey, gritty smell crept into her nostrils, of smoke blowing down from chimneys along bleak terraced streets in some desolate city where she was a stranger.

She began to wash up again, tears brimming in her eyes, and remained in a curious mood all day, on a knife-edge between tears, and exaltation at her readiness for tears. When she fetched Damian from nursery-school she took him to the recreation-ground and played with him in a strange, wild way. She threw him up in the air and swung him round and kept laughing. Every time he stopped playing and became thoughtful, as if about to recount an incident from the life of Jack, she clapped her hands and chased him off on another game. The sudden intensity of all this fun unnerved him slightly. He became over-excited, then querulous, and finally so tearful that she had to take him home.

It occurred to her during the afternoon that the odd strand of excitement which was woven into her mood might have something to do with Bob. She at once felt guilty for even thinking such a ridiculous thought, which somehow seemed to discredit her feelings about John's absence, and about separation in general. She also felt more excited still. She immediately began to imagine getting a baby-sitter and going out for dinner with Bob in some small restaurant in Soho. They would have wine – a whole bottle between them – and talk about this and that. Not about anything very deep or significant. They'd just gossip – but easily and intimately. They'd tell each other how they *felt* about things. She had feelings about everything today. She longed to tell them. She thought of Bob leaning on the table listening, looking at her with his mild, familiar eyes.

She had her hand on the phone to ring him at the office and suggest dinner when she remembered Tessa. How *awful* that she hadn't thought of her before! She bit her lip, shocked at herself. But after she had got used to the idea she began to think that it would be almost as good even with Tessa there. She would invite them both to dinner at the house. She saw herself being astonishingly kind to Tessa – astonishing Tessa, astonishing Bob, and even astonishing herself. They would all talk together with great ease and openness. Tessa, who was always so shy and unforthcoming with her, would start to feel secure in her friendship. All three of them could be friends, close friends. She wanted to be very close to Bob and Tessa. She wanted John to be close to them, too, of course.

She rang Bob, but even while she was waiting to get through her excitement ebbed, and she realized how awkward it might turn out to be, if Tessa didn't warm to her any more than she had on previous occasions. And when Bob answered he sounded preoccupied; he said Erskine was waiting for him to finish some job in hand. She talked about a house which she thought Tessa ought to see, then couldn't think of anything else to say, and in the end didn't invite him at all.

She watched the television again all evening, in fact, doing the *Times* crossword simultaneously to persuade herself that she was not being entirely supine. Once she thought she heard rubbish being thrown over the wall. Probably; the garden was full of rubbish now. She would make an effort and clear it all up. She'd do it tomorrow. No, she'd do it when John came home. She'd be able to start getting things done again when John came home.

* * *

At Beirut the Magic Carpet party's advance bogged down and stuck. The Scandinavians had got there ahead of them, and left again already. But the main party was unable to follow. According to Starfield there was a minor technical fault in the plane which would be rectified within the hour. But the hour passed and another hour followed it, and they were still in the transit lounge drinking down the compliments of Magic Carpet. They would be taking off very soon indeed, Starfield assured them. The warm Mediterranean dusk thickened outside the windows. The landing lights glowed brighter and brighter as the sky faded – red on the approaches, blue on the runways, green on the taxiways, like some dream vision of the jewelled Orient. It was the French who forced Starfield to get them all into hotels for the night; the rest were too reduced by alcohol and travel-weariness to argue. It took a great deal of argument. Starfield threatened them that the plane would take off as soon as it was ready, and that anyone not aboard it would have to get himself repatriated at his own expense. He pleaded with them, begging them to consider that they had consumed some £5,000 worth of Magic Carpet's hospitality already. He swore he would report them all to their respective Press Councils for infamous professional conduct. He beseeched them to consider his own position. But the French were adamant, and in the end Starfield found hotels for everyone. Which was just as well, because when they got back to the airport next morning they found they were no nearer taking off than they had been the night before.

It turned out that the fault the aircraft had developed was not a technical one; it was financial. At some time in the past the aircraft's operators had failed to pay a bill for landing dues at Beirut, and now the Lebanese authorities had distrained upon the aircraft, and impounded it until the bill was settled. At first Starfield denied this. But as the day grew hotter, and the drinks at the bar, compliments of Magic Carpet, flowed more and more like water, he shifted his ground slightly, and denied only that the debt was in any way the responsibility of

Magic Carpet. It had been incurred, he said, by Nederlandse Zonnenvaart Luchtbedrijs of Amsterdam, the company from which the plane was chartered, and he implored them to be patient, because they would be taking off just as soon as N.Z.L. had paid the necessary sum into the Lebanese Government's account. He spent the morning hurrying from telephone to cable office to police headquarters, and just before lunchtime was able to report that N.Z.L. disclaimed all knowledge of the debt. Apparently they didn't even own the aircraft. They were operating it on long-term charter from another company, Overland en Overzee N.V. of Rotterdam. It had become uncomfortably hot in the lounge; Starfield mopped his brow and pressed his palms together, and then had to mop the palms, explaining all this to the journalists. But he had already cabled O & O, he assured them hoarsely, and he expected the matter to be settled within minutes.

It was only halfway through his seventh lager that Dyson realized he was sitting exactly opposite a poster with the girl from Schiphol on it. She was still just stepping out from the side of the swimming-pool into empty air; she still had the same anxious smile on her face; and she had still not got her toes wet. He got up and moved to another seat, so that he had his back to her. It brought him face to face with Mounce instead.

'I mean,' said Mounce, chinking the ice about in a large glass of whisky, 'it'll all have simmered down by the time this lot's finished, won't it?'

There were drops of sweat running down Mounce's temples. He looked tired; the strain of fetching drinks and keeping an eye on his publicity folder seemed to be telling on him. Whenever he asked Dyson yet again if he thought things would have simmered down or blown over by the time he got back, Dyson realized how much he preferred it when Mounce explained to him about intending to have it away with one of the model girls as soon as they got to Sharjah; though as soon as he started to explain about having it away with the model,

Dyson immediately realized that it had been the topic of simmering down and blowing over which he had really preferred all the time.

'I mean,' said Mounce, 'what do you think personally?'

Dyson rested his head against the back of the chair, gazing up at the ceiling. 'Even if we take off for Sharjah immediately,' he said, 'I don't see how I'm going to be back in London in time for my television programme on Friday night. I just don't see it.' He fanned himself meditatively with his publicity folder.

'I mean,' said Mounce, 'have you taken a look at the one they call Daisy-Claude? Haughty and naughty – that's how I like them. You wait till we get to Sharjah. First night in a proper hotel and I'll be away.'

Dyson watched the shadow of Mounce's chair creep millimetre by millimetre nearer the toe-cap of his right shoe. 'If I miss that television programme,' he said, 'I swear to God I will take Starfield and his crapulous company to court and sue them for every penny they've got.'

Mounce swirled the bits of ice round at the bottom of his empty glass until they shot out over the side and fell on the floor. 'I wish you'd stop crapping on about your spotty television programme,' he said. 'You're getting a real bore about it.'

Starfield did not reappear until teatime. Apparently Overland en Overzee knew nothing about any bill for landing dues at Beirut. At the time of the alleged tort they had been chartering the plane to Lineas Aereas Pan-Balearicas of Palma, a company whose affairs now seemed to be in the hands of the receiver. The French were very firm with Starfield when he had explained all this. Magic Carpet, they insisted, would simply have to settle the debt itself and sort everything out later. The Belgians agreed. So did the Germans and the Dutch and indeed everyone who was not too drunk to express an opinion, except Starfield. Magic Carpet couldn't settle the debt, he explained, until it had received the subsidy it was getting towards the cost of the press trip from the Joint Tourism Committee of the Trucial Sheikhdoms. And when would that be? demanded the French, with the full support of the Dutch, the British, and everyone else. When it had delivered its cargo of journalists into the Committee's hands in Sharjah.

Slowly the sun settled towards the west, and the airfield was covered once again in red, blue, and green jewels. Starfield hurried desperately in and out, telephoning his directors in London and trying to placate the French. 'Listen, boys! . . .' Dyson could hear him pleading haggardly. 'Gentlemen, I beseech you! . . . We shall be taking off any moment! . . . Friends, I beg of you to facilitate proceedings by remaining calm! . . . I implore you! . . . I give you my solemn oath! . . . For God's sake talk English – I can't understand a word you're saying! . . . Oh, go and jump in the sea, you stupid ignorant Frogs, I'm sick of the sight of you! . . .'

Another night in a Beirut hotel, with windows open once again on the soft Levantine air, and the noise of Beirut's traffic. Dyson liked the noise of the traffic. It soothed him as he lay on top of his bed, unable to sleep, because it was tangible evidence of the real and romantic world which existed outside the confines of international airports. He hoped he would never see another airport in his life after this trip. Every time he closed his eyes the blank waiting faces of the passengers came back to him, and the roaring and whining of jets and turbo-jets, and the characterless international voice of the loud-speaker system announcing the departure of Flight ME 731 to Baghdad and Tehran, the further delay in the arrival of Flight ME 491 from Istanbul and Ankara . . . Oh God, how he hated airports!

And in the morning – back to the airport. But there was a surprise awaiting them. Starfield – unshaven, exhausted, and triumphant after sitting up all night telephoning and negotiating – had found them a fresh and unencumbered plane. It was older and even more visibly second-hand than the one they had arrived on; it had piston engines, which caused Mounce to start predicting a stinking sticky end for it even before they were aboard. Prudently, Starfield waited until they were airborne before he pressed his palms together and announced where they were going. The stewardesses would be coming round immediately with drinks, he said, compliments of Magic Carpet, and they were on their way back home to Amsterdam. Having said which he at once helped himself to a bottle of whisky from the galley and locked himself in one of the lavatories with it, while the French beat on the door in vain. For Starfield the war was at last over.

Mounce made a few indignant noises about Starfield's stinking cheek. But they sounded mechanical; Dyson had the impression that even Mounce was privately relieved. Everyone was relieved, except the French, who had a great sense of responsibility. The trip had been one long series of disasters. God clearly did not want them in Trucial Oman, and there was nothing for it but to retire to Amsterdam in good order, drinking to keep their spirits up as they went.

Dyson felt a deep content. He would be back in Amsterdam by evening, and on his way to London first thing Friday morning, in plenty of time for his programme. It was television he was cut out for, not travelling. He felt the sort of happiness he had always expected to feel when he had been a homesick Boy Scout at interminable summer camps in waterlogged meadows, if only he could have found an excuse for getting himself sent home early.

The feeling persisted until teatime, when in front of his incredulous eyes the starboard outer propeller came spinning to a halt, and they landed in some haste, with fire-engines and ambulances standing by, at Ljubljana.

12

Everyone thought that Bob ought to do the programme if Dyson wasn't back in time. They kept ringing him at the office all through Friday morning to urge him.

'It's not just my idea, Bob,' said Jannie. 'John wants you to do it, too, if he's not back. He made a great point of it when he rang from Ljubljana this morning.'

'How did he sound?' asked Bob. 'Was he in a great state?'

'No, he was surprisingly calm.'

'Poor old John.'

'He'll almost certainly be back in time, Bob. You'd just be standing by in case. It's really simply that this Samantha Lightbody woman at the BBC has got in a great tizzy about it. She keeps ringing up to ask if I've got any more news.'

'She keeps ringing me up, too.'

'What did you tell her?'

'I said I didn't know anything about race relations.'

'Oh, Bob! Don't be so feeble. You know as much about them as John does.'

'I can't think why you're so keen for me to do it, Jannie.'

'I'd just like to see you on television, Bob. I just think you'd be terribly good.'

Bob sighed. 'Yes, well,' he said, 'I've got some work here that Erskine's waiting for.'

Ten minutes later Samantha Lightbody rang again to say that she gathered Bob *did* know something about race relations – she understood he'd shared rooms in college with a Siamese. Bob gazed longingly at some layouts for the new pre-teen page which Erskine had asked him to look through. There was nothing he wanted more in life, he realized now, than the chance to get on with a little quiet work.

'Who told you about the Siamese?' he asked.

'Mrs. Dyson,' said Samantha Lightbody. 'She's just very kindly phoned about it. Honestly, we're absolutely scraping the barrel. Every expert on race relations in London seems to be sick, or away at some conference.'

'I'm very sorry . . .'

'We'd only use you in the very last possible resort.'

'All the same . . .'

'Can we leave it that you'll think about it?'

'Well . . . all right, I'll think about it.'

As soon as Samantha Lightbody rang off, Tessa was on the line.

'Your friend Mrs. Dyson's been ringing me,' she said. 'She told me to try and persuade you to appear on this television programme.'

Bob slipped a peppermint into his mouth and rubbed a galley between finger and thumb. He liked the coarse, soft texture of newsprint. 'Go on, then,' he said.

'How do you mean, go on?'

'Go on and persuade me.'

'Well, do you want to do it, Bob?'

'I don't know. Do you think I ought to do it?'

'Bob, I don't want you to do anything you don't want to do. You know that.'

'Yes.'

'I only want you to do what you want to do. I only think you ought to do it if you think you ought to do it.'

Bob felt suddenly exasperated. 'Tess, you never have any opinions of your own! There's never anything you actually want yourself!'

'Bob, that's not true! I want you to be happy and do what you want. I don't want to stand in your way. Bob, you're the man! You've got to run your life and decide things for yourself.'

It embarrassed Bob to argue on the phone in Morris's

presence. Morris gave no sign of hearing. He typed on behind the wavering blue tape of cigarette smoke, then wrote odd sentences in longhand, clipped bundles of paper together, and tossed them onto Bob's desk.

'Erskine, do you think I ought to do this damned programme?' Bob asked him.

'Sure,' said Morris soothingly, without breaking off his work.

'I knew you'd say that,' said Bob gloomily. 'You really think I should?'

'Sure.'

Mrs. Mounce rang. 'Darling, I just had to ring. Tess has told me. Sweetest, you're not going to turn a chance like this down, are you?'

'I'm thinking . . .'

'I mean, it's nothing to do with me, sweets. But, Bob, do be *serious* about it, darling. Opportunity doesn't knock twice, you know, and you are going to have a family to support. I know what it's like, I can tell you, trying to live on the money that paper pays.'

'I'm thinking . . .'

'You've got to start making a career for yourself, darling. You've got to get *on* – you've got to try and make a teeny weeny bit of progress. Think of Tess, Bob . . .'

'Well, I am thinking of her . . .'

'Now, sweetest, will you promise me you'll ring the television people at once and say yes?'

'I honestly am thinking about it . . .'

'Well, will you promise me you'll think about it very very very very seriously? . . .'

At one point in the morning he had Samantha Lightbody back on one line, asking if he had made up his mind yet, and Tessa on the other, worrying if she had said the right thing earlier.

'Perhaps I ought to push you more, Bob,' she said miserably. 'I suppose you're someone who needs rather a lot of pushing.

Mrs. Mounce thinks I should push you. I'll certainly push you if you think that's what you need to get the best out of yourself, Bob. But I don't want to push you into being pushed. Do you see what I mean, Bob?'

Jannie rang back, too. 'Bob, you'd be terribly *good* on television,' she said. 'I only want you to go on because I'm sure you'd do it well. You remember how I hated it when John went on – I knew he'd overdo it and just be embarrassing. But you'd be a natural, Bob!'

Bob gazed out of the window at the great whiteness of the sky. 'I honestly don't feel I'd be much good, Jannie,' he said.

'Bob, you make me so *mad* sometimes, the way you underestimate yourself! It's not proper modesty – it's something really horrible and pathological.'

Bob felt hounded. 'I *am* thinking about it,' he said. 'I've agreed to do that. I wish everybody would let me get on and think about it in peace.'

'But, Bob, it might be your chance!'

'My chance? What chance?'

'Well, for heaven's sake, Bob – your chance to break out of that office, for a start. You don't intend to stick there for the rest of your life, do you, just being John's dogsbody?'

'I don't know. I suppose I'll move on eventually . . .'

'*Eventually*? It'll be too late, *eventually*! You'll be there when you're forty, Bob, you really will. You and John – you're both getting stuck in the rut. But at least John makes an effort to get out. You won't do anything! You just plod along taking everything for granted, waiting for people to come and bring you your life on a plate.'

Bob doodled on the edge of a galley – a little bald eggheaded man putting his tongue out.

'You're in a funny mood today, Jannie.'

'I'm always in a funny mood when John's away.'

'It's not like you, going on about things like this.'

'Well, I *am* going on about this particular thing, Bob.'

'You're mothering me, Jannie.'

'Somebody's got to mother you, you poor orphan boy.'

She sounded both cross and tender – perhaps cross at her own tenderness, thought Bob, rather as a mother might be.

'I'm sure your mother would say just the same if she were alive. She'd push you on and make you do something with your life.'

Bob sighed, watching the endless blue smoke rising from Morris's cigarette. 'Perhaps you're right,' he said. 'Anyway, I'll think about it.'

Jannie *was* in a funny mood, she knew it herself – an even funnier mood than the one she had been in earlier in the week. Her tense anxiety for John to return and her excited longing to help Bob and Tessa had both turned to irritation now that they were frustrated. She was irritated with John for so typically getting himself aboard a plane which had a defective oil-feed system in the starboard outer engine. She was irritated with Bob for being so wet and unhelpable; it was like trying to mould milk-pudding. Above all she was irritated with herself, for allowing herself to be so pointlessly and inappropriately irritated.

Because she was irritated, of course, everything around her conspired to irritate her further. The phone kept ringing. Each time she heard it she literally ran to it, thinking it might be John in Ljubljana, or Bob ringing to say that he would do the programme after all. But each time it was someone banal, with some entirely banal message. It was the BBC wanting to know if she'd heard anything more from her husband (she'd told the stupid woman she'd let her know as soon as anything happened), or John's brainless sister-in-law chattering about children's illnesses, or the bank manager pestering on about their overdraft. Most irritating of all, because so entirely meaningless and irrelevant, was some stupid old woman with a condescending voice who kept calling long-distance and asking to speak to a Miss Pennycuick. Nothing Jannie could say seemed to convince her that she didn't have a Miss

Pennycuick concealed about the house. Apparently poor old Miss Pennycuick had gone off to stay with friends in London, and had written back to say that their number was VINcent 4763. Jannie could imagine the poor old soul peering with maddening short-sightedness at VINcent 4673 on her hostess's telephone, or seeing it correctly and transcribing it with infuriatingly slow, methodical wrongness, never guessing that what she was doing would cause some innocent stranger to be pestered almost out of her mind.

'For the last time,' Jannie snapped, when that terrible condescending voice came back on the line yet again, 'you have the wrong number. The name of the people in this house is Dyson. There is no Miss Pennycuick here. There is no maiden lady of any sort living or staying here, and there never has been. Now will you *please stop ringing me?*'

Oh, thought Jannie, the chaos and fragmentation of life! On a day like this nothing fitted. Nothing made any continuous sense or pattern. John should have been home and wasn't – not for any reason which arose out of his character, or which had any significance outside itself, but because a small part had failed in one engine of a plane he shouldn't have been on in the first place. Bob should have agreed to take John's place on the programme if necessary, but wouldn't – for a reason which undoubtedly arose out of his character, but which was so tangled and obscure and unsatisfactory that even a broken oil-feed would have been better.

And even if you fitted all this lot together to make some sort of sense, what about the wrong numbers, and the garbage collecting in the garden, and the slates falling off the roof? She roamed through the house doing nothing, waiting for the telephone to ring, waiting to collect Damian from school. Life was all thumbs, she thought, a long series of wrong numbers.

'I suppose perhaps I ought to, oughtn't I?' Bob asked Morris, unable to concentrate on the pre-teen page for indecision.

'Sure,' said Morris, typing.

'I mean, I don't want to do it, Erskine. I'm honestly just not interested in this sort of thing. But I suppose it's an opportunity I ought to take, isn't it? What do you think? I suppose one ought to try and make some effort to get ahead in life and so on, oughtn't one?'

'Sure.'

'Of course, I know you think that. But would *you* do it? Would *you* appear in this programme?'

'Surely. Like a shot.'

Bob opened a new tube of chocolate caramels and slipped one into his mouth. 'I suppose you would,' he said.

It was not in the first place the condition of the starboard outer engine which detained the Magic Carpet party at Ljubljana; it was the condition of Starfield. Starfield had to be got into normal negotiating condition before work on the engine could even start.

He had not envisaged a stop at Ljubljana, of course, when he had retired to the lavatory with a bottle of whisky after take-off from Beirut, and the first difficulty was to get him out of the lavatory again, since he was sitting on the floor inside with his back against the door, and seemed unresponsive to all entreaties to move himself. When they had extracted him from the lavatory they had difficulty getting him down the steps, and when they had got him down the steps it was the ground that proved too much for him. He was propelled slowly across the tarmac with Dyson holding him up on one side and the man from the *Telegraph* holding him up on the other; there was a general feeling among the party that as a British citizen he was a British responsibility. 'Beseech you, boys and girls . . .' he said vaguely as they went. 'Implore you, folks . . .'

A group of Yugoslav officials had appeared on the apron, and the Magic Carpet party advanced to meet them from the direction of the plane, parading Starfield in front of them like some sacred relic or regimental mascot. The two parties halted face to face. Silently the Western press held Starfield up for inspection, so used by now to his authority that they somehow assumed it would be self-evident. Silently, the Yugoslavs inspected him, giving little sign that any impression of authority was registering.

Dyson and the man from the *Telegraph* hurriedly conferred together.

'Know any Serbo-Croat?' asked the man from the *Telegraph*. Dyson shook his head.

'I'll try them in German then,' said the man from the *Telegraph*, and turned to the silently gazing Yugoslavs. *'Dies ist unser Führer,'* he said, pushing Starfield a little farther forward.

The officials examined him even more curiously. *'Ever Führer?'* they repeated musingly. *'Ah, so.'*

'Be taking off in a few minutes, folks,' said Starfield, his eyebrows going up, his glasses coming down, and his eyes focussing on a spot some five feet through the other side of the Yugoslavs' heads. 'Give you my solemn oath.'

'Er ist ein wenig, oh, what's the word?' said Dyson. 'Well, *malade.'*

'Ah, wirklich?' said the Yugoslavs, inspecting Starfield again.

'Nein, nein,' said the man from the *Telegraph* frankly. *'Die Fakt ist, unser Führer ist ein wenig getrunken* – no, *getrinken . . . getranken . . .'*

'Betronken,' said Dyson.

'Betrunken,' suggested some of the German journalists helpfully.

'So, *so,'* mused the Yugoslav officials.

'Drinks will be served in the bar,' said Starfield. 'Compliments of Magic Carpet . . .'

But for once drinks were not served in the bar. The Yugoslavs insisted on examining all their passports, and then took a representative selection of the party, including Starfield and his supporters, and the captain of the plane, who was Lebanese and spoke neither Serbo-Croat nor German, into the airport offices to discuss the situation. Starfield, the only one with any powers or experience to negotiate on their behalf, sat in the position of honour in the middle with his head dangling very slightly to one side.

'If this is Amsterdam,' he said indistinctly, 'I'm a Dutchman.'

The Yugoslavs displayed a clear sense of priorities.

'*Nun*,' they began. '*Wer zahlt?*'

'Who pays?' translated the Germans.

'Him,' said everyone at once, pointing to Starfield. '*Er, lui.*'

'*Jawohl*,' said the officials. '*Seine Papiere, bitte. Seine Ermächtigung, seinen Kreditbrief.*'

'His authorization and letter of credit,' translated the Germans.

Someone went back to the plane and fetched Starfield's briefcase. The officials opened it and spread the contents out over the desk. Very slowly and patiently, with the assistance of everyone present, they went through them all document by document.

'Per-son-al Assid-ent In-soor-ance,' they would read slowly aloud.

'*Personalunfallversicherung*,' the Germans would translate, and slowly, regretfully, the officials would lay the document aside and take up another one.

When a collection of documents had at last been assembled which satisfied the authorities, a number of Yugoslav forms were run to earth in distant offices and laboriously completed by the officials. Dyson and the man from the *Telegraph* had to wake Starfield up to sign them, because he had fallen uncomfortably asleep with his head on his chest. It was difficult to wake him; it was more difficult still to get him to write. His eyes were bleary, and his hand moved waveringly over the paper. The officials compared the marks he had produced with his signature on the documents from his briefcase, and shook their heads regretfully.

'*Nein, nein*,' they said. '*Nicht gut.*'

They tried again with the man from the *Telegraph* steering

Starfield's hand, but the result was worse. Dyson asked if they would let him forge a signature. '*Ja, ja!*' they said, quite eagerly. But when they had seen the result they shook their heads again. '*Nein, nein,*' they said sadly.

'*Er kann in die Morgen unterschreiben,*' said the man from the *Telegraph* hopefully. '*Er wird in die Morgen ganz O.K. sein.*'

'*Nein, nein,*' said the Yugoslavs dogmatically.

Dyson and the man from the *Telegraph* took Starfield outside and poured cold water over his head. The British party took turns at walking him up and down the carpark, trying to exercise the alcohol through his system faster.

'Honestly,' said Mounce, as he and Dyson sat resting in some grass at the edge of the car-park, 'it's a bit stinking much when the stinking organizer of the expedition gets stinking himself.'

'Bang goes my television programme,' said Dyson bitterly. 'Bang goes most of my life, in fact.'

'It's stealing the booze out of *our* mouths, for a start,' said Mounce. 'It's just downright selfishness.'

From time to time Starfield was taken back to the office to try another signature. Most of the officials had gone home for the evening by this time, but the ones that remained shook their heads politely. Dyson and the young British humorist with the hair all over the place held Starfield up while he was sick next to the taxi-rank. 'Now he'll be all right,' said the humorist. But the wasn't; he was worse. He groaned and rolled his eyes and was sick again in the middle of a flower-bed. After that he refused to be walked any more. He lay down in a quiet corner behind some oil-drums and went to sleep. They covered him with his own silky blue showercoat, and he slept for several hours. When he woke up it was dark. Dyson, who was keeping watch at a discreet distance, heard him sit up, and groan, and blow despairingly through his teeth several times. He got up, and a moment later there was the noise of a thin but powerful jet booming against the side of an empty oil-drum and trickling away across the tarmacadam. Starfield emerged into the moonlight and washed himself under a tap sticking out of a wall. Then he lifted his head and gazed thoughtfully upwards for a long time. Dyson supposed for a moment that he was staring at the moon, then followed the direction of his gaze more carefully and realized that he was studying the sign on the side of the control-tower which said LJUBLJANA.

Starfield hurried into the departure lounge, where the rest of the Magic Carpet party was scattered, lying on benches and propped up in armchairs, trying to snatch a few hours of cramped and fitful sleep.

'Boys and girls!' he cried, pressing his palms together as anxiously and operatically as ever, and waiting till everyone had woken up. 'We regret this delay, folks, which is due to unavoidable causes beyond our control. I do assure you that we are doing everything in our power to facilitate our speedy departure, just as soon as it can be arranged. Meanwhile, drinks will be served at the bar, compliments of Magic Carpet. Thank you.'

They heard him in silence, perhaps because they were half asleep, or perhaps because, like Dyson, they were all lost in astonishment and admiration. The bar, of course, was closed, and remained closed. There was no possibility of starting work on the plane that night, and there was no one left in the Putnik office to arrange accommodation. So eventually everyone settled back to spend the night on the seats in the departure lounge – too beaten down by fate now even to curse, too weary in mind and body even to mutter to themselves.

Just before dawn Dyson got up to stretch his aching legs. He walked outside into the road in front of the airport. It was cold, and he shivered violently. Slowly his eyes got used to the grey pre-dawn light; he made out the shapes of cars parked by the roadside, covered by a thick white dew, and soft banks of mist lying motionless in the fields all round. Beyond the mist the dark grey of the surrounding hills was just detaching itself from the lighter grey of the sky. Everything was quiet, and completely still.

He turned up his lapels, and cringed along the road with his hands in his pockets, feeling cold and miserable. The banks of mist in the fields showed whiter as he looked at them, and odd little hills loomed between them. A whiff of manure lingered on the air – human manure, taken brown and liquid and disconcertingly acrid from farmyard tanks. Gradually he began to warm up and feel more alive. He stopped and pissed into the ditch with a great sense of satisfaction, shivering pleasingly as he did up his trousers. Then he ran along the road as fast as he could, until his heart was pounding, and getting his breath was like dragging rocks into his lungs, and his eyes were streaming from the effort in the cold air.

He slowed down and let his pulse return to normal. On and on he walked through the grey light, thinking about Jannie and the boys, and whether he would be able to get any breakfast at the airport, and about his boyhood, and night exercises in the army, and poor old Eddy Moulton, and how he had once walked all night, when he had been an undergraduate, from Murat to Salers, over the Peyrol pass. That was fifteen years ago now. Fifteen years! Perhaps a quarter of his life.

There was a section of drystone walling to the left of the road. He hoisted himself up onto it and sat down. On the other side was a field full of weeds and erratic patches of mist, with a small windowless brick building in the middle of it, surrounded by barbed wire and warning notices, which presumably housed either a transformer or some outlying piece of airport radar equipment.

What had he done with that last quarter of his life? He had married; had fathered two sons. He had made some progress in an honourable career; had considerable prospects of success in various fields; was happy. He was having a good life, undoubtedly. And yet ... Half of it had gone – gone like a dream, slipped through his fingers. He couldn't give any account of it. He had spent his youth as one might spend an inheritance, and he had no idea what he had bought with it.

Except himself, as he now was. He hunched up and pursed

his lips and gazed at the little brick building without any windows. He was rather a silly man, he could see that. Vain and splenetic – passionately devoted to futile objectives. He remembered the television programme he was so anxious to get back for, and couldn't help grinning to himself at the thought. Here he was, at daybreak, sitting on a wall in the grey morning light, looking at a field full of weeds and a meaningless brick structure of unknown function somewhere in the middle of rural Slovenia – and that evening he was supposed to be in a television studio in London, sitting in a pool of unnaturally brilliant light and greasing up to the second Baron Boddy, who was if anything a sillier tit than he was himself. He could not see himself managing such a sudden and total transformation, whatever happened to the plane. They were in two different worlds, and there was some much vaster gap between them than could ever be bridged by a battered old DC-6, even with all four engines working. About these weeds, this wall, and this ugly brick box in the middle of Slovenian nowhere there was something indissolubly solid and smelly and tangible. The second Baron Boddy, and the views which he might or might not exchange with the second Baron Boddy, and the gin-and-tonic and smoked salmon sandwiches which he might or might not share with the second Baron Boddy beforehand, were as factitious and insubstantial as fairyland. He could not help laughing aloud to himself at the optimistic presumption of the universe in thinking that it could contain both Dyson-here and Dyson-there. He remembered with rueful amusement that there had been earlier states of Dyson-here – such as Dyson-yesterday and Dyson-the-day-before – which had worried themselves raw in their anxiety to become Dyson-there. For a few short minutes, at any rate, Dyson-here occupied him completely.

Somewhere behind the mist and the grey hummocky landscape there was a noise of aircraft engines starting up. It was a long way away, but in the still, quiet air it carried clearly. Dyson sat up rigid. It couldn't possibly be the Magic Carpet plane, of course. It needed only a moment's reflection to realize that it couldn't conceivably have been repaired yet.

The noise grew faint, then boomed out loud again through the mist, and died away almost to nothing. The plane was taxiing. Dyson strained his ears. It couldn't possibly be . . . The engineers couldn't possibly be at work yet . . . There was not the slightest need to worry . . . Dyson held his breath, trying to work out what was happening on the airport field. Once again the engines were run up, then died away, then roared out again, and grew steadily louder and louder. A moment later the plane passed almost over Dyson's head – a twin-engined Dakota climbing into the opalescent sky, its navigation lights winking with reassuring calm.

But Dyson was still sitting rigid with anxiety, even after it had cleared the hills to the east and disappeared in the direction of Zagreb. Dyson-here was once again no longer enough. He jumped down from the wall and began to walk quickly back towards the airport, and the possibility of smoked salmon sandwiches with the second Baron Boddy.

None of the usual crowd in the Gates realized that Dyson was overdue. They had scarcely realized he was away in the first place. 'Where's John, then, Bob?' they had asked vaguely earlier in the week. 'In the Persian Gulf,' Bob had explained at least a dozen times. Now that he proved not to have been in the Persian Gulf at all, but at Beirut, and was now no longer at Beirut but at Ljubljana, and should not even have been at Ljubljana, but here sinking half-pints of bitter in the Gates, people had at last got used to the idea that he was in the Persian Gulf. 'John still in the Persian Gulf, then, Bob?' they asked today. Dyson had disappeared from their lives almost as completely as poor old Eddy Moulton. They were like a self-sealing petrol tank; when sections were shot away they closed up automatically and filled the gap, spilling not a drop of the precious communal spirit. But then no one – not even Bob – had noticed Mounce's absence at all.

Still, they were amused by Bob's account of Dyson's slow progress to nowhere, with bits dropping off the plane every time it got into the air. 'Trust old John,' chuckled Bill Waddy, 'to get himself on a plane which falls to bits in the middle of Yugoslavia!' 'Poor old John!' said Gareth Holmroyd. 'He'll never live this down.'

And everyone, when Bob asked them, assured him that he ought to do Dyson's programme.

'Oh, definitely,' said Ted Hurwitz. 'I don't think there's anything wrong with – incidentally, Bob, what are you drinking? – I don't think there's anything wrong with doing a spot of television on the side.'

'It might be sensible when you come to think about it, Bob,' said Mike Sparrow. 'You've got to reckon on getting out of this job – bitter, please, Ted – by the time you're forty.'

'Hey, steady on, Mike,' said Bill Waddy. 'I'm thirty-eight, you know. Thanks, Ted. I'm thirty-eight, Mike.'

'I'm forty-six,' said Gareth Holmroyd.

'I didn't mean . . . Well, I mean, you're both specialists,' said Mike Sparrow. 'What I really meant was, you've got to either get out or specialize by the time you're forty. Is this my bitter, Ted?'

'What about Laurence Evenden?' said Gareth Holmroyd. 'He doesn't really specialize, and he's in his fifties.'

'Well, Laurence is an exception,' said Mike Sparrow.

'Old Laurence is all right,' said Bill Waddy.

'Laurence is different,' said Andy Royle.

'What about old Harry Stearns?' said Gareth Holmroyd. 'He's not really what you'd call a specialist.'

'Old Harry's rather an unusual case, of course,' said Ted Hurwitz.

They all sipped their beer in reflective silence.

'I mean,' said Mike Sparrow, 'I'm thirty-two myself, for heaven's sake.'

'I'm thirty-four,' said Ted Hurwitz. 'How old are you, Bob?'

'Twenty-nine,' said Bob. 'I'll be thirty next month.'

They relapsed into silence again, some looking into their beer, some at the floor, and some over everyone's heads at the advertisements round the walls. The last time they had had this discussion, about a month ago, thought Bob, Bill Waddy had been thirty-seven. And Bob could remember a similar occasion in the past when it had been Bill Waddy himself who had talked about the need to get out of journalism by the time one was forty. He had been thirty-five then, Bob seemed to recall. Bob was still thinking about this when he realized that he had definitely decided to do the programme.

Hammersmith was solid with evening rush-hour traffic. The taxi edged along yard by yard, and Dyson craned haggardly forward in his seat trying to spot some break in the jam ahead. 'Oh God, oh God, oh *God*!' he cried. 'We've only got thirty-five minutes before the programme actually starts! Suppose it takes us ten minutes to get through this lot, then say five minutes to get up to Shepherd's Bush . . . Shepherd's Bush will be solid, of course . . .'

'You spent the whole stinking morning,' said Mounce, 'telling me that you didn't care about this snotty programme any more.'

'Oh, for God's sake!' snapped Dyson. 'That was in Ljubljana!'

The traffic in the lanes on either side of them began to flow forward without obstruction.

'Oh *God*!' shouted Dyson. 'If we don't start moving within the next minute I swear I'll smash this taxi to pieces with my bare hands!'

'You went on and on,' said Mounce, 'about how you'd seen through the whole spotty business.'

Dyson wriggled his fingers tapped his feet and drummed his clenched fists up and down on his knees. 'If only we'd been twenty minutes later leaving Ljubljana!' he groaned. 'We'd have missed the connection from Amsterdam and everything would have settled itself!'

'I don't know,' said Mounce. 'For stinking consistency you just about take the stinking biscuit.'

They reached the Television Centre in Wood Lane some ten minutes or so before the programme was due to go on the air. The sight of the place brought on a new spasm of anxiety in Dyson.

'Oh God!' he cried. 'I haven't even thought what I'm going to say! I haven't got anything prepared at all!'

He sprang out of the taxi as it drew level with the entrance and rushed up to one of the girls at the desk inside as if he were going to strangle her.

'*New Perspectives*!' he shouted. 'Which studio? Which studio?'

The girl examined a list. Very slowly she ran her finger down one page, then turned over and ran it down another.

'Oh, for God's *sake*!' cried Dyson. 'It's starting in ten minutes!'

'Here we are,' said the girl. '*New Perspectives*. They don't do that one at the Centre – it's Lime Grove. Out the back gate – down Frithville Gardens. It'll only take you five minutes, if you run all the way.'

It was in effect a race between Bob and Dyson, though neither of them was aware of it as such, which perhaps didn't matter greatly in the event, since it was won by Erskine Morris.

Morris was actually on the screen when Samantha Lightbody showed Dyson and Mounce into Hospitality Room Number 8 at Lime Grove. They were both panting hard.

'My God!' gasped Dyson. 'Not *him*!'

The room was full of people sipping gin-and-tonic and nibbling smoked salmon sandwiches. 'John!' cried several of them, turning at the sound of his voice. Bob was the only one Dyson took in at first.

'Bob!' he cried. 'You mean to say you let them put that unspeakable little tit on my programme?'

'John,' said Bob quickly, 'do you know Erskine's friend Lake?'

Dyson scarcely glanced at her. 'Honestly, Bob,' he said, 'couldn't you have stood in for me yourself? You are a rotten swine. You really are.'

'John, I can't explain now,' said Bob. 'Why don't you say hello to Jannie?'

Dyson turned round in surprise. 'Jan!' he said. 'What are you doing here?'

'Sh!' hissed a number of people sitting in one corner of the room – the friends and relations of the other performers, perhaps – who were gazing at the monitor screen as if they actually wanted to see what was going on.

'I came to watch Bob on the programme,' whispered Jannie. 'He was supposed to be on it.'

'We all came to watch him!' cried Mrs. Mounce. 'Didn't we, Tessa?'

'Well, well,' said her husband. 'I didn't expect to see *you* here.'

'Reg, darling! Where have you sprung from?'

'Bei-bloody-rut and Ljub-stinking-ljana, if you're interested.'

'Darling! How super!'

'Sh!' hissed the viewing faction.

'Let me get you both drinks,' whispered Samantha Lightbody to Dyson and Mounce.

'If Bob was supposed to be on the programme,' said Dyson, trying to keep his voice down too, 'why isn't he on it?'

'That's a long story,' said Bob.

'I'm afraid there was a slight misunderstanding,' said Samantha Lightbody. 'Let me get everyone drinks.'

'Bob just let himself get shoved out of the way like a booby, as usual,' said Jannie.

'Sh!'

'Jannie, that's not really fair,' said Bob. 'Erskine must have thought I was inviting him to do the programme instead of me. I couldn't really insist on his standing down again after he'd gone to all the trouble of coming out here.'

'You were shoved out of the way, Bob,' said Jannie.

'Sh! Sh!'

'It was just one of those balls-ups,' whispered Samantha Lightbody. 'Let's all have stiff drinks and forget about it.'

Dyson sank down into the chair next to Jannie's with his glass of whisky and put a hand over hers. 'Jan,' he whispered, squeezing her.

'John,' she said, putting her other hand on top of his.

They gazed at the screen. Morris appeared on it again, talking about certain social developments he had noticed in the Western Region of Nigeria when he had been out there earlier in the year. His voice flowed on like the smoke rising from his cigarette, steady and unemphatic, but definitely hypnotic.

'There goes my future,' said Dyson sadly.

Jannie rubbed his hand.

'Bob's future, too,' he said. 'We're both washouts, Jan.'

Morris cut Lord Boddy off in mid-reminiscence with a deftly-placed Sure sure, and put the chairman right on a couple of points of fact.

'He's good,' whispered Bob.

'He's a nasty little prick,' said Dyson.

Mounce leaned across to Bob. 'How are things at the office these days, Bob?' he asked in a low voice. 'Has all that Other Arrangements business blown over yet?'

'Haven't you been in this week, then?' asked Bob.

Mounce thoughtfully eased some shreds of Yugoslav ham sandwich from between his teeth.

'Perhaps I'll stay away permanently and see if anyone notices,' he said. 'Really give it a month or two to sort itself out.'

Lake was talking to Mrs. Mounce. 'My feet feel as if they've been put in a vice,' she whispered. 'Do you suffer with your feet at all?'

'With me it's my glands,' whispered Mrs. Mounce. 'Honestly, darling, you'd never believe the amount of time I've spent seeing specialists . . .'

The door opened, and a commissionaire ushered a tall, gaunt woman in a hat into the room. 'Miss Pennycuick?' called the commissionaire. 'Is there a Miss Pennycuick in here?'

'Mummy!' said Tessa jumping to her feet and going bright red.

'Hello, Mrs. Pennycuick,' said Bob, getting up too.

'Mrs. Pennycuick?' said Jannie in an appalled whisper.

'What are you doing here, Mummy?' asked Tessa.

'I've come up to town to look for you, Tessa. We'll talk about it afterwards, outside.'

'Oh, my God!' said Jannie. 'This is entirely my fault! I simply didn't know that Tessa's name was . . . I mean, I didn't realize . . . It didn't occur to me that . . .'

'Shush!' hissed the enthusiasts.

'I'll talk about it privately with my daughter afterwards, if I may,' whispered Mrs. Pennycuick.

'Yes, but for heaven's sake don't think . . .' said Jannie. 'I mean, don't imagine that . . . I mean, after all, they are *engaged*.'

Mrs. Pennycuick stared at the television screen, as if unwilling to commit herself to looking at any of the people in the room. Tessa gazed at it, too, to hide her confusion, and after a few seconds Bob and Jannie turned their heads towards it as well. Everyone in the room found it a convenient place to rest the eyes, except Lake, who had drawn her right foot up into her lap to examine the condition of her toes, and Dyson, who had his head back and his mouth open and was falling asleep. In silent conciliation, Bob held out his tube of peppermints to Mrs. Pennycuick, half turning his head towards her, so that he could see Lake with her slim white knee drawn up to her ear, and the long bleached hair tumbling around it.

Morris gazed impassively out at them all, the flesh bagging judicially along the line of the jawbone. 'Sure,' he said, with the suggestion of a cryptic smile. 'Oh, sure, sure.'

faber and faber

Headlong
Michael Frayn

Shortlisted for the Booker Prize 1999

Martin Clay, a young would-be art historian, suddenly sees opening in front of him the chance of a lifetime: the opportunity to perform a great public service, and at the same time to make his professional reputation – perhaps even rather a lot of money as well. To obtain the treasure he thinks he has identified involves him setting up a classic sting and risking everything that is valuable to him – and so he finds himself drawn step by step into a moral and intellectual labyrinth.

'Elegant, witty and sparklingly knowledgeable . . . there is no doubt about the sureness of Frayn's achievement in this black and brilliant comedy of uncertainties.' Peter Kemp, *Sunday Times*

'The precision of plot is as sparkling as ever; but Frayn's dissection of his characters – social, intellectual, ethical – is even more dazzling . . . Michael Frayn is outstanding.' Caroline Moore, *Sunday Telegraph*

faber and faber

The New York Trilogy
Paul Auster

The work that made Paul Auster's name, **The New York Trilogy** is the ultimate postmodern thriller – a series of brilliant variations on the classic detective story. Auster stakes out the well-traversed terrain of New York City and makes it over anew as a strange and compelling landscape where identities merge and nothing is what it seems.

City of Glass: Quinn, a writer of detective fiction, becomes enmeshed in a case more puzzling than any he might have written.

Ghosts: Blue has been forced by White to spy on Black. From the window of his rented room, Blue watches Black in his room across the street. But Black is staring out of the window. Who is watching whom?

The Locked Room: When Fanshaw disappears, leaving behind a wife, a baby and an extraordinary cache of novels, plays and poems, his boyhood friend is lured obsessively into the life that Fanshaw left behind.

'A shatteringly clever piece of work . . . Utterly gripping, written with an acid sharpness that leaves an indelible dent in the back of the mind.' *Sunday Telegraph*

faber and faber

Jack Maggs
Peter Carey

Jack Maggs, raised and deported as a criminal, has returned from Australia in secret and at great risk. What does he want after all these years, and why is he so interested in the comings and goings at a plush townhouse in Great Queen Street? And why is Jack himself an object of such interest to Tobias Oates, celebrated author, amateur hypnotist and fellow-burglar – in this case of people's minds, of their histories and inner phantoms?

'A master of storytelling . . . Vivid, exact, unexpected images and language match the quick, witty intelligence flickering through this novel, and make it a triumph of ebullient indictment, humane insight and creative generosity.' *Sunday Times*

'When you have a Peter Carey novel open in front of you, dinner and doorbell count for nothing . . . For its scope and intelligence, the whole story is so compulsive that readers will leave skidmarks on the pages.' *Evening Standard*

'Future reprints of **Oscar and Lucinda** may well bear the legend "by the author of **Jack Maggs**".' *London Review of Books*

faber and faber

The Poisonwood Bible
Barbara Kingsolver

Shortlisted for the Orange Prize

Told by the wife and four daughters of Nathan Price, a fierce evangelical Baptist who takes his family and mission to the Belgian Congo in 1959, **The Poisonwood Bible** is the story of one family's tragic undoing and remarkable reconstruction over the course of three decades in post-colonial Africa. They carry with them all they believe they will need from home, but soon find that all of it – from garden seeds to Scripture – is calamitously transformed on African soil.

'There are few ambitious, successful and beautiful novels. Lucky for us we have one now in **The Poisonwood Bible**.' Jane Smiley

'**The Poisonwood Bible** shows what happens when one of the most talented writers of our generation comes to maturity . . . [It] ranks with the most ambitious works of post-colonial literature and it should at last establish Kingsolver's reputation in Europe as one of America's most gifted novelists.' *Independent on Sunday*

'Brilliant. Now, that is no sort of measured critical reaction but it is how I feel I must begin – with a one-word shout of praise for this superb epic novel.' Margaret Forster, *Literary Review*

faber and faber

Our Fathers
Andrew O'Hagan

Shortlisted for the Booker Prize 1999

Jamie returns to Scotland with his grandfather, the legendary social reformer Hugh Bawn, now living out his last days on the eighteenth floor of a high-rise. The young man is faced with the unquiet story of a country he thought he had left behind and now he listens to the voices of ghosts, and what they say about his own life. It is a story of love and landscape, of nationality and strong drink, of Catholic faith and the end of the old Left. Jamie Bawn's journey home will leave him changed beyond words – beyond the words that darkened his childhood.

'By any standards **Our Fathers** is a powerful novel. As a first novel, it is very remarkable indeed.' *Independent*

'I have scarcely read so silvery beautiful a style when it comes to Scots landscape, nor one so tender when it comes to matters of life and death.' Candia McWilliam, *Financial Times*

'The tang of truth, the irreducible core of humanity lies like a shock in the shuddering heart of this great fiction debut.' *Scotland on Sunday*

'A beautiful, elegiac work . . . required reading for everyone.' Ian Rankin, *Evening Standard*

Please send me

	title	ISBN	Price
_____	The New York Trilogy *Paul Auster*	15223 6	£6.99
_____	Jack Maggs *Peter Carey*	19377 3	£6.99
_____	Oscar and Lucinda *Peter Carey*	15304 6	£7.99
_____	Red Earth and Pouring Rain		
_____	*Vikram Chandra*	17456 6	£7.99
_____	Pig Tales *Marie Darrieussecq*	19372 2	£6.99
_____	Hullabaloo in the Guava Orchard		
_____	*Kiran Desai*	19571 7	£6.99
_____	The Last King of Scotland *Giles Foden*	19564 4	£6.99
_____	Headlong *Michael Frayn*	20147 4	£6.99
_____	Lord of the Flies *William Golding*	19147 9	£6.99
_____	The Remains of the Day *Kazuo Ishiguro*	15491 3	£6.99
_____	The Unconsoled *Kazuo Ishiguro*	17754 9	£7.99
_____	The Poisonwood Bible *Barbara Kingsolver*	20175 X	£7.99
_____	Immortality *Milan Kundera*	14456 X	£7.99
_____	The Unbearable Lightness of Being		
_____	*Milan Kundera*	13539 0	£6.99
_____	The Buddha of Suburbia *Hanif Kureishi*	14274 5	£6.99
_____	Aunt Julia and the Scriptwriter		
_____	*Mario Vargas Llosa*	16777 2	£7.99
_____	Amongst Women *John McGahern*	16160 X	£6.99
_____	A Fine Balance *Rohinton Mistry*	17936 3	£7.99
_____	Birds of America *Lorrie Moore*	19727 2	£6.99
_____	Our Fathers *Andrew O'Hagan*	20106 7	£6.99
_____	The Bell Jar *Sylvia Plath*	08178 9	£6.99

**To order these titles phone Bookpost on 01624 836000
Or complete the order form below:**

I enclose a cheque for £ _____ made payable to Bookpost PLC
Please charge my: o Mastercard o Visa o Amex o Delta
o Switch Switch Issue No_____

Credit Card No _____ Expiry date _____

Name _____

Address _____

_____ Postcode _____

Signed _____ Date _____

Free postage and packing in the UK.
Overseas customers allow £1 per pbk/ £3 per hbk.
Send to: Bookpost PLC, PO Box 29, Douglas, Isle of Man, IM99 1BQ
fax: 01624 837033 email: bookshop@enterprise.net
http://www.bookpost.co.uk